THE RAVEN'S PRICE

A MARGARET OF SCOTLAND MEDIEVAL MYSTERY

J. G. LEWIS

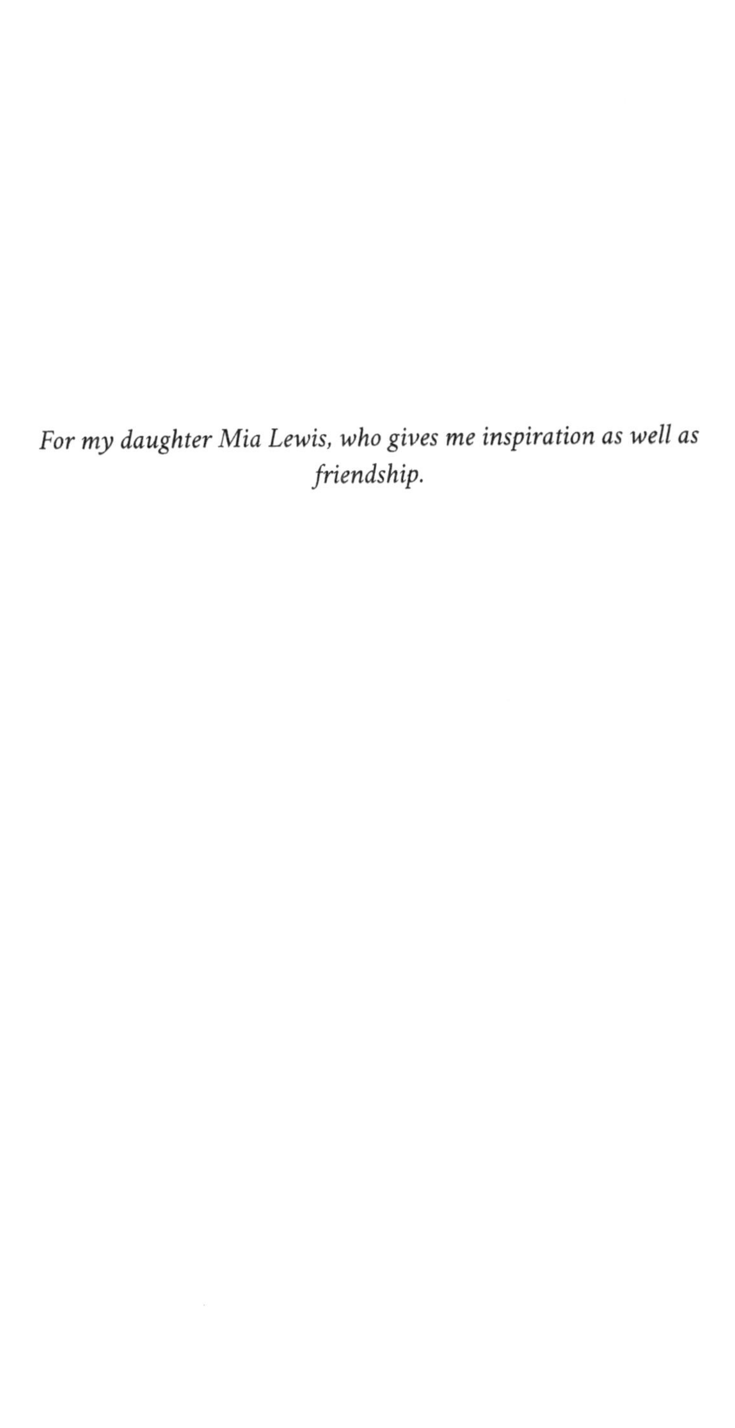

For my daughter Mia Lewis, who gives me inspiration as well as friendship.

ACKNOWLEDGEMENTS

Many thanks to the kind people who read this story in various stages, including Betsy van der Hoek and Dan Rothman. All remaining errors are mine.

"Allow me to lead away the freemen again, the children of nobles, into their native land, into their deserted towns, the women and the boys and the wretched widows."

Old English version of Genesis, *Junius 11*, Bodleian Library

CHAPTER 1

Dunfermline, May 1071

"The gray one's a stunner, can I try it?" Young Duncan stood next to his father, King Malcolm, on the open plain, watching unfamiliar horses go through their paces. Great fanfare had preceded the horse trader's arrival, and almost the entire household stood outside on this bright May morning watching horses of various sizes and colors fly around the field. Queen Margaret watched with her friend Aelgith beside her.

Malcolm's eyes followed a dark dapple gray horse as it galloped past them, mane flying. "Always let the trader's lad ride it first. Then you'll see any quirks it has before you climb aboard."

"I can ride a rearing horse, Dad. You've seen me."

"That doesn't mean you should." Malcolm patted his son affectionately on the shoulder. Margaret was glad of the time he spent with his sons from his first marriage. It bode well for how he would treat their own children.

A small red horse with a flaxen mane suddenly spun hard. The lad riding it grabbed a fistful of mane and almost rebalanced himself, then the horse bucked, going almost vertical, and the lad hit the ground with a thud.

"See? Do you want to get on that one?"

"I bet I can ride it," said Duncan, with a shade of doubt in his voice.

"There are plenty of good horses out there. Don't buy one with a vice when you don't have to. I do like the look of the gray, though." The dappled gray gelding went thundering past them again, great hooves sending the sod flying. "See how steady it is. There's a nice rhythm to its paces."

"So, can I?"

"All right, lad." Malcolm muttered something to the horse trader, a tall man with dark hair and a beaky nose. The man called out to the rider in a strong Irish accent. The gray horse turned and galloped toward them. It stopped short less than ten yards from where they stood, in a dramatic maneuver that caused both Margaret and Aelgith to jump backward a step. Aelgith even let out a tiny shriek.

"As you can see it's very highly trained," said the trader.

The lad riding it was a boy of about fourteen with a mop of blond curls. He jumped down and handed the reins to Duncan, on the trader's instructions.

"How did you ask for that stop?" asked Duncan, of the lad.

"Sit back and a tiny tug on the reins. He's very sensitive."

Duncan put a foot in the stirrup and sprung up into the saddle with no apparent effort. He'd left in a hail of clods before another word was spoken.

"Where do these horses come from?" asked Margaret. They rivaled anything she'd seen in the royal court at Westminster.

"All over, my lady. I've got my scouts here and there looking for the best horseflesh to bring here to the king."

"Are they all young?"

"Oh no, some of them are well aged with plenty of battle experience. See that black one over there?" He gestured to a magnificent steed showing off a measured and intentional rear of the kind used to crush an enemy in battle. "One of King Harold's horses, God rest his soul."

"How did you come by it?" asked Margaret. Harold Godwinson had been king for a few short months in 1066 before William invaded.

"I bought it off the man who captured it in the battle and had it turned out in a field—his men couldn't do anything with it. I know how to spot a good horse, even if it's gone sour. The best war horses can be spirited and high strung and don't always take well to change. They'll need retraining if they've been in the wrong hands for a while."

"You train them yourself?"

"Yes, my lady, though I had an English lad who's twice the rider I am. He put the stop on this gray."

Duncan was now struggling a bit with the massive gray horse. It kept exploding forward, then the lad would rein it in, soon it became angry and started trying to snatch the bit from his hands. The horse trader ran off toward him. "Light hands, lad, light hands!"

"My son used to do that." Aelgith spoke so softly that Margaret barely heard her over all the thundering hooves. "Make the horses stop instantly as if by magic. He had a gift for training horses."

Aelgith rarely spoke of her son, who'd been killed at the Battle of Hastings five years earlier. "He learned it from his father who was a great horseman, but dear Oswin surpassed even his father's skills."

Margaret could hear an edge of tears rising in her friend's voice, and she reached for her hand and held it.

The trader came marching back. "You have to stay out of

that one's mouth. But he's trustworthy. See how he didn't throw the lad?"

"He was trained by an English lad, you said?" Margaret looked around. "Is he here?"

"No, sadly I was forced to part with him since he was property of one of my clients. He'd lent him to me but once he realized what he was capable of he's taken him back."

"Property?" asked Margaret, hackles already rising. "Do you mean he's enslaved?"

"Yes, my lady. Captured years ago, they said. I'd have paid good money for him but you don't argue with the Lord of the Isles."

"What did he look like?" asked Aelgith, with an odd tone to her voice.

"Who, the boy?" asked the trader. "A tall lad. Thin as a whip. Doesn't look like he could lift a pile of kindling but he can ride a horse like nobody's business."

Margaret felt Aelgith's hand tighten around hers.

"Does he…by any chance…have a birthmark?" asked Aelgith, sounding even stranger.

"Aye, right near his nose." The trader pointed to his own face. "Red as wine and distracting to look on but you don't see it after a while. Wait, how did you know that?"

But Aelgith didn't answer because she'd crumpled to the ground.

For a moment Margaret was too shocked to react, then she bent down and felt her chest under her cloak. A light mist of rain suddenly dusted them all with droplets. "She's breathing but…we need to bring her inside."

Guards hurried over and gathered up Aelgith. As soon as one had lifted her up in his arms she awoke and started to struggle.

"Help!" She kicked her legs. "Help me!"

"Don't panic, it's me, Margaret." Margaret reached for her

hand. Poor Aelgith was probably recalling the awful time that she and her daughter were captured and sold into slavery.

"Put me down!" Aelgith's increasing panic alarmed Margaret. She asked the guards to put Aelgith gently on her feet.

"You're fine. No one's stealing you away again," said Margaret, trying to reassure her.

"The boy with the birthmark…" Aelgith turned to her and grasped both her hands. "I think it's my son."

Margaret froze. Aelgith's son was dead. Killed in the battle of Hastings along with her husband. Still holding fast to Aelgith's hand, she excused the guards and told them to return to Malcolm. "How is that possible?"

"We were told he was dead. My daughter and I. One of our neighbors returned from the battle injured and in a panic. He told me that all was lost and that he'd seen my husband and son killed with his very eyes."

Margaret squeezed her hands. "A terrible day."

"But what if they were just injured? What if they pretended to be dead so the enemy wouldn't slay them?" Aelgith's blue eyes were wide. "What if my son is alive, right now, wherever this gray horse came from?"

During this exchange they'd moved far enough away from Malcolm and the horse trader that they were out of earshot.

"We must ask the trader where the boy lives and go look for him," said Margaret.

"His name's Oswin. Tall and thin as a whip. That description fits him exactly. And how many men have a wine-colored birthmark on their face?

Margaret could think of at least two that she knew. Still, that all these features co-existed in one person… "And your son had a way with horses?"

"Always. He could stay balanced atop a horse before he was even five years old. I couldn't keep him away from the stables. All he wanted to do was ride. He used to creep from his bed at night to sleep in there with the horses!"

Aelgith was more animated than Margaret had ever seen her. "He's alive!"

A frisson of excitement shivered through Margaret, and she almost felt like it came directly from Aelgith. "It does seem possible." She glanced back at Malcolm and the horse trader. "I think we should be careful with this information. You know how people are these days. If the boy is highly valued they may sell him or hide him away before we can reach him."

Aelgith's brow lowered. "Yes, the Mormaer of Fife refused to part with my daughter. He wanted to keep her for her fine stitching. How can men be so cruel?"

"We managed to free your daughter. If your son lives, we'll free him as well."

She drew in a steadying breath. "Calm yourself and keep your own counsel. We'll return to viewing the horses and try to gather as much information as we can."

She gave Aelgith's hand one last squeeze, then walked back to where Malcolm and the trader were now negotiating a price for the gray horse.

"He's a fine beast," said Margaret in Gaelic, with all the breezy cheer she could muster. "Where did you say he came from?"

"I bought him off the Lord of the Isles but I couldn't say for sure where he came from before that," said the trader cheerfully. "For all you could say about these troubled times they've brought a lot of very good horses onto the market."

Margaret's gut clenched at the thought of all the death and horror that had befallen the prior owners of these horses —her fellow Englishmen.

Margaret could see that Aelgith could barely hold herself together. She kept staring around her, and Margaret could see that she wasn't seeing the scene before her eyes, but past scenes where her son rode boldly on his own horses, on their manor now stolen by the enemy.

"You look ill," she said quickly. "I think we should get you inside for a rest before you collapse again. You might be coming down with something."

"But..." Aelgith stiffened and looked ready to protest. Margaret shot her such a sharp look that it stilled her tongue.

Once they were halfway back to the tower, Margaret leaned in. "He said the boy belongs to the Lord of the Isles. My husband will know where he lives and likely where he keeps his horses for training."

"Will you tell your husband the truth?" Aelgith knew that Margaret had used secrecy and subterfuge in her efforts to free Aelgith's daughter Osgifu, keeping the purpose of their rescue mission a secret even from the king.

"I believe I will. He hates what the war has done to our people as much as anyone."

"Can I tell my daughter that her brother lives?" Aelgith's cheeks, once drawn and hollow with starvation, now flushed pink.

Margaret bit her lip, wondering how careful they needed to be. "I think so. The family can know but let's not have all the guards or other nobles find out. Some of them travel across the country to take messages and for various reasons. We don't want the information to reach the boy's captor."

"I understand." Aelgith was practically running back to the tower.

"Wait for me!" Margaret's dress was longer and trimmed with weighty gold thread. It required some management for her to navigate up the wooded hillside to the tower. Her servant Grizel, who often helped her with it, was inside the tower with the wet nurse and Margaret's new baby.

"Oh my goodness, I quite forgot myself!" said Aelgith, suddenly horrified and hurrying back to Margaret. "Running ahead of the queen like a foolish child."

"I understand," said Margaret with a smile. "You have good reason to be distracted and excited. I pray that you'll soon be reunited with your son."

She hoped that the lad truly was Aelgith's son. How crushing it would be to find the lad and have him be a different half-starved, lanky English boy with a birthmark. Still, there was a very good chance that it was Aelgith's son and she vowed to rest at nothing until they found the lad and retrieved him.

"Aelgith, you look as if you've just seen a ghost." Christina, Margaret's sister, looked up from her embroidery.

"I feel as if I have seen a ghost." Aelgith took up a seat near the fire where the women usually gathered.

Margaret's baby had fallen asleep at the wet-nurse's breast. Mairi stuck a finger gently in his mouth to break his hold on the nipple and handed the babe to Margaret. Little Edward was still too young to hold his head up, so Margaret cradled him in the crook of her arm. Grizel held her chair still while she lowered herself into it.

"We think that Aelgith's son might still be alive," said Margaret quietly. "And in captivity in the Western Isles somewhere."

Aelgith's daughter Osgifu gasped. "Oswin alive? But we were told he was killed alongside Papa." The girl had just turned fifteen. Since being rescued from captivity five months earlier, she'd filled out and grown almost two inches and looked like an entirely different person. "Is it true, Mama?"

Aelgith, still looking dazed, nodded. "I saw one of the horses stop exactly the way your brother used to train them. The horse trader then spoke of an English boy who'd trained the horses, tall and thin. I asked if he had a birthmark—" Tears sprang to her eyes. "Am I dreaming? Can my son be alive?"

"Reports of death in battle are usually accompanied by the return of the bodies," said Margaret. "But you never saw it?"

"No, the battle at Hastings was different...the greatest battle ever, they said. Hundreds—perhaps thousands—of bodies left scattered across the fields with no one to carry them home. All the defenders of our homes put to flight...." Aelgith's words caught in her throat.

"A terrible day," said Agatha, Margaret's mother, in her continental accent. "The end of the world as we knew it."

Margaret would have crossed herself but for the baby nestled against her chest, still fast asleep. His tiny hand rested on her arm. Her baby son had no idea that the future of the great House of Wessex—a five-hundred-year legacy of English kings—lay cupped in his chubby palm.

"Oh, Mama!" Osgifu flew to her and wrapped her arms around her mother's neck, long light-brown braids draping over her mother's slim shoulders. "Oswin still alive? It seems too much to hope for."

"He'd be twenty-one by now," said Aelgith. "A man. He was training to be a knight."

Margaret knew what it was like to have all your hopes and dreams vanish before your eyes. Her father had died—suddenly and mysteriously—only days after arriving in England to reclaim the throne of his ancestors at the invitation of Edward the Confessor. With his death the entire future planned for her and her family had vanished like smoke in a breeze.

But for them to come back to life? For an instant she imagined what it would be like if her father—known to most as Edward the Exile but to her as simply Papa—was to walk up the stairs and into the hall right now, with more gray in his hair but still tall and proud, with excitement in his kind eyes—

"How do we find out if it's him?" asked Aelgith, suddenly more animated than Margaret had ever seen her.

"I wish we could write to where he is and inquire for details but you know how things lie. He's clearly of great value to whoever commands his service and thus I fear we must be more circumspect."

"Like you were in finding me," said Osgifu.

"Yes. I've never met the Lord of the Isles and I know little about him."

"Is he one of the mormaers, like the Mormaer of Fife, who captured me?" asked Osgifu.

"I believe he's even more important than that. In fact as I understand it, his territory is not even part of my husband's kingdom, but a separate domain. This will have to be handled very carefully. I'll tell my husband everything and ask him how best to proceed."

"Perhaps he could lead a raiding party and seize him back?" said Osgifu hopefully.

"God forbid," said Margaret. "The last thing we want is to start a war between my husband and one of his allies. William the Bastard would love nothing more than that."

"So true," murmured Agatha, looking up from her stitching. "He might seize the opportunity to invade Scotland. But your husband is a master of diplomacy, despite appearances to the contrary."

With this barbed comment, she went back to her stitching.

"Mother! My husband is a fine-looking man."

"Did I say he wasn't?" said her mother with a smile. "I just said that he didn't look like the simpering toadies in the court at Westminster who'd divide the kingdom between them with a carving knife if given half a chance." She looked up at Margaret. "I like a man with a beard."

"Do you think your husband can arrange to go visit him?" asked Aelgith, looking frantic. She probably didn't like this urgent conversation veering off course.

"We shall see," said Margaret. "It's late spring and a good time to travel—if there is such a thing in this rainy land—so I plan to suggest that we arrange to go there as soon as possible."

"Oh my goodness," Aelgith fanned herself. "I can hardly believe it."

"This would be excellent news indeed," said Christina. "But perhaps it's best not to get your hopes up too high." Her sister was an expert in having one's dreams crushed.

Still, there was no reason to dampen this flame of hope in such dark times. "Surely there aren't that many people with a wine birthmark on their face who are also tall and thin and an expert rider? I think there's good reason to hope that your son Oswin lives." The tricky part would be extracting him out of slavery. "Let me talk to my husband and see what he suggests."

CHAPTER 2

$\mathcal{M}$argaret went back out to watch the horses, this time bringing Grizel as her attendant and leaving Aelgith inside to fuss over her baby. She didn't trust Aelgith to hide her feelings. The horses cantered back and forth in the open field, occasionally rearing up or dancing sideways under their rider to show their battlefield maneuvers.

Malcolm still stood next to the horse trader. Now she paid more attention to the man, who had a ratlike face and a cap that covered his hair. Short and wiry, with a weathered face, he could have been any age between thirty and sixty. In a yellowish tunic and leggings he was dressed more like an Englishman than a Scot or Irishman. "What is your name?" she asked in English.

"Eochaid, my lady," he answered, in heavily accented English. "I'm from Kells in Ireland," he continued, as if sensing her question. "But I've found the trade in horses to be very profitable here in these last few years."

"I can imagine." No doubt the trade in seized and stolen horses was as brisk as the trade in humans, and more openly practiced. For all the pour souls dispossessed by the Norman invasion, there were those who reaped a harvest from all the destruction—and this man was one of them.

"I have a fine black palfrey," he said, looking more at Malcolm than at her. "Safe and quiet and smooth as silk for a lady to ride." He gestured to a pretty black mare standing off to one side, held by a boy of about eleven. The boy started walking the horse toward them.

Margaret wondered which of her displaced country-women used to love this horse and kiss its soft nose and feed it handfuls of sweet grass. "What's her name?"

"Her name?" The rat-faced man looked amused. "Whatever you want it to be, I suppose."

"You don't give them names?"

"No, my lady. We don't get attached to them. Buying and selling is the game." He was speaking Gaelic now, and hers had improved to the point where she understood him quite easily.

The mare had a kind eye and a very long, thick dark mane. "She's a beauty," said Margaret softly, sliding her hand under the horse's mane to stroke her.

"What will you call her, my love?" asked Malcolm.

"You think we should buy her? We have some nice palfreys already."

She looked back at the pretty mare, wondering where she'd go and who would own her if she didn't buy her today. Would she end up tugging a cart of peat up and down slippery hillsides for the rest of her life?

Probably not, since she was likely quite expensive. Still… she could guarantee this beautiful horse a life of ease and comfort—such as those things could be had in these times. "I like her. I think I'll call her Maud. Her color reminds me of the night sky between Matins and Lauds."

Malcolm chuckled at this. "We'll take her."

"Should one of the lads put her through her paces?" asked Margaret.

"I trust Eochaid not to sell the King of the Scots a dangerous horse for my wife. He knows that would be bad for business. Still, Duncan!" He called out to his son, who sat on top of a chestnut mount nearby. "Come here and ride this horse so Margaret can see how she goes."

"Can I pull you aside for a moment, husband?" She wanted to make sure they gathered all necessary information from the horse trader before he loaded up his sacks of silver and left Dunfermline.

"Yes, my dove." He kept one eye on Duncan, who rode the palfrey around the edge of the field. She was a smooth-gaited horse, very quick and quiet, just as promised. "What's on your mind?"

Once they were out of earshot, Margaret spoke low. "Remember how Aelgith asked him if the lad who trained the gray horse to stop like that had a birthmark?"

Malcolm looked confused for a moment, then seemed to remember. "Yes, and then she fainted. Has she recovered?"

"Aelgith's son is a tall, lean lad with a gift for training horses and a birthmark on his face."

Malcolm frowned. "I thought he was killed in battle."

"She never saw his body. It was just a report from a man who claimed to see it. What if her son lives and was captured and taken to where the gray horse was retrained?"

"And you want us to go there and obtain his freedom at any price?" said Malcolm brightly.

"You understand me so well, husband." Was he mocking her? "Aelgith has become a dear friend to me. Can you imagine if you thought one of your sons was dead then you received news that he lived—and labored in captivity?" They both watched as Duncan rode the black horse by and gave them a cheerful wave. "She's lovely!"

"Thanks, my lad, you can take her to the stables."

Malcolm turned back to Margaret and drew in a deep breath. "Eochaid said the gray horse came from the Lord of the Isles."

"Yes," said Margaret cheerfully. "So we know where to find the lad. Can you arrange for us to visit him? The weather is perfect to start the royal progress."

"I'd planned to go north to drain the coffers of those troublesome but entertaining men of Moray this summer."

"Surely a trip to the Isles would be an interesting diversion? I'd love to see more of this beautiful and wild country."

He laughed. "It's wild all right, out in the far west. And a lot of water and hills to cross. You may find the journey to be more than you bargained for."

"I doubt it will top the journey from Hungary to England, every night wondering if our royal procession would be attacked by bandits." Margaret still had nightmares about the long and fearsome voyage made when she was an impressionable girl.

"Bandits know better than to harry the King of the Scots. The Lord of the Isles, however, may present more difficulties than an entire gang of bandits."

"Why's that?"

"His father died the same year that you and I were married so he's new to ruling and likely wants to prove himself. His father was a force to be reckoned with. If the lad learns that he has something I want—someone I want—he may drive a very hard bargain."

"Do you have something he wants?"

"My kingdom," said Malcolm cheerfully. "I haven't met with him since he's taken hold of the reins, but being young and brash—by all accounts—he probably considers himself capable of ruling it."

"Oh dear. Will it be unsafe to travel there?"

"We'd be far safer at home in our stone tower but what is a king who stays safe in his feather bed? Perhaps my concerns about him are a good enough reason to enter his territory and establish my authority."

"I don't like the sound of this at all. Could it start a war?"

"Sometimes convincing someone you're going to start a war is the best way to prevent a war. In truth I need him as an ally against William."

"That sounds like rather risky diplomacy." Margaret glanced back at the horses. Would all their lives be at risk if they traveled into this fearsome lord's remote and barely accessible territory? "Perhaps you could simply send a messenger with an offer to buy the boy and see what he says."

"No, my dear. You've put the idea into my head and we shall act on it. I shall request an invitation to visit him and you shall have an opportunity to see the ragged westernmost edges of my kingdom, where it meets his."

Margaret's stomach was tying itself in knots. "I'm not sure this—"

"Do you trust me?" Malcolm took her hands in his.

"Of course, husband." As if she could say anything different. In addition to being her wedded husband, he was King of the Scots. One thing still concerned her. "Are his lands very great in size?"

"If you count the watery parts of them," said Malcolm with a grin. "His main courts are on the Isle of Man and the Isle of Islay."

Margaret wasn't sure where either of these lay but she didn't like the sound of them at all. "So we'll have to travel over sea? And what if we travel all the way there and Oswin is in a different part of his territory?"

"Hmmm….Let me ponder this and I shall find a way to make sure that he meets us near the border of my own lands

—in a place accessible by foot and hoof—and that the boy is there as well."

AELGITH GREW impatient as the days went by and they'd heard nothing back from the Lord of the Isles. Malcolm had sent him a long letter, written by a scribe on the finest vellum and carried by a contingent of four of Malcolm's trusted men.

"Did he ask about my son in the letter?" she asked anxiously, looking up from her embroidery as they sat by the fire one evening.

"I don't know what he said in it."

"He didn't read it to you?"

"He didn't discuss it with me at all until after it was dispatched. He composed it alone with his scribe." Margaret found that rather irksome. Why had he not consulted her as to the wording? "He told me to trust him."

"Ah, yes," said her sister Christina, looking up from her prayer book. "A woman must always trust her husband, even as he leads them over a cliff. That's why I'd rather be a nun."

"Christina!" said their mother, Agatha, sharply. "Trusting in your husband is little different than trusting in the Lord."

"Which is why you trusted Father to bring us to England only to have him die a few days later," said Christina. "You trusted him to bring us safely to the royal court where he'd become king. Instead he lead himself and us into a trap."

"His illness was very unfortunate," admitted Agatha, for the hundredth time. "But he was not poisoned!"

"Some people say he was," said Christina. "Not in front of us, but I've heard there are whispers. If Papa had lived he'd have been Edward's successor as king, and old Earl Godwine couldn't have put his son Harold on the throne in his stead.

King Edward's wife Edith was Harold's sister…does that not strike you as rather coincidental?"

"Are you accusing dear Queen Edith of killing our father?" asked Margaret, horrified by the turn this conversation had taken. While the subject of their father's untimely demise did get broached from time to time, Christina had never gone this far. All the men were away feasting at a local thane's hall and the servants, other than Grizel, were downstairs so they had a rare chance to speak freely. "Edith was like a mother to us."

"Only because she had no children of her own," said Christina. "She tried to push our dear mother out of the way so she could guide and shape us in her own image."

"Nonsense, darling," insisted Agatha. "I was quite happy to welcome the queen into our lives. I refuse to believe she had any ill intent toward your dear father."

"I suppose you have to tell yourself that or you'd go mad," said Christina softly, and without a hint of malice. "Such a cruel twist of fate is hard to survive."

"Mother has raised us to possess her rare resilience," said Margaret. "And I feel sure that a certain amount of optimism is a crucial part of it. Aelgith, you must fan the flames of your optimism and keep hope alive that your son will soon be here with us in Dunfermline, safe and well."

Aelgith attempted a smile. She wasn't good at fakery and her delicate features tended to show every emotion. "What if we never hear back from the Lord of the Isles?"

"Then perhaps my husband will invade and seize his lands," said Margaret cheerfully. "But that won't happen. We shall hear back."

"Well, I'm not going with you on this voyage to the back of beyond," said Christina. "If we could go in a wagon I wouldn't mind but having to sit in a saddle for hours every day makes my behind hurt just thinking about it."

"Christina!" said Agatha again. "Don't say such crude things. You'll do whatever Malcolm wants you to do."

"He's not my husband."

"No," said Margaret. "But he is your king."

MALCOLM'S MEN finally returned about two weeks later with a reply from the Lord of the Isles. Shortly after dusk, when the family was gathered around the table for the evening meal, a guard climbed the stairs to the hall with a scroll in his hand.

"A sealed scroll," said Malcolm. He took it and broke the wax seal. "I was rather expecting a verbal message of invitation."

"What does it say?" asked Margaret impatiently, after he'd read it and had a moment to ponder it. His furrowed brow did not offer reassurance. "Can we go visit him at once?"

Malcolm drew in a breath and looked up from the scroll. "Why yes, we can. There's a surprise, though."

"What's that?"

"He's made a proposal of marriage for your sister Christina."

Silence descended on the table as everyone turned to stare at him.

"What? How does he even know of her?"

"Well, I mentioned the members of my family that I intended to bring with me. In the past I've visited one of his father's households with a party of men and the accommodations and entertainments were....unsuitable for a visiting delegation of noblewomen. So naturally I mentioned your mother and your sister—" He paused and licked his lips. "I wasn't anticipating that he'd see this as an opening for a marriage proposal."

Margaret now looked at Christina, who stared at him in wide-eyed horror. "He knows nothing about me," she said, almost breathless. "Why would he make this strange offer?"

"You're a princess of the ancient house of Wessex and sister to the Queen of the Scots," said Agatha cheerfully. "Which makes you a marvelous marriage prospect."

"But for all he knows I could be two foot tall and covered in warts!" protested Christina.

"I may have used the word lovely to describe you and your mother."

Agatha smiled at Christina. "You are lovely, my dear."

Christina looked doubtful. "Who even is this man?"

"He rules over a mighty fiefdom," said Malcolm. Margaret could almost see his thoughts running wild under his thatch of hair. "Some call it a kingdom. He's not an unsuitable match. A marriage between our houses would be advantageous. Most advantageous."

Christina's spoon had fallen from her fingers and clattered on the table. "You can't be serious."

Margaret wanted to grab her sister's hand and reassure her but she sat across the table from her. "Don't be so quick to reject this proposal. Perhaps it would be sensible to meet him and assess his qualities as a husband." She turned to Malcolm. "Right?"

Malcolm pursed his lips in an odd manner that she hadn't seen before. "Indeed."

"What do you know of this man?" asked Christina. "What is his name when he's not being called by his title?"

"Fingal Mac Gofraid."

"What a peculiar name." said Margaret. Christina looked like she was about to cry. "We need to make this journey to find Aelgith's son," said Margaret. "Or at least to see if the lad really is Aelgith's son and Osgifu's brother. Why not at least get to know this Fingal and see if he would make a suitable husband?"

"I feel like I'm being sold into slavery," said Christina. "What if I don't want to marry him?"

"If you don't want to marry him, you won't have to," said Malcolm.

"What if that risks starting a war?" asked Margaret. Some said that Malcolm was so furious when Margaret wasn't delivered to him as originally promised when she was a teen, that he'd invaded Cumbria to express his anger. She'd never risked asking him because the question sounded too conceited.

"Peace in the Kingdom of Alba does not depend on your sister Christina's marriage prospects," said Malcolm. "I consider it a rather interesting offer."

"What does he look like?" asked Christina.

"It's been some years since I've seen him, truth be told," said Malcolm. "I'm more familiar with his father. But I think I remember him being tall, with dark hair. He's probably only two or three years older than you."

"I suppose that's encouraging," said Christina.

"Shall I take that as an insult?" asked Malcolm cheerfully. "Your sister says she appreciates the maturity that comes with my great age."

"I'm less concerned with his age than with his character," said Christina primly.

"Oh, so that's why you asked how he looks?" said Margaret with a smile. She could see her sister Christina's horror fading as her mind opened to the prospect of at least meeting this tall, dark youth.

"What if he doesn't find me to his liking?" asked Christina. "He may think I'll be as beautiful as Margaret and then be disappointed when he sees me."

"You are every bit as pretty as I am," said Margaret. "Oh

dear, that sounds awfully vain, doesn't it? I'm sure many would say you're far prettier than me with your thick dark hair and those soulful eyes of yours."

Christina had larger breasts, for one thing, and curvy hips, but Margaret certainly wasn't going to mention those at the table within hearing of the servants and guards. "Most men prefer a petite beauty to a tall stick-figure like myself."

"I prefer the term willowy," said Malcolm. "But she's right that you're a great beauty in your own right. I'm sure Fingal will be delighted with you."

Color now filled Christina's cheeks. Margaret couldn't tell if she was embarrassed or delighted by this onslaught of compliments.

"This proposal of marriage," said Agatha. "Must it be accepted before we visit?"

"Oh no," said Christina. "Surely we can wait until I meet him."

Malcolm unfurled the scroll again. "I would like to propose marriage to your wife's sister, Christina. If the marriage is acceptable to you, the wedding can take place during your visit to my lands."

An uncomfortable feeling unfurled in Margaret's gut. "Is he suggesting that we can only visit if we agree to this marriage?"

"No," said Malcolm definitively. "The Lord of the Isles does not set terms for my friendship with him. I am King of the Scots. I'll send word that our party will arrive and take up marriage negotiations."

"What if I don't agree to this?" said Christina in a sudden panic. "I might still want to be a nun."

"Either you have a vocation, or you don't," said Agatha. "That you're suddenly considering marriage tells us that you're not fully intent on being a bride of Christ."

"I'd rather be a bride of Christ than the bride of some rough warlord living on a windy crag."

"I might have said the same," said Margaret sweetly, with a wry glance at her husband. "But the crag isn't even all that windy thanks to the tree cover."

Malcolm laughed. "And we rough warlords have our finer qualities."

"We must prepare a trousseau," said Agatha, suddenly animated. "Thank goodness those two French tailors are still here. I shall put them to work on it at once."

Margaret glanced at Christina to gauge her reaction to this. She looked stunned, staring into the fireplace. Her whole life path had changed in an instant. But had it changed for the better?

CHAPTER 3

The following day, Agatha launched into preparing the trousseau. She held long conversations with the tailors, two impish brothers from the lands where France met Flanders. They protested with horror at the idea that such a wealth of vestments be prepared in just a week or two.

Margaret sat with Christina, listening to her read from a book of psalms. Their mother interrupted without ceremony. "Preparing the trousseau will take some time," said Agatha. "Perhaps we can put the journey off for some months."

"But that will delay our finding Oswin," said Aelgith, who sat nearby embroidering a length of ribbon for the abbot's vestments. "What if he's sold to Ireland or worse?"

"Aelgith is right," said Margaret. "Time is of the essence if we're to find Oswin and free him. The trousseau can follow us. Surely the marriage preparations will take a few weeks and they'll arrive by then."

"What if I don't want to marry him?" asked Christina, for perhaps the twentieth time.

"Try to look on the bright side and stop worrying about

what could go wrong," said Margaret. "You may find him delightful and look forward to the marriage. I hope my own happy example inspires you."

Christina looked skeptical. "I'm honestly amazed that you and Malcolm get along so well. You seem so different."

"Becoming a wife is a journey. I have to consider my husband's needs before my own, which is a blessed mortification to my sometimes willful spirit."

Christina now looked even more doubtful. "You have him wrapped around your little finger."

"I most certainly do not. And besides, perhaps soon you'll have the Lord of the Isles wrapped around your little finger." She studied Christina's unadorned hands. "We need to put some rings on those fingers. Here, try this one." She pulled a gold band set with a tiny ruby off her middle finger.

Christina took it with some reluctance and tried it on every finger to learn that it only fit on her left pinky. "My fingers are fat."

"They are not! We shall have some new rings made for you. I've already asked the goldsmith to melt down some rather ugly old cups I found in my husband's trunks and—"

"His chests of stolen treasure?" asked Christina.

"Yes," said Margaret, rather defensively. "Raiding for treasure to share with one's loyal men is just an unfortunate aspect of being a king." She was still trying to convince herself of this. "And some of it will be made into a marvelous cup and paten for the new abbey we're building. But there will be plenty left to make a few pretty rings for your lovely fingers."

"You know I don't like ornamentation as much as you do." Christina looked at her plain hands, where the one ring looked rather incongruous. "I rather hope the Lord of the Isles is plain and pious and would prefer a less decorated bride."

"That's a fair point," said Margaret. "We know so little about him. But let's try to be prepared for all eventualities."

"I shall miss you terribly," said Osgifu to Christina. Everyone turned to stare at her since Osgifu didn't speak often. She was still traumatized by her experience of being captured and enslaved. But she and Christina had grown close while stitching together, and she said she enjoyed listening to Christina read aloud from her prayer books. Sometimes when they sat quietly she said she could imagine that William's invasion of England had never happened and she was still sitting quietly by her hearth in Hampshire.

"I don't know why you should miss me," said Christina, suddenly animated. "You could stay with me as my lady-in-waiting."

Osgifu's eyes widened. Her mother, Aelgith, gasped and looked like she wanted to say something, but held her tongue.

"Why not? It's not a crazy idea. Aelgith is my mother's friend and lady-in-waiting and you shall be mine."

"I'm not sure Aelgith and Osgifu want to be parted so soon after their reunion," said Margaret. "They've only been reunited since Christmastime. Let's not get ahead of ourselves. They shall both come with us and any such decisions can be made once we have a better idea of how things lie."

THE BIGGEST DILEMMA THEY FACED, and one that caused Margaret more grief even than the prospect of her dear sister marrying a foreign warlord, was whether little Edward should come on the journey. Still only a few weeks old, he was past the lying-in period when he must be kept away from strangers, but he was still very small and delicate.

Edward had a dusting of golden hair and had recently started to dazzle them with a glorious toothless smile, but he wasn't close to being able to sit by himself. He would have to be carried in arms. If they were able to travel by carriage, Margaret and the nursemaid and her mother and sister and Grizel could have sat together in relative comfort, out of the wind and rain.

But here in the northern lands there were almost no roads to support carriage wheels, especially over long distances. Around Dunfermline, some farmers used hand-carts to bring their goods to market but most used pack animals. Malcolm had laughed at the idea of trying to navigate a wheeled vehicle through the steep and marshy terrain they'd encounter on their journey west.

Agatha was insistent that Edward stay behind. They'd gone into Margaret's chamber to speak in confidence. "He'll be fine. I left all of you children at our estate for weeks at a time when your father and I attended the summer court or the winter court in Hungary."

"Perhaps you could stay behind to take charge of him?"

"And not meet the man your sister is all but betrothed to marry? I'd be failing in my duty as a mother if I don't take the measure of this Fingal Mac Gofraid."

Margaret sighed. "I understand. Truly I do. I can't imagine marrying little Edward off one day, but the prospect of leaving him with the servants does frighten me." The nursemaid and even Grizel were out of earshot. Margaret didn't want the staff to get an idea that she didn't trust them. "Aelgith is the only one of my ladies-in-waiting who's raised a child, and she must come with me. The other girls are young and silly. They dote on Edward, but would they know when to call for the doctor?"

"The nursemaid is a mature woman who reared five of her own children."

"Two of them died."

"Of scarlet fever. That was hardly her fault."

"What if a deadly sickness sweeps through Dunfermline while we're away?"

"With the king and queen gone and not a soul visiting the hall? Little Edward will be safer than if you were here."

"I suppose you're right. Still, it feels awful! Like I'd be leaving my own arm behind." Her breasts still ached and occasionally—when Edward cried—they'd suddenly dampen her shift. She'd nursed him for his first two weeks, and enjoyed it thoroughly, but then her mother had told her that it was time to hand him to a wet nurse.

She'd protested but her mother had warned her that her breasts would keep leaking until she weaned him and how could she entertain a table full of grand guests, or go on a journey, if her breasts had a mind of their own? Margaret, who took her royal duties very seriously, was forced to agree.

Now, several weeks later, her breasts still occasionally protested their separation from her baby. And her heart and mind recoiled from the prospect of spending weeks away from him. "I can ride in a sidesaddle and hold him," she suggested.

"Malcolm's warned us that the terrain is difficult. What if he falls from your arms? He's safer here."

"Perhaps I could wrap him to my back like the peasant women do when they're out in the fields with their babes?"

"You are not a peasant woman. And what if you were to fall off and land on top of him?"

"Could Grizel and the nursemaid travel on foot alongside our party?"

"In that case it might take us weeks to get there instead of days. In fair English weather that wouldn't be so bad, but you've been here long enough to know that the weather is changeable and prone to rain squalls at almost any time of year. And Malcolm said it's even more so in the west."

Malcolm had made it seem as if it rained there every day and was blowing a gale half the time as well. She wondered if he was trying to stop Christina from getting too excited about her prospective marriage.

Now that she and her mother were alone, Margaret seized the opportunity to ask a question that had been bothering her. "Do you think this could be a good marriage for Christina?"

Agatha's noble bearing had carried her through many a crisis and Margaret always admired it. Her mother lifted her chin. "I think it might be. With England fallen, and her enemies swarming to savage the corpse, there's a shortage of suitable husbands for an English princess. I'd rather have her living a few days overland journey to the west of us than far away over the rough sea in Norway, married to some fish-smelling jarl."

Margaret couldn't help chuckling at this description. "You do make a good point. Malcolm insists that it's a short journey if we travel fast. We could see her regularly, which is never guaranteed when a sea voyage is involved."

"I shall see what I make of this Fingal Mac Gofraid when we get there. If he's a nobleman and not a savage, and if Malcolm is in favor of the match, I'm inclined to support the marriage. I'd like to see Christina have the joys of marriage and family rather than be locked away in a cloister. Wouldn't you?"

Margaret inhaled slowly. "There's safety and security in a cloister. Marriage is more of a gamble."

"Well, I think we've managed to throw a very fine set of dice in getting you married to Malcolm." Her mother took hold of her arms and rubbed them. "And perhaps your sister is destined for such happiness as well."

~

THEY'D ARRANGED to meet the Lord of the Isles at his easternmost manor, a place of very ancient habitation called Dunnad Fort. Apparently one of his favorite hunting grounds, it lay just past the border of Malcolm's kingdom and could be reached without crossing any large bodies of water.

Their journey to the far west edge of Malcolm's realm set out on a rainy Tuesday morning at the beginning of June. "We could wait until the rain stops," suggested Margaret, as moisture sparkled on the manes of the horses gathered in the courtyard. "Won't our baggage get drenched?"

"It's wrapped in waxed cloth," said Malcolm. "If we wait until it stops raining here it will only be raining on the far side of the next hill we cross. This is but a light mist."

Margaret hated leaving her newborn babe behind, but she didn't want him out on the windy moorland, exposed to the elements.

"Edward is so tiny that he won't know whether you're there or not," said Malcolm. "We'll be back long before he speaks his first word."

"I know." She knew that as a queen she had to keep her motherly sentiments tucked away behind a facade of duty. A guard helped Margaret into her saddle. Due to the length of the journey and difficulty of the terrain they'd decided that the women should ride astride and command their own horses. While this was somewhat unconventional for a royal party, Malcolm assured them that they'd encounter few people on their journey other than the ones he'd arranged to stay overnight with. They'd be able to travel farther and faster than if all the women sat in awkward sidesaddles and their horses had to be led. Sitting astride had required some adaptation of their clothing which had drawn the attention of the tailors away from Christina's trousseau.

Margaret turned back to Aelgith and Osgifu. "Are you comfortable on your mounts?"

"Yes, my lady," they both replied in unison. Aelgith continued: "Osgifu learned riding from the same old knight who taught Oswin to have such a deft hand with horses."

They moved out of the courtyard and down the wooded hill away from the tower. Their procession consisted of five and twenty horses bearing the household and her husband's trusted knights. A phalanx of servants and sturdy ponies brought up the rear with their baggage. The servants wouldn't be expected to keep up the pace but would follow in their footsteps and likely arrive at their destination a day or two later.

Margaret rode on her new black mare, Maud. She'd been thoroughly tested by both Malcolm's sons and her brother Edgar, who threatened to steal her because he liked her so much. Her brother Edgar now rode beside her on a fancy bay charger, another new purchase. He'd insisted on coming to meet the Lord of the Isles and have a say in his sister's marriage.

Margaret wasn't thrilled about Edgar coming. He had a way of turning every conversation to his seemingly futile quest to regain the throne of England. Malcolm had become good at managing his expectations. She'd learned to keep her thoughts to herself and let the men handle him.

They walked for a good deal of the journey, up and down hills, through shallow streams and shadowy forests, across stony ground. When they came to an open plain or a gentle valley, they picked up speed and gained time. Margaret's smooth-gaited horse covered the ground without bouncing, and she enjoyed the freedom of feeling the wind whipping against her face as she flew through the countryside.

That night they rested in the hall of a local thane. Malcolm had sent an advance guard out to secure nighttime accommodations for them along the way. The lady of the household welcomed them with cups of warm ale and freshly prepared meat stew. The hall was damp and drafty, despite a blazing central fire and the relatively balmy spring temperatures, but their bed was warm and dry. Margaret slept like a babe in her husband's arms.

In the morning her first thoughts were of her own babe, and whether his tiny chubby arms would reach for her and find her absent. Instead she tried to turn her thoughts to God and ask his blessing for their journey and the safe return of Oswin to his mother's arms.

The second day of travel went less smoothly. Christina's horse went lame and she was mounted on Osgifu's instead. Osgifu was moved onto one of the guard's horses and the guard onto a pack horse, like a dance of switching partners. The lame horse was left to rest and be cared for in a local household, where they'd retrieve him on their return.

Still, they made it to their appointed resting place and again enjoyed the rustic hospitality of the local nobles.

As the journey wore on, both the weather and the terrain grew wetter and wilder. The hills became rockier and steeper and the need to find and follow passes in between them meant that each mile of journey took longer. They went an entire day without seeing a single soul and Margaret wondered if they'd even find the settlement where they were supposed to sleep that night.

But sure enough, a bearded thane and his household awaited them, took their soaked cloaks to dry by the fire, and entertained them with music, stories and well-cooked fare.

Margaret watched the people serving them food and sweeping the floor and shooing the dogs away from the table, and wondered if any of them were enslaved or refugees like Aelgith and Osgifu. The mother and daughter were very quiet, intimidated in this strange household, almost as if they might suddenly be put to work washing the dishes or mending the linens.

At no point was Christina's impending marriage mentioned. That night, as she lay in bed with Malcolm behind heavy curtains, she voiced her curiosity.

"Is the marriage proposal a secret?"

"If news of it travels, it will become a matter of pride for the Lord of the Isles to secure the marriage. Christina's refusal would become cause for great offense and possibly start a war."

"Did you really invade Cumbria when King Edward didn't send me to marry you as he'd promised?"

"I don't want to talk about it," he whispered. She could hear a hint of humor in his voice. "But a man does not like to be jilted any more than a woman does. All's well that ends well."

"Perhaps you convinced William to invade England so I'd finally fulfill the pledge?" she teased.

She felt Malcolm's chest shake with silent laughter. "Even I'm not that much of a risk-taker. Though I am grateful to him for delivering you into my waiting arms."

"Surely Fingal Mac Gofraid will be offended anyway if Christina refuses him."

"No doubt, but his shame will be private and thus less hot and fearsome."

Something else had been nagging at Margaret. "Is there a possibility that he'll refuse her after he meets her?"

"No." Malcolm nuzzled against her.

"You sound so sure." Was she a faithless sister to doubt Christina's ability to win over her prospective husband? "She can be prickly and difficult. And for all her beauty she doesn't perhaps fit the image he may have in his mind of an Anglo-Saxon princess."

"He proposed to your sister for her status, not for any of her personal attributes, about which he surely knows nothing."

"Word doesn't spread among the men of your kingdom about myself and my family?"

Malcolm seemed to consider this for a minute. "His lands are far away and there's little contact between his men and mine."

"The horse trader's movements suggest otherwise."

"Well, if he knows more of her than I suspect, he may have invited the proposal for her personal qualities. Though I suspect his aims are purely political."

"That sounds awful. Like she's a pawn."

"Are royal marriages ever different?"

"You married me for my status alone?"

"Not just your status." He squeezed her, stirring warmth inside her. "Also your royal bloodline, so I might enrich the heirs of Scotland with the cunning and courage of wise King Alfred."

Margaret pushed him away, half playful and half offended. "You cared nothing for my heart and mind?"

"I knew little of them when I asked your great uncle for your hand in marriage. They've been a delightful surprise."

"I suppose peasant women are luckier. They at least get to know their swain and are more likely to be pursued for who they are rather than what lands or titles they bring."

He chuckled. "Don't be so sure. I suspect many a peasant bride is married in the hope that she'll bring her mother's talent for weaving or her father's prized cow with her."

She sighed. "I suppose you're right. Poor Christina's so anxious. She's panicked that he'll want her and she'll have to go live the rest of her days in a remote settlement, far away from all of us. And she's equally terrified that he'll meet her and reject her and she'll never live down the shame of it."

"Such is the fate of all noblewomen."

She swallowed. "You can see why many of us prefer the cloister. It's a way to avoid the extremities of fate that pursuing a marriage can thrust us into."

"Is it better to spend your life locked away from the world, and never to know the joys of marriage and children?" Malcolm kissed her softly.

"I don't know." She wrapped her arms tighter around him. "I miss little Edward horribly. And I don't even know how long I'll have to be parted from him. I feel like I left a piece of my heart behind in the castle of Dunfermline. What if he sickens and dies while I'm away?"

"Don't say such terrible things. Look at all that you and your sister and brother and mother have survived—and you're all here today, hale and hearty, under this strange thatched roof."

"Losing my father so suddenly, and just as he was about to fulfill all his fondest dreams and become King of England, has robbed me of any lasting sense of safety."

"Well, I intend to restore it by bringing you a long and happy life in my arms." He held her close. "And I wish only the best for your mother and sister and brother, as well as our children. Our babe is thriving, I'm sure of it. And I myself shall decide if the marriage is suitable for your sister."

"How will you know?"

"Trust me."

Can I? Part of Margaret wanted to relax into her husband's reassuring strength and let him take control of everything. But her busy mind always tried to seize the reins and guide events.

She inhaled slowly. Her husband had two decades more

life experience than she did. He knew his country and his countrymen.

But she did not intend to let Christina enter into any marriage unless she could be confident that it served her sister well.

"Relax and get some sleep," whispered Malcolm. "We have hard travel tomorrow."

"Harder than today?" How was this supposed to relax her?

"The beauty of the scenery will enchant you." He squeezed her gently.

"While my horse is scrambling down the face of a cliff?"

His chest rocked against her as he chuckled. "Possibly."

THE NEXT DAY'S ride took them along the seemingly endless shores of a shimmering lake named Loch Awe. It also brought wind and rain—both in far greater quantities than they'd seen thus far. When they stopped for the night—at another remote settlement of mossy thatched huts that passed for a nobleman's domain in this country—they were all drenched and chilled to the bone.

The hall was a long, narrow one, of Norse design. The men were welcomed to the high table next to a roaring central hearth. Platters sat piled high with roasted meat and servants poured flagons of ale.

Margaret begged for some time for the ladies to dry and change their clothes before they feasted. The lady of the house—a middle aged woman in a veil and wimple that covered almost everything but her warm hazel eyes and a parsnip-shaped nose—ushered them to a quieter area of the long hall where a brazier warmed the air.

Servants rubbed their hair dry with clean cloths, then

combed it out and re-braided as they warmed themselves by the fire. "Does it always rain this much here in the west?" asked Christina. The lady of the house had returned to the high table to pour out the ale, as custom required, and no one among Margaret's women or their servants seemed to know the answer. None of them had ever been this far west before.

"Poor Oswin," said Aelgith. "To think of him out in this chill, wet weather, day in and day out."

"Don't worry about things we're not sure of, Mama," said Osgifu. "For all we know he may have a comfortable place to sleep near the fire if he's a respected horse trainer."

"And we're not even sure if the lad we seek is your son," said Margaret. She didn't want Aelgith and Osgifu to have their hopes risen so high that dashing them would crush their spirits. "Though I certainly hope it is."

At the high table, Margaret gathered that this thane's domain was the westernmost fiefdom in the Kingdom of the Scots. By midday tomorrow, at the latest, they would leave the safety of Malcolm's realm for the lands controlled by the mysterious Lord of the Isles. "Is it true that we'll rest in Fingal Mac Gofraid's hall tomorrow night?"

"Indeed we will," said Malcolm. "We're so close we could call out to him with a ewe's horn."

"I'm scared." Christina took hold of Margaret's hands.

"Your fingers are ice cold! I've never seen you like this before."

"I've never risked being married off to a stranger who lives in a land dangling half-way off the edge of the earth."

"Trust in the Lord," said Margaret, trying to remind herself to do the same.

Christina pouted. "Our father trusted in the Lord to accompany him on his journey to Westminster, only to find himself poisoned and—"

"We have no proof that he was poisoned. All we know is that the Lord called him home to Heaven. Is that such a terrible fate?"

Christina blinked. "I shall remind myself of that. But somehow being called home to Heaven seems an easier fate than being married off to a stranger. What if I'm a terrible wife? What if I can't bear children? What if his mother hates me and finds fault with everything I do?"

"I believe both of his parents are dead, so at least that last concern can be banished from your mind," said Malcolm.

"Oh dear, then who shall guide me in the customs of the place?"

"Stop looking for things to worry about! Remind yourself that our foremost purpose in this journey is to search for Aelgith's son, Oswin. If a favorable marriage for you can also arise from these circumstances, then that is an added bonus. By the end of the day tomorrow, we shall know more."

CHAPTER 4

*R*ain dogged them for the rest of the journey into Fingal's lands. As they drew closer, the drops sliced at them like cold knives. "I can't say I'm excited about moving here," said Christina, as water dripped off her eyelashes and the constant wind whipped at her cloak.

"I'm sure it's not always like this," said Margaret, trying to be reassuring but wondering if she'd ever be warm again. "Malcolm, how much farther from here?"

"We're almost there."

A sweeping glance across the rugged landscape showed no sign of human habitation, not even a single wet sheep. Suddenly, however, about twenty horsemen appeared from behind a crag, cantering toward them and sending clods of earth flying into the air.

"Halt!" cried Malcolm, to his own party.

"Are they brigands?" asked Margaret, in a sudden panic. Even well-trained guards might easily be bested on unfamiliar turf.

The men slowed to a trot and rode right up to them, barring their path. "The Raven welcomes you to his lands,

King Malcolm," cried one of them. "Follow us and ye shall soon be warm and dry."

Margaret shot a glance at Christina, not sure whether to be relieved or alarmed.

"I can't have him see me like this, soaked to the bone," said Christina, looking down at her rain-darkened cloak.

"Don't worry, I'm sure we'll have time to prepare before you meet him. But why did they call him The Raven?" Her second question was for Malcolm.

"I've not heard him called that before," admitted Malcolm. "Maybe he's taken on the new name to sound more fearsome."

They rode along a high treed ridge, then a strange thing happened. One by one, the men leading them dropped out of sight, over the brow of the ridge.

"I'm glad we're riding astride," she muttered to Christina. "How steep is this hill going to be?" Malcolm, leading the party, disappeared next, and didn't turn to shout a warning, so she rode boldly on, albeit at a walk. As they crested the ridge and descended over it, she saw a wide, spreading valley in stark contrast to the dark heather-clad hills they'd just crossed.

Green and verdant, the valley floor stretched out before them. Smoke rose from a large cluster of thatched dwellings. Around them Margaret could see cows and sheep, some grazing and some in small enclosures.

The path they rode down led them sideways along the face of the hill, so the going wasn't too steep. As they descended toward the valley, the wind let up, blocked by the surrounding high ground.

The lord's long hall was clearly visible, with smoke rising from the steep thatched roof. As they drew closer, a tall man emerged from it and walked, quite slowly and casually, toward the approaching party.

"It's him," whispered Christina. She looked excited; which cheered Margaret, whose optimism that a marriage could be made had diminished with each rain-soaked and windswept mile they rode.

As they descended to the valley floor, carpeted with lush green turf that looked nothing like the surrounding landscape, the rain suddenly stopped. Margaret wondered if a golden ray of sun might emerge through the dense bank of gray clouds to complete this miracle, but perhaps that was too much to hope for.

The tall man walked up to Malcolm's horse and greeted him. Malcolm jumped down and shook his hand—using both hands—and then turned to introduce Margaret and Christina.

Margaret held her breath as he looked at Christina. Would he betray disappointment or otherwise dash Christina's hopes and poison this first meeting? He was indeed a young man, with bold, beardless features. But he didn't look juvenile or foolish. His long face and aquiline nose gave him a noble and imposing appearance. Raindrops sparkled in his hair, which was almost jet-black.

"You are even more beautiful than rumors suggest," he said, staring at Christina as if smitten. "Allow me to help you dismount."

He held out an ungloved hand. Christina looked panicked, as she was usually in need of considerably more help to dismount with a great weight of wet cloak around her. Luckily the guards rushed into position and managed to ease her to the ground where she took his hand in her gloved one, and he kissed it extravagantly.

Margaret glanced at Malcolm, who watched the proceedings with a satisfied smile. Margaret dismounted, also with considerable help, and The Raven led them all into his hall. Margaret begged for a few moments for the ladies to refresh themselves, and they were shown to a private area behind a carved screen, where servants waited with cloths to dry them and combs and bowls of warm water.

"He's anticipated our needs," whispered Margaret. "And I'm not sure we need to whisper since I doubt many of the servants speak English."

"Unless they're enslaved English nobles," whispered back Christina.

"You're so right!" Margaret glanced back at Aelgith and Osgifu, who stared around them, trying to take in the strange hall. Aelgith hurried forward to help Grizel remove Margaret's wet cloak and wring it out. Osgifu was already unbraiding Christina's hair and asking the servants to bring her dry ribbons and a dry gown. "I didn't see many horses. Where are they? I hope his horse trainer is here. I had Malcolm ask that we be able to meet him."

"Fingal is very handsome," said Christina, looking rather dazed. Two servants re-braided her hair and wrapped it in fresh white ribbons ornamented with silver thread. She'd donned a sky blue gown that complemented her complexion and her cheeks were a flattering pink from exposure to the wind.

"You look lovely." Margaret kissed her on the cheek. "And he's not too hard on the eyes, either."

Christina giggled. "I got a little…frisson…when he touched me to help me off the horse."

"Oooh, that's a good sign. I felt the same when I met Malcolm. It shocked me! I was only expecting to sacrifice myself for the family honor, not feel my body come alive under his touch." Margaret had whispered the last part, and looked around. "Are you ready?"

"I think so."

Margaret had also donned a new gown, a modest gray so as not to outshine her sister, and Aelgith and Osgifu were also coiffed and radiant in new dresses she'd had made for them. They presented an elegant royal party, as she intended.

Back in the hall, her brother Edgar roared with laughter, apparently at something The Raven had said. Ale flowed freely and the high table was laden with plates of unfamiliar delicacies. Their host rose and greeted Christina like she'd just descended from a cloud surrounded by angels. He seated her in a great throne-like chair next to his own, along one side of the table. Malcolm welcomed Margaret into a similar seat next to his own and the rest of their party found their places around the table or hovering nearby.

The Raven...Margaret found the strange appellation suited him better than his given name, with his beaky nose and dark shining eyes and glossy almost-black hair. Christina glowed in the light of his admiration as he showered her with compliments. Margaret thought he was laying it on a bit thick but her sister seemed delighted and filled her plate with proffered morsels.

Margaret helped herself to a piece of white fish and some braised parsnips, which were the only things she recognized on the table. Her stomach was in knots worrying about both Christina's future and their prospects of finding and retrieving Oswin.

The Raven asked both Margaret and Christina questions about their childhood in Hungary. He seemed fascinated by the sound of the Hungarian language—coaxed out of them with some embarrassment on their part—and wanted to know about the famed horses and the great wooden castles of the region. Christina even sang him a little Hungarian song that seemed to charm him. Agatha, quiet as usual in strange company, watched with a contented smile on her face.

The Raven regaled Edgar with tales of the wild exploits of his countrymen—originally hailing from Dublin, it seemed—

and the ferocious battles his family had fought to secure his territory. Edgar grew increasingly excited, probably at the prospect of harnessing this race of fearsome warriors in his quest to retake the throne of England.

Were any of his tales true? She couldn't claim to understand the politics of this region where Vikings and Gaels fought over the most remote and rocky outcrops as if they were Jerusalem itself. Still, Malcolm also looked pleased with how things proceeded as the evening wore on.

A bard recited a long epic poem while a lad strummed on a small harp, and Margaret rejoiced in the absence of piercing pipe music. Lulled by smooth ale and the warmth of the fire, she found herself growing sleepy and wondering when they could all go off to their beds.

A woman's angry voice cut through the fog of sleepiness. Margaret looked up to see a tall woman, with long pale braids like her own, berating their host at his own table.

"What is she saying?" she whispered to Malcolm. Who didn't respond. He was listening intently. The woman spoke fast and with an unfamiliar accent, so Margaret, couldn't grasp the words.

The Raven barely acknowledged her, and gestured for his guards to remove her. "I don't even know how she got in here," he said to Christina. "I apologize for the disturbance."

The woman struggled against her captors, voice rising. Margaret noticed that her gown was of fine quality, and she wore gold rings on her fingers and a thin gold band around her head, over her veil. "She's a noblewoman," whispered Margaret to Malcolm. "What's going on?"

After the woman had been removed, Malcolm cleared his throat. "What was all that about?"

The Raven waved his hand dismissively. "You know how women can be."

Margaret's spine instantly stiffened. "How exactly can

they be?" The words shot from her tongue before she could stop them.

"I know just what you mean!" chimed in Edgar. "Making assumptions that have no basis in fact."

Christina's glow of passion had dimmed significantly after this exchange. Margaret could tell she wanted to ask some probing questions, but could hardly do so without seeming to pry.

Margaret felt no such compunction. "What did she say to you?"

"Oh, a lot of nonsense!" The Raven waved his hand and now the dreaded pipes struck up a tune that drowned out further conversation. He leaned and whispered something into Christina's ear that restored her smile and soon her eyes were sparkling again.

Margaret looked at Malcolm. "Could you understand that?" she whispered.

"A jealous woman," said Malcolm softly. "Nothing more."

This did not soothe her particularly. Of course a powerful man like The Raven would have women interested in becoming his wife. He was five and twenty, perhaps, so likely not a virgin.

"Have you been married before?" she asked, over the cacophony of pipes, as the question occurred to her.

"Never, my lady," he replied, with an easy expression. "I've been waiting for the right woman to come along."

Malcolm patted Margaret's thigh as if to tell her to calm down, and she put her hand on his to reassure him that she would. The Raven returned to sweet-talking Christina, who now seemed unperturbed by the interruption.

Margaret sat watching the assembled company. Like her husband's, his court was a mix of men from various parts of the region, though speech was mostly in Gaelic. His hall was large and well built, with carved beams and woven hangings that gave it some aspect of a palace. Servants heaped and stoked the central hearth and kept the air warm and dry despite the constant rain that she glimpsed every time someone opened the door.

Aelgith looked tense as a pulled bowstring and barely picked at her food. Osgifu glanced around her as if bandits might spring from the shadows at any moment. No doubt she'd do the same if her child or her sister was held captive somewhere close by.

In her own hall, she could bid everyone adieu and head for her chamber to retire and pray, but as a guest it was polite to remain at the table until their host decided the evening was done.

Finally the evening wound down, with The Raven kissing Christina's hand and wishing her a pleasant sleep with beautiful dreams. Margaret managed not to roll her eyes. The Raven's extravagant flirtations were falling very flat on her but seemed to be having their intended effect on Christina, who sparkled like a polished gem in the candlelight.

At least Christina would be sharing a bed with Aelgith so there was little chance that The Raven would try to make a guest appearance in her "dreams." Still, Margaret was more than a little tense as Grizel undressed her for bed. With the hall quiet as a woodland glade now everyone had retired, she waited until she was in bed and behind the curtains to speak to her husband.

"I don't trust him."

"You don't trust anyone," said Malcolm. She couldn't see his expression in the dark but she could imagine his look of amused resignation.

"There's nothing wrong with being wary."

"Your sister seems to like him."

"He's making an effort to woo her. Still, that does nothing

to soothe my fears. What did that woman say when she came in? Could you understand her speech?"

"She spoke of broken promises," said Malcolm, his whisper more serious. "Which is concerning, I agree."

"Do you think she was betrothed to him?"

"Breaking a betrothal is a very serious matter," he murmured. "I don't imagine he'd have taken such a step."

"Unless he spied a better opportunity, such as the sister-in-law of the King of the Scots."

Her husband's silence spoke volumes. "I could hardly fault him in this instance. And the girl is young and beautiful and will make a new match."

They lay in silence for a while. Then Margaret leaned closer to him. "A man who'll break a promise to one woman will do it to another."

"If he breaks any promises to your sister, he'll have me to answer to. He knows that. He's not a fool."

"How do you know?" Margaret had learned to be wary of male charmers—including her brother and her husband's brother—who were used to toying with women. Sometimes their exploits were nothing short of foolish and reprehensible, despite neither of them lacking in intelligence. "You knew his father but you know little of him other than what we've gleaned today."

"No promises have been made yet. We're here to get to know him better. For your sister to evaluate the life he promises her."

"That reassures me." She knew how quickly these contractual marriages could progress. She even knew women who'd been betrothed and married to men they never met before their wedding day. "My sister's happiness is as precious to me as my own."

"I suspect you'd sacrifice your happiness in an instant to feed the poor of the parish."

Margaret shoved him gently. "You give me far too much credit. But speaking of the poor, it would be interesting to see how our host cares for them. That would teach us about his character and his commitment to the teachings of Jesus."

"I'd imagine that caring for the poor is entrusted to the abbot and his almoner and at best our host contributes funds to pay for such."

"Then it would be interesting to see how well-funded they are. My first concern is to locate Aelgith's son—if he's here, that is—and perhaps we can ask to explore the local area to see what kind of environment my sister would be living in."

"Our host may well have a program of activities planned for us."

"Indeed. And I shall begin my own program by rising before the household to pray in peace."

She looked forward to the quiet pre-dawn hours as an opportunity to pray for the safe discovery—and retrieval—of Oswin.

Malcolm pulled her close. "Get some sleep. We've had a long journey and need to restore our energy."

Margaret didn't want to admit that she was too impatient to sleep. Anxious for her sister and fearful for Aelgith and Osgifu's hopes, she suspected she'd be counting the moments until she could rise.

But somehow the inviting circle of Malcolm's arms around her back relaxed her. His breath, warm on her neck and growing slower as he drifted into sleep, lulled her and soon she found the cares of the day drifting up to the thatch like smoke.

~

MARGARET ROSE in the dark to pray and found Grizel already waiting outside the bed curtains. Grizel helped her dress and together they picked their way through the hall by candlelight. The fire had burned almost out and the boy charged with stoking it woke as they passed and rubbed his sleepy face. One of the hounds by the fire stirred and growled and Margaret cringed at the possibility of waking the entire household, but luckily he turned his head and went back to sleep.

The guard by the door startled awake, opened the door for them and pointed them toward the chapel. A thin curl of smoke rose from the thatched hut that looked just like another house.

"No church bells?" The predawn silence was eerie, and a light mist of rain dampened their cloaks during the short walk. She was relieved to find several holy brothers preparing for the early service. The abbot welcomed them to the front of the small space and gave Margaret a cushion to kneel on. All this reassured her that this might be a place Christina could live a decent Christian life.

Still, her heart ached at the thought of losing her sister's constant company. Rather than saying a prayer that her sister's progress toward marriage would proceed as smoothly as possible—as one might expect—she instead prayed that today they'd see into the heart of The Raven.

Was Fingal a man who could be entrusted with her sister's life and future happiness? Malcolm had reassured her that his status was high enough to make him a suitable match in that regard. And she knew that an alliance with the Lord of the Isles would go a long way to securing peace between this realm and her husband's kingdom.

Still…Christina had suffered a lot during her short life, especially the sudden and agonizing loss of their beloved father. Since the fall of England and their flight to Scotland, her sister had retreated into herself. She seemed to have given up all hope of a happy future and rather wished to hide herself in a cloister, the better to escape the trials of the world.

They emerged from the chapel into an eerie purple predawn mist that cloaked the entire settlement. They could barely find their way back to the hall through it, and the wind blew out Grizel's candle. "This primitive place makes Dunfermline feel like Westminster by comparison," whispered Margaret.

"The servants seem to be well treated," said Grizel, clearly hoping to reassure her.

"Are any of them slaves?"

"I don't know. I didn't like to ask."

"Did you find out anything about the horse-boy?"

"I learned that he's staying over the river where the grazing is better for the horses at this time of year."

They were now within hearing distance of the hall so Margaret turned the conversation to the fog, which was now starting to lift and transform the collection of low thatched structures into something resembling a fairy kingdom.

A guard had already started to open the hall door for them, when an eerie sound pierced the silence. "What was that?" Margaret turned and looked behind her. "It sounded like a scream."

Another sound, a thin wail, rose through the air. It was coming from the direction they'd just left, behind the chapel. Margaret glanced at Grizel and they both started running toward the sound.

CHAPTER 5

The wailing noise came from a woman running through the morning mist into the settlement. "She's dead!" she cried. "Face down in the water!"

People emerged in the doorways of surrounding huts. Margaret glanced back to see guards stirring out of the hall. They pelted past her and Grizel as yet another eerie shriek from someone out of view rent the foggy air.

All around them people were donning their cloaks and coming out into the mist, to follow the haunting cries.

"She's dead," cried a woman's voice, thick with pain. "Dead in the river!"

Margaret gathered her long skirt and hurried after the crowd of people now heading off into the fog. She picked her way over the unfamiliar ground in this eerie scene, crossing a flat field of sheep until they arrived at the banks of a river that seemed to wind around the flat open field where the settlement lay.

People gathered on the near bank, huddled over and blocking her view as she approached.

"Make way, make way," cried Grizel, doing her duty. They

turned to stare at Grizel—a stranger with an unfamiliar accent—then at Margaret whose embroidered cloak marked her as—not one of them.

The guards roughly pushed the people back, barking orders, and Margaret could now see the fully clothed body of a young woman lying on the bank of the river.

She had an unsettling sense of recognition. "Is that the girl from last night?" The intruder had only interrupted their dinner briefly, then been whisked away, so Margaret hadn't paid close attention to her features. The long pale braids were similar though—and the ribbons wrapped in a criss-cross pattern down their length. "I think the woman last night had pale green ribbons like this." Though she couldn't be sure as the hall was so dark and smoky.

"I think you might be right," said Grizel, peering at her. "Though I admit I didn't get a good look at her since I was just coming back from brushing out your cloak and only saw her leave."

The dead girl's face looked ghostly white and her pale eyes stared unseeing at the clouds above. Margaret crossed herself at the chilling sight. "May God rest her soul." She was young, probably under twenty, and beautiful. "Her gold circlet and finger rings are gone."

"I wonder if they were swept away by the river," said Grizel.

"Who pulled her out?" asked Margaret, of the local people. Though she asked the question in Gaelic, they all stared at her as if she'd started speaking in tongues. "I know I'm a stranger, but I'm wife to the King of Scots, who is visiting your lord."

She glanced behind her to see if Fingal or Malcolm had been summoned. What was taking so long? She had no authority to take charge of an investigation. "Who pulled her from the water?" she asked again.

"I did, my lady," said a lad of about eleven. "But I couldn't do it by myself, so Cormac helped me. He pointed at an older man with white in his hair. Both were soaked from the waist down and the lad was shivering in the chilly spring air.

"Where did you find her?"

"She washed up near the bank of the river. I think her dress or cloak caught on the rocks here." He pointed at a stony area of shoreline.

Finally, Malcolm strode up with Fingal. "What's amiss here?"

Margaret turned and explained what she'd learned so far.

"A cruel sight for a fine lady to rest her eyes on. You can go inside now," said Fingal.

"My wife has a keen eye for detail," said Malcolm. "You might wish for her to help discover what came to pass."

"I think we can all see what came to pass," said Fingal. "A woman has drowned."

"Is she the woman who interrupted our evening meal last night?" asked Margaret.

The thin morning light illuminated the dead girl's expressionless face and some wet tendrils of hair around her brow.

Fingal peered at her for a moment as if trying to decide. "It is."

"Who is she?" asked Margaret, wondering what kind of story he might tell. The woman had been an embarrassment and an annoyance last night. If he'd made promises to her, did she represent an obstacle to his prestigious marriage to Christina?

"Agnhilda Finnsdottir," said Fingal. "She's the daughter of a local thane."

"Why was she here last night?"

"This is a private matter that should not be discussed in front of all," muttered Fingal.

"She was wearing gold last night, and now it's gone," said Margaret. "Perhaps someone killed her for it."

"Or perhaps she fell in the river and drowned on her journey home, and they were washed away by the water," said Fingal. He was looking anywhere but at the dead woman's blank, staring face.

The villagers peered into the water, perhaps looking for signs of the missing gold.

"She might have drowned herself on purpose," said Fingal. "Some women do that."

Margaret stared at him. He was making a great effort to blame her for her own death. Did this point the finger of guilt at him? Margaret felt a wave of sorrow for the poor, dead young woman who'd come between a powerful man and his ambition.

Did he kill her himself to get her out of the way? If so, she must prove it to be sure Christina didn't marry a killer.

"Have her carried to the counting house," he said. "And lay her on the table there until she can be prepared for burial."

"Where's her family?" asked Margaret.

"I shall send for them."

"Surely she didn't ride here by herself last night?" asked Margaret again. It was extraordinary for a woman to interrupt a meal in a noble's household but it would be far stranger if she'd arrived in the dark of night by herself.

"I don't know." Fingal looked around, seemingly confused by the whole situation himself. Perhaps he's not guilty. She resolved to keep an open mind. Her fears for Christina's future mustn't sway her judgement. "Let's go back inside and break our fast."

"First let's examine the bank for any sign of a struggle or to see if she fell in." Margaret didn't want to abandon the scene so quickly. "If she was going home wouldn't she be on a horse?"

"No," said Fingal. "This river is too deep. A horse would have to swim it, so the rider must dismount and get wet along with it. She'll have crossed by boat."

"Where's the boat for her crossing?"

Fingal pointed to a wide wooden vessel tied to a dock further down the bank toward the settlement.

"Who manages the boat?"

"There's a boatman." Fingal frowned. "Where's Cormac the boatman?"

A man emerged from a hut near the boat and Margaret saw at once that he was the older man who'd helped the lad pull her body from the water.

"I was just drying myself off, my lord," he said quickly.

"Did she cross over the water in your boat last night?" asked Fingal.

"Aye, she crossed twice last evening, coming and going."

"Was she alone?"

"She was. And we made it safely to the other side, and then I returned to my bed."

That's very odd, thought Margaret. Did this young woman—adorned with gold—intend to cross these rugged moors in the dark by herself? "You let her walk off into the night by herself? Did you not think it odd that she was alone?" she asked the boatman.

"Not really. Plenty of people pass alone over the river, men and women."

"In the dark?"

"In winter it's dark much of the time, so yes."

"A man wouldn't dare rob a woman in my territory," said Fingal suddenly. "I'd have his throat slit as soon as look at him. Safest kingdom in Christendom."

Margaret felt this as a slight to her husband. Still, she wasn't sure she'd recommend that lone women wander about her husband's kingdom after dark with their gold on display. Almost every month there were reports of pilgrims on their way to the shrine to St Andrew being set upon by robbers. The culprits were rarely caught.

"You carried her safely across the river, in your boat?"

"Aye, my lady," said the boatman. "And returned home to sleep in my bed."

Unless the boatman was lying, the girl had been killed on the other side of the river. "Please take us to the other side to see if we can find where she was killed."

"She probably slipped on the bank and fell in," protested Fingal. He looked at Malcolm. "Surely your wife would prefer to break her fast in the hall while my men investigate?"

"I'm afraid that my wife is unlikely to enjoy a bite of food until she's satisfied with seeing all the important details." Margaret wanted to kiss him but restrained herself.

Fingal looked irritated but ordered the boatman to take them across. The boat was big enough to hold six or eight people sitting on two benches, so Margaret, Malcolm, Fingal and two of Fingal's men climbed in. The boatman steered them across, using a long pole to propel them. The river was wide but shallow—only a few feet deep at the deepest part of the crossing—and the current slow, so Margaret reasoned that it likely didn't bring the body from too far away.

Fingal offered Margaret his arm as they disembarked on the slippery bank on the far side. Despite yesterday's constant rain there was a good deal of foot traffic visible. "What settlements lie in this direction?" she asked.

He reeled off three long and incomprehensible names. She hoped Malcolm understood them. "And is the woman from one of those places?"

"She's from Slockavullin."

"Someone must tell her family that she's died," said Margaret. She hadn't heard Fingal issue such an order and was starting to wonder at it.

Fingal looked surprised, but told one of his guards to deliver the message. The man did his best to hide his dismay at the task, and set off toward the nearby hills. Margaret could see smoke rising from behind them against the white sky.

They walked along the bank looking for signs of footprints, but there weren't any, just a straightish track of churned earth and mud heading in the direction that the guard had gone. "Everyone walks directly toward the hills?"

"Unless they're fishing along the banks," said Fingal.

"She wasn't killed here from the looks of it." There was no sign of a scuffle and she didn't see a single footprint beyond the well-trodden track. "Who are her family?"

"She lives with her brother Drostan, his wife Gyda and their two children. Her brother inherited the estates when her father died four years ago."

"What of her mother?"

Fingal paused. "I think she went away to a convent when her husband died."

"Are there other siblings?"

"She had an older brother who drowned on a voyage to Ireland and her older sister is married to a minor thane who lives on one of the islands."

Margaret steadied herself before asking the next question. "Did you ever make a promise of marriage to her?"

Fingal stopped walking and looked at her. "Do you think I would ask for your sister's hand in marriage if I was bound by verbal agreement to another woman?"

Yes.

She managed to keep her expression neutral. Or at least

she hoped she did. Malcolm was quiet, but she could feel his reassuring strength beside her. She also knew that Fingal was likely only bothering to respond to her questions because he was there.

"Sometimes there can be misunderstandings," said Margaret cautiously. "Where an idea is floated—a marriage imagined—but no formal agreement arrived at. Is it possible that there was some confusion over your intentions toward the girl?"

"Her father wanted me to marry her, back when he was alive, but there was never any agreement." Fingal looked ahead at the hills.

This answer told Margaret everything she needed to know. The girl believed that The Raven was her intended husband. She'd likely got wind of his proposal to Christina and turned up in a desperate effort to salvage the prestigious marriage her father had planned for her.

Except that was not how these things were handled. The girl's brother should have arrived, perhaps with an armed party, and threatened war and bloodshed over her honor. Perhaps her brother had refused to challenge his overlord.

She glanced at their host. Even on short acquaintance she could tell that Fingal Mac Gofraid was not a man to be trifled with. And his threat about slitting throats was likely not a hollow one. Perhaps the girl's family had decided that sending her alone—as if on a girlish whim—would offer less of a threat to their lives and property. But what had they hoped to gain? A payment of some kind?

Or had the girl developed a foolish fancy for The Raven? That was perhaps more likely to explain her rash behavior than a broken contract. And it might even explain her taking her own life by jumping into the river…

But it didn't explain where her gold jewelry had gone.

"She could have been killed anywhere," said Fingal suddenly. "And I won't let a king starve while wondering about it. We'll return to my hall and break our fast."

Margaret couldn't really argue with his logic. And she hadn't forgotten their true purpose in being here—to look for Aelgith's son. She nodded her agreement and they walked back to the ferry boat.

"I'm sorry that your visit has been marred by such a sad event," said Fingal. "Don't worry, though. I shan't rest until the woman's killer has been found and punished."

I shan't either, thought Margaret. Especially since The Raven himself was at the top of her list of suspects. He had good reason to make a former betrothed disappear in a hurry to clear the way for a royal marriage. He might even have stolen her gold—because why not?

AFTER THE MORNING MEAL, Malcolm had arranged for them to go look at some horses, in the hope that their trainer would prove to be Aelgith's son, Oswin. Instead of them all venturing out over the same river in the same ferry boat to the good spring grazing where the horses were being kept, The Raven had arranged for the horses to come to his hall.

The horses arrived wet and stamping, having apparently swum across the water, and the men with them were partially wet as well, perhaps from sitting astride them during the swim. The horses were corralled, and rubbed dry by servants, and the men came into the hall to dry off in front of the fire. They'd removed their boots and hose to ford the water and now put them back on again.

There were three of them but in the dim light of the hall and with their backs to her, Margaret couldn't make out their faces or even tell how old they were. She'd told Aelgith and Osgifu to hide themselves in the shadows far from the fire, and to master their emotions and be sure not to let out a cry of recognition or otherwise betray their connection.

Heart pounding, Margaret walked up to the lads and addressed them. "My husband bought a fine gray gelding recently and was told that one of you trained him to stop so fast that you could ride him hard to the edge of a cliff."

The three of them looked at each other and two of them gestured to the third. "I'm glad you find the horse to your liking," said the man. He spoke Gaelic, not the English she'd hoped for. Aelgith's son was from Hampshire.

Still, she spoke Gaelic as well these days, so that didn't mean much. And he did have a reddish birthmark that covered part of his nose. "How did you teach him to stop like that?"

The young man had light brown hair and a kind face. "I just convince the horse to listen to me and practice until he understands."

The other two men muttered something about how even he doesn't know how he does it. That he had a gift. Margaret ached to turn and look at Aelgith's expression to see if she recognized the lad. She was almost sure this boy must be her son. She wanted to get them busy so she'd have a chance to whisper in Aelgith's ear. "Could you show us the horses you brought with you?"

"Give the boys a chance to dry off!" said Malcolm. "The horses aren't going to gallop away."

Fingal agreed. "Come lads, come have ale and oat cakes." As the men were led to a table over to one side of the hall, Margaret snuck a glance at Aelgith—who was frozen like a statue, staring. Osgifu had taken herself away into a corner, hiding her face, perhaps overcome by emotion.

It's him.

She had to handle everything so carefully. If The Raven knew how much Oswin meant to them, he might drive a very hard bargain to part with him.

"Aelgith, could you help me re-pin my veil?" she asked, as if it was pulling on her hair.

"Yes, my lady," managed Aelgith, clearly barely able to manage herself.

Margaret led her behind the screen to where she and Malcolm slept. Aelgith started to unpin her veil and Margaret leaned in. "Is he the one that spoke to me?"

Aelgith nodded. Her face was taut. "It's odd to hear him speaking a foreign language, and he's very thin, but it's certainly him—you can see the distinctive birthmark."

"When I saw that I was sure it must be him. God be praised," whispered Margaret. "My veil is fine. We shall find a way to bring him home with us, but we must be very circumspect."

"Should I let him see me?" asked Aelgith. "I want him to know we're alive and that I've come to find him."

"We don't want to endanger him or have him moved away from us. I suspect you should stay hidden for now."

"But how I long to look on his dear face again!"

"I understand." She took Aelgith's hands in hers and squeezed them. "You shall stay right by my side." Together they re-pinned Aelgith's veil so that it hid her face well before they rejoined the group.

Malcolm sat at one end of the long table with her mother, who was twittering on about something to make polite conversation. The Raven and Christina sat at the other end. She couldn't quite hear what passed between them but it left a smile on Christina's face. The Raven reached for her hand, looked into her eyes, then studied her fingers like a fortune-teller. Christina blushed and giggled like a foolish girl.

Margaret cringed inwardly. How many other girls had he

practiced this studied charm on? Everything about this man rubbed her the wrong way. She was already sure he hadn't led a life of monkish celibacy, and now she suspected he might have left a trail of broken-hearted women with ruined reputations in his wake.

After the horsemen were fed, dried off and dressed again, they all headed outside. Malcolm took her arm and they walked to an open area of heath to watch the men put the horses through their paces. The Raven already led Christina in the same manner, as if she were his wedded wife.

They watched the three boys—or men, really—ride the horses around, showing off the airs they'd trained into them —rearing and spinning, as you might in battle to evade or attack an enemy, galloping and stopping suddenly, maneuvering sideways and backward.

All the horses and riders showed considerable expertise, but the one they'd identified as Oswin was in a class of his own. He governed his horse with invisible skill, coaxing it to feats of speed and athleticism that outshone his companions.

"Is it the horse that excels, or its rider?" asked Malcolm, after seeing each of them perform the same movements at The Raven's command.

"Let's ask them to trade mounts, and we shall see," said Fingal.

The men switched horses, rode around a few times to adjust to their mount, and then Fingal asked them to each perform a different maneuver. Once again it was clear that Oswin—who had not yet been introduced to them by name —was the superior horseman.

"I'd like to take that skinny lad back home with me," said Malcolm. "The one with the rose on his nose." Margaret's heart leaped as he spoke. Malcolm knew exactly why they'd made this journey past the rugged western edge of his kingdom. "I should like him to train my horses."

"As you can see, he's a trainer of great value, who can turn a horse into a fearsome weapon of war. And he's a slave, with no rights of his own, so mine to control. Such a slave has considerable worth to me, as you can imagine."

"What is your price?"

CHAPTER 6

Margaret held her breath. She could imagine the mix of hope and terror that must be surging through Aelgith's veins right now. She wondered if Oswin had recognized his mother or sister, and if he knew how close he was to leaving this place with them.

The Raven lifted his chin and shone an almost-smile on Malcolm. "I shall gift him to you upon my marriage to the lovely Christina."

Margaret froze. How dare he equate the life of a lowly slave with that of a royal princess, as if this might be some kind of even exchange? She glanced at her sister's face to see if she felt the sting of the insult as sharply as herself.

Christina stood there wearing a beatific smile, apparently ready to receive the priest's blessing on her marriage to a man she'd only just met.

Even Malcolm seemed rather stunned by his statement, and stared at the boy in silence.

"He's a nobleman by birth, you know," said Fingal. "English, though he's picked up Gaelic like a native speaker. Sharp as a whip, he is. Could probably command an army if given

"

half a chance, which he certainly won't be!" The Raven burst into laughter as if this was a hilarious joke.

"He's a skilled rider indeed but I hardly think that his worth is equal to that of a royal princess of ancient lineage," said Malcolm finally. He'd voiced her thoughts exactly. No doubt he was as offended as herself by the proposed trade. Still, she could see how it wouldn't help any of them to insult The Raven or make him defensive or angry.

"A nobleman, you say," said Margaret. "From where does he hail?"

"God only knows," said The Raven. "But I suppose we can ask him." He beckoned the boy over to them. Margaret's heart beat faster as he rode toward the group. Aelgith and Osgifu stood behind her. Would he recognize his mother and sister? Or had the last five years changed them beyond recognition?

"Lad, what town or county do you hail from?"

"Chester, my lord." He spoke in Gaelic, even though The Raven had asked the question in English.

Chester? He was lying. That was nowhere near Hampshire. Margaret wondered why he might have developed a false identity.

"Do you speak English?"

"Yes, my lord." Now he spoke in English. He was starting to look nervous, and the horse, sensing this, shifted beneath him.

"Tell us about your noble family, lad." The Raven commanded sharply. Perhaps he was growing impatient with the young man's brief and dismissive answers.

"My father owned a manor that had been in the family a long time, probably hundreds of years. Our family was ancient but not titled."

Margaret knew that this part was pretty accurate based on what Aelgith had told her. If he'd been from a grander family, he'd have been wise to downplay it. The ancient enmity between the various peoples of this region could turn to cruelty very easily. And there was no question of a large ransom being paid for his safe return. Oswin knew as well as anyone else that the Hampshire and the England he knew had been smashed to pieces and his family along with it.

"How did you come to know so much about horses?" Margaret now regretting asking about his origins, which he'd apparently learned to obfuscate. She wanted to steer the conversation in a safer direction.

"I learned all I know from my father," said the boy. She heard a quiver of emotion in his voice. Now he looked past her, to where Aelgith stood, watching him from beneath her hooded veil. She saw something flash across his face —recognition?

Margaret needed to create a quick distraction. She wasn't sure how Aelgith would handle this mention of her dead husband, let alone her son seeing her for the first time in years. She hurried up to his horse and made a fuss of patting its neck.

Malcolm cleverly asked to see some more riding and soon the men were galloping around and Malcolm was bargaining for one of the horses. Margaret glanced at Aelgith, who now stood still as a statue, eyes fixed on her once-dead son who'd come back to life before her eyes.

AT THE MIDDAY MEAL, Fingal continued his campaign to charm Christina. He asked her for all sorts of details about their childhood in Hungary and she delighted in answering him.

"How come I didn't know half of this?" asked Malcolm to Margaret, at one point.

"I suppose you never asked."

Christina described the fine-boned, athletic Hungarian horses they'd grown up with and how different they were from the sturdy ponies and warhorses of England and Scotland. She even sang another little song about the Hungarian countryside that seemed to delight him. Christina did have a lovely voice.

Is he really falling in love with her? Despite her skepticism about Fingal's motives, Margaret found herself starting to wonder. Christina seemed happier and more engaged than she'd seen her in years.

The servants brought dishes that surprised her with their variety and sophistication: roasted fowl, rich sauces, honeyed pies and cakes and a sweet fruit compote. "Your cook is wonderful," said Margaret, after tasting a particularly delicious sweetmeat. "These dishes are as fine as anything we ate at Westminster."

The Raven grinned. "That's because my cook used to serve in the king's kitchens."

Margaret's heart sank. Another Briton conquered and enslaved to serve in foreign lands. "Ah, that explains it," she managed politely. "And spice traders travel to your lands?" She tasted seasonings that she knew came from the continent, if not even further away.

"They do indeed. They sail here after they stop near Dublin. Your sister shall not want for luxuries here."

Margaret looked at Christina, who looked back at her with a glow of excitement that awakened a flare of alarm low in Margaret's gut.

"Is there any news of the dead woman, Agnhildha Finnsdottir?" She said the name as if to remind everyone that she was a real person with a whole life story that had just been extinguished.

"My guard has informed her family and they will make

arrangements for burial," said The Raven, before taking another swig from his cup of ale.

"What of the investigation into her manner of death?" she asked. "We never examined the body for signs of how she died."

Fingal looked irritated. "Surely such details would upset her family. They can't bring her back to life."

Margaret looked at Malcolm in horror. "But if she was killed, her killer would then go unpunished."

"For all we know, she slipped into the river and drowned."

"I should like to take a closer look at her," said Margaret calmly. "And undress her to examine her body."

"Surely such a sight would—" The Raven trailed off, unable to even formulate a reply.

Margaret could feel Malcolm stirring next to her, wanting to tell her to leave well enough alone. Everything in her rebelled against letting this woman's manner of death be buried along with her in a cold grave.

If this man is a killer I must find out before he marries my sister. "Who will be summoned to look for evidence to present in a trial?"

"A trial?" The Raven looked mystified. "I can pronounce judgement on the matter myself."

Of course, thought Margaret. "Surely you don't settle every squabble between a miller and his customer, or between two farmers fighting over a spring?"

"My local thanes take care of such matters in their own territory. If the law is complicated then the Brehons preside. This particular settlement—a seat of the ancient kings—and the villages within a day's ride of it are under my direct control." He said it proudly as if he dared anyone to defy him.

Do I dare to defy him?

Her duty as queen was to support her husband. Her husband wanted good relations with this man who controlled the lands to the west of his own kingdom. She bit her tongue.

AFTER THE MEAL, Fingal wanted to take them for a walk to show Christina the beauty of his lands or some such. They donned their cloaks and headed out into a mercifully rainless and only slightly windy afternoon. Outside the hall, they found a commotion.

An older woman seemed to be arguing with the guards, as if she wanted to gain entrance to the hall but they wouldn't let her. She was well dressed, wrapped in a hooded cloak with a plaid pattern, which gave her an old-fashioned appearance, like a rustic peasant, except that her cloak and shoes were of good quality and not worn.

"What is she saying?" Margaret asked Grizel. They spoke too fast, in their heavily-accented Gaelic, for her to understand.

Grizel frowned. "I think I heard her say that a terrible crime has been committed and someone needs to do something."

Since the guards seemed to have no intention of letting the woman near their master—and since he was busy helping Christina don her gloves while describing the magical beauty of a nearby waterfall—Margaret approached. "My dear lady, what's amiss?"

The guards, who knew that Margaret was Queen of the Scots, took their hands off the woman. She tugged at her cloak to straighten it. "I'm the old nursemaid of Agnhilda Finnsdottir. I begged to see her before they wrapped her in the winding sheet. They said that she drowned but she has marks around her neck as if she was choked to death—bruises in the shape of great fingers!" The woman's gray eyes pleaded with her. "They want to bury her and told me to hush about it, but my dear little girl has been murdered!"

"This is shocking news." Margaret took the woman's hand. "Malcolm, Fingal! This woman has seen marks on the neck of the girl found in the river that suggest she was strangled!"

The Raven looked up from his ministrations to Christina with a look of mild annoyance. Malcolm walked toward her. "This is concerning news indeed. If she was killed there must be a proper investigation." He turned to Fingal. "Surely you agree?"

"Absolutely," said The Raven. He apologized to Christina that their promenade by his mystical lake must wait a short while. He strode over to the woman, who introduced herself again as Maeve and explained her role in the family.

"What does your master think of this?"

"He says she's dead and nothing can be done to raise her. But justice must be done if someone has taken her life. I was so worried about her. She left the hall last night saying she was going to the chapel to pray, then she never came back inside. I searched everywhere for her and she didn't return home at all. I sat up all night wondering what could have happened to her, and in the morning we searched all around the manor. And that's when they brought the terrible news."

"She was here in the hall last night," said Margaret, before anyone could fabricate another story. "She burst in while we were eating dinner."

"What?" Maeve seemed shocked. "Why would she do that?"

"I was hoping you would know," said Margaret. She glanced at Fingal. "She said something about broken promises."

Maeve looked confused. "She said she was going to ask

God for guidance. She never said anything about coming here to the hall."

Margaret wished she could get the woman aside to find out what she knew about a history between her and The Raven. She turned to Christina and Fingal. "Why don't you two go on your walk and I'll find out what she has to say." She said it brightly as if it was a matter of little importance.

Fingal looked hesitant—and frankly, so did Christina—but he suddenly decided that was the best course of action and invited Malcolm and Edgar to join them. Malcolm looked at Margaret, who nodded for him to go. This was an opportunity to gain more knowledge about her sister's intended husband, and the fewer people who were there to overhear, the more probing questions she could ask.

"I can see that you're upset," she said to Maeve. "Why don't we go for a little walk ourselves, so you can settle yourself and tell me what you saw." She smiled at the guards and asked for some space.

"Who are you?" asked Maeve.

"I'm Margaret," she said simply. "And I want justice for Agnhilda as much as you do. It's a terrible thing for such a young woman to lose her life before it's even truly started."

Maeve looked rather doubtful. Why should she trust her thoughts to this obviously foreign stranger? Margaret asked her a few questions about Agnhilda's childhood and family to get her talking.

Finally she approached the topic of keen interest. "Was Agnhilda ever betrothed—even in an informal way—to Fingal Mac Gofraid?"

"Well…" She and Maeve had walked a little way from the hall. The guards watched them but hadn't followed, so they were out of earshot except for a few nearby sheep. "There was talk of them marrying one day. I do remember that being the fond hope of her father. And her brother promoted the idea as well." She hesitated.

"I'd imagine he'd like his sister to be married to the most powerful man in the realm. What man wouldn't?"

"Exactly," said Maeve. "And they were becoming anxious to secure a marriage for Agnhilda since she was of age."

"How old was she?"

"Twenty-three. An age at which she should take a husband or risk losing the glow of youth and being called an old maid."

Margaret thought this was ridiculous. A woman was hardly teetering on the brink of cronehood at twenty-three, but both her mother and sister had expressed the same worries about Christina's prospects since she was the same age.

"Was he ever betrothed to anyone else?" she asked innocently.

"I'm sure I don't know, my lady," said Maeve. "Not that I've ever heard of. He was still young and seemed to enjoy the life of a single man, if the stories are true."

"What stories?" asked Margaret way too fast. Had The Raven bedded woman up and down the western coast?

"Well, I mean…" She looked like she regretted her words. "He's a handsome man and a great lord."

"He keeps a mistress? Or concubines?" She wasn't sure what word to use in Gaelic. This wasn't a topic that came up in her language lessons.

The woman swallowed and looked about. "I don't know, my lady. It's not my business."

"Do you think he might have…taken advantage of her youth and innocence?" She wondered if he'd taken liberties that might have led to her feeling entitled to him in some way.

"I can't say, my lady." Maeve looked unsettled. Perhaps

she didn't want to betray the confidences of her dead mistress.

"She came alone to the hall and the boatman said she crossed back over the river alone and in the dark."

Maeve's face turned pale. "She never!"

Margaret swallowed. "Did her family send her to plead her case, perhaps?"

"They'd never have let her go out alone at night."

"So it was her own idea."

Maeve looked down at the ground. "Don't tell anyone I said it, but I do think he'd whispered sweet nothings in her ear."

"And more?"

Maeve squeezed her eyes shut. "I can't believe she's gone. All that youth and beauty vanished in one night."

"I want to make sure that the one who killed her is identified and punished." Margaret turned and glanced toward the settlement to make sure no one had moved closer to listen. She could see The Raven, Christina and Malcolm standing off in the distance, backs to her as they admired a view.

Did it matter if Fingal had kissed Agnhilda, or fondled her? He'd clearly led her on and given her reason to believe she could be his bride. She must have got wind of Christina's arrival and its portents and hurried to plead her case before it was too late.

But who had killed her? Had The Raven wanted her dead so she couldn't claim him? If he'd taken her innocence, her family could force a marriage using the law.

Except that in his own lands Fingal Mac Gofraid was the law.

"Tell me more about the marks you saw on her. Did you see her whole body?"

"I did. I washed it with a soft cloth and combed out and re-braided her hair." Tears now filled the old woman's eyes.

"I can't believe I'll never look on her pretty face again. "The only marks I saw were the ones around her neck."

"Were there any signs that she'd fought with someone? Scratches? Her nails torn?" Margaret had sat through trials—at Westminster and in her husband's hall—and knew some of the details that were discussed as evidence.

"I didn't see anything like that, my lady. Just the bruises around her neck. Two big thumb marks right at the base." She pointed to the back of her own neck—wrapped in a scarf and her cloak—and shuddered visibly. "Great big man's hands, they must have been."

Margaret inhaled slowly. As a tall man—like her husband—The Raven certainly had large hands. But then so did many of his guards and no doubt others in the area. The boatman, for example, was a short but stocky fellow, with big hands callused by working his pole to punt the boat across the water.

Something struck her as odd. "The thumb marks were on the back?" Maeve nodded. "So whoever killed her was behind her when they strangled her." She'd never heard of that before. She did know of a case where a court page was garroted from behind by a jealous rival. "He must have been very sure that he could overpower her."

Another worrisome idea occurred to Margaret. She leaned in to whisper it. "Is there a possibility that she was pregnant?"

Maeve gasped. "How would a young maiden girl be pregnant?"

Margaret swallowed. "Perhaps...someone took advantage of her."

Maeve frowned. "Her belly was somewhat swollen...but I took it to be from the water she was found floating in."

"I'm sure that was it," said Margaret, not at all sure of it. She crossed herself. "My heart is breaking for you, and for her family. Trust me, I will make sure this matter isn't swept aside." Especially since Christina's happiness was at stake.

"When Agnhilda came into the hall she was wearing a gold band around her head."

"Yes, that used to belong to her mother. Very old it was, and very valuable. Where is it now? I'm sure the master will want it."

"I don't know. It was missing when they found her. And her gold rings as well. I noticed them when she interrupted our meal as they instantly marked her as a noblewoman."

As queen, her constant and often tiresome phalanx of guards and attendants announced her status. Still, as a representative of the royal house of the Scots—and of the great and ancient house of Wessex—she always made sure to attire herself appropriately. The girl had clearly wanted to signal to everyone in the hall that she was the daughter of an important family.

"Do you think someone killed her to steal her gold?" asked Maeve.

"It's certainly possible." *Or they may have stolen her gold to conceal their true motive.* "Can you think of anyone who may have wanted her dead?"

CHAPTER 7

Maeve stared at Margaret as if wondering what could have possessed her to ask such a question. Margaret wanted to ask her if she thought Fingal Mac Gofraid was capable of ordering her killing to clear the way for his marriage to Christina, but such an accusation would be a grave insult to her host and might even start a war between him and her husband.

"She lived with her brother and his wife. Did they get along well?"

"Very well, my lady," said Maeve sharply, as if insulted. Margaret wondered whether to believe her. As a loyal retainer who still lived in their household she'd hardly be likely to slander her benefactors, who perhaps seemed more like family members than masters to her.

"Did she have any male admirers who might have been jealous of her attentions?"

"I'm sure there were many men who admired her, but I can't think why they would take her life. If her gold jewelry was missing, it seems more likely that someone killed her to steal them."

Margaret wasn't so sure. Most bandits and robbers weren't looking for a murder charge. A lone woman in the dark, hampered by a long dress and cloak, would be easy to steal from. "Do you know of any bandits in the area?"

"The Raven would never allow such lawlessness to go unchecked."

Or would he? He didn't exactly seem to be combing the countryside looking for a killer.

Margaret glanced over to where Fingal, Christina, Edgar and Malcolm were walking back toward the hall. Right now Fingal was—perhaps wisely—making Christina his priority.

All the more reason for her to pursue justice for the poor dead girl. "Thank you for coming to report that you saw marks on her neck. That's certainly a significant finding. Let's go back to the hall."

"IT'S SO BEAUTIFUL HERE," gushed Christina. "We saw a waterfall dancing with rainbows."

For once it wasn't raining or blowing a gale, but Margaret kept that thought to herself. She liked seeing her sister so happy. She didn't think she'd seen Christina smile like that in…. Her heart sank when she realized she couldn't remember her sister glowing with such joy since their father died all those years ago.

She's falling in love.

"Let me guess," said the Raven, as they walked closer. "The girl's family is seeking compensation for their loss from the perpetrator?" He spoke half to Margaret and half to Maeve.

Maeve sniffed. "I came here of my own accord, my lord. The family is mourning. I wanted you to know that her neck was bruised as if she'd been choked to death. She didn't drown in the river but someone killed her and threw her in there."

"I shall have my guards ask everyone in the area if they saw a stranger in the vicinity. You may go home to the grieving family now." He waved her away.

Maeve wrapped her plaid cloak tighter around herself. She nodded to Margaret and started walking quickly in the direction of the ferry crossing.

"A very sad business," said Fingal, not looking very sad at all. "Let us call for some ale and a merry tune to brighten the afternoon."

Margaret glanced at Malcolm, whose face betrayed nothing of his thoughts.

~

Margaret was relieved to find Aelgith and Osgifu still sitting inside the hall. Both rose as she entered. "It's so dark in here I can't see to sew," said Osgifu. "Can we go outside?"

"Not yet," said Margaret. She was still afraid they'd try to sneak off to find Oswin. She glanced over at The Raven who was now commanding Malcolm and Christina's attention with a story about a recent hunt involving a mysterious white hind.

"I want to talk to my son," said Aelgith, eyes pleading.

"You can't, it would jeopardize everything." Margaret spoke in a whisper.

"But why would it? They already know you want him to return with us. Is it so necessary to keep a secret?"

"Yes, because otherwise our host may suspect—rightly— that we came here to retrieve your son rather than to pay our respects to him."

"But I don't even know if he's seen me."

"I fervently hope he hasn't, or he might start asking questions and jeopardize his own safety. You can see that he's adopted a false identity for some reason."

"But my heart aches for him to know that I'm still alive! And that I know he's still alive."

"I know." Margaret glanced at Osgifu. "And I'm sure you're yearning to hold your brother again. But we must act very cautiously." She hesitated for a moment. "Perhaps I could speak to Oswin, and let him know that you're alive and that we're working to bring him back with us. It's probably a good idea to let him know our plans in case he resists being sold to Malcolm and away from his friends here."

Aelgith nodded frantically.

"I'll go speak to them while they're still here." She suspected the horsemen would return to their quarters over the river before nightfall. "Grizel, come with me."

Margaret and Grizel went outside again and headed for the enclosures where the horses were now penned.

The pens had low turf walls that an athletic horse could jump quite easily, but the fine animals rested inside peacefully. She spotted the horseman sitting on the close-bitten grass a few yards away—unfortunately all three of them together.

How could she peel Oswin away from the others? She hazarded a guess. "Do any of you speak English?"

Oswin stared at her for a moment, looking reluctant, then perhaps remembered she was a queen. He rose to his feet. "I do, my lady," he responded in perfect English.

"Please attend me for a moment. I have some questions about the horses."

He glanced at the other young men as if to say, "what now?" then followed her as she walked away, asking innocuous questions about what the horses were fed and how they were kept. He explained that they kept them on the other side of the river as the grazing on this side had been eaten down by the milk cows and flocks of sheep.

Once they were out of earshot she stopped and turned to him and very quietly spoke. "Oswin?"

His eyes widened. "How do you know my old name?"

"I have your mother and sister here with me. I worried that you might recognize your mama so I had her pin her veil and wimple to cover her face. We're trying to arrange for you to come back to Scotland with us. Our host knows nothing about this, so you must keep it entirely secret and not tell anyone."

He swallowed. "I can do that." His face showed panic and worry rather than the joy she'd expected.

"Do you want to leave your life here?"

He hesitated. "It was a long, hard road to find myself here, so I do fear for my future in another place."

"My husband is the King of the Scots and has seen your skills. He wishes to give you a place training horses there." They hadn't actually discussed this, but surely it would make sense? A gift for training war-horses was like a bubbling spring of gold since a well-trained destrier was worth more than a fine house.

"I would dearly love to see my mother and sister again," he said tentatively, as if this was too much to hope for.

"She begged to come see you but I told her we must keep everything secret. We traveled to this area for the purpose of finding you, but our journey has taken on…other aspects and we'll likely be here for at least a few more days, maybe even weeks."

He looked confused.

"It's a big secret to keep, but I know that you're a knight of old England and can be trusted—"

"I'd finished my training and was soon to be made a knight but Hastings extinguished my hopes."

"You're a knight in your heart. As a princess of England, and now Queen of the Scots, I need your loyalty and your trust."

He bowed his head. "They are yours, my lady."

"Excellent. I suspect you will soon be Sir Oswin at my husband's court. But until then we must move carefully. Go about your duties as usual and don't breathe a word of this to anyone. Can you do that?"

"Yes, my lady. I am at your service." He did look more cheerful now she'd basically promised him a knighthood. She would have to convince Malcolm, but she was confident in her ability to do it. Her promise seemed to have given the boy faith that he might have a brighter future in Scotland than here.

"If the lads ask you what we spoke of, just say that I wanted confidential information about the skills of each horse so I could choose one for myself, or something like that."

"I shall." His inhaled a ragged breath. "This is a lot to take in. My mother lives! And dear Osgifu! I hardly dared to hope for it."

"You shall learn the full story of their journey into my household, but not yet. For now we must remain quiet and carry on as if none of this is known."

He nodded. They were now walking back toward the horse pen. About half way there, Margaret thanked him for his time and turned toward Malcolm and Christina, who were standing, watching her.

She approached them with a calm smile on her face. Neither Fingal or any of his men or servants were within earshot. "That was Oswin. I told him that his mother lives and that I intend for him to return with us. I might have mentioned something about the knighthood he was deprived of in England."

Malcolm burst out into laughter. "You never fail to surprise me."

"Surely he deserves one for fighting so bravely at Hastings. And his skill with horses is exemplary, and—"

"Hush, woman," he said softly, still laughing. "From slave to knight in the blink of an eye! Such is the stuff of fairytales."

"My sister always loved fairytales when we were growing up," said Christina.

"I did," Margaret admitted. "And so did you! We used to dream of the handsome princes who'd come to sweep us off our feet on their white chargers."

"And here I am!" said Malcolm cheerfully.

"And now I have a handsome prince as well," said Christina, with a smile. "Who's whisking me away with his charm."

"I can see that," said Margaret. "And I really want to be happy for you—" She leaned in, having checked that no one else was too near. "But aren't you concerned about that girl from last night? She came here to accuse him of breaking a promise…then was found dead this morning."

"You don't mean to suggest he had anything to do with her death?" Christina hissed back.

"I don't know," whispered Margaret.

Christina stared at her for a moment. "You don't want me to get married. You want me to stay at home and wait on you as your handmaiden, like Aelgith."

"I don't, I promise—"

"Ladies, a subject for another time," said Malcolm calmly. "Your voices are rising."

"What do you think?" asked Margaret. "About our host."

"I'm enjoying his hospitality and conviviality," he looked at Christina. "I suspect the girl met with an unfortunate accident."

"She accidentally got strangled?" asked Margaret, incredulous. "Her nursemaid, who I just spoke with, said she had bruises around her neck."

"Perhaps she got tangled in her cloak when she fell in the river," said Christina, obviously irritated that this unpleasantness was casting a shadow over their day. "We didn't see her neck because her cloak was still fastened around it. Did you think of that? And what was she thinking interrupting us in the hall like that? She must have been a madwoman."

"I think we should rejoin our host," said Malcolm. Fingal had come outside, cup in hand, and was issuing instructions to two of his guards.

"But the nursemaid said she had thumb marks on the back—" Margaret's protest was met with a glare from her husband.

"Don't ruin this for me," hissed Christina. "This might be my one chance at happiness."

Chastened and silently furious, Margaret followed them back toward The Raven. Her sister was apparently willing to marry a murderer just to get out of her household! Well, she couldn't be sure that Fingal Mac Gofraid was involved in Agnhilda's death, but he seemed the most likely suspect.

THE DAY CONTINUED with various entertainments. The Raven must have summoned musicians and bards from all over the region, and there was no denying their talent and mastery of their arts.

The Raven continued to charm Christina with his almost undivided attention and he was making an effort to win the rest of the family over as well. Her brother Edgar seemed to be almost in love with the man, showering him with flatteries. No doubt he hoped for his participation in some future foray to reclaim England from William.

And now he turned to her. "Margaret, you'll be pleased to hear that I've sent some of my men to look into the sad situation of this morning." She had to admit that him leaving her to talk to the old woman—quite unattended and overheard by his men, as far as she could tell—suggested that he wasn't concerned about her learning anything bad about him.

Which did promote the idea of his innocence.

Still, his men would surely come back with whatever news their master wanted to hear. "I'd imagine her family would at least be concerned about the disappearance of her gold jewelry," said Margaret.

"Perhaps they're still too overwhelmed with grief to think of their material losses," said The Raven. "Such a tragedy."

"Indeed, I can't stop thinking about her. Such a beautiful young woman, cut down before her life could even start."

What was the broken promise she spoke of?

She couldn't ask, though. The Raven was not one of her husband's subjects, but an ally whose friendship he needed to cultivate.

She could feel Christina's hostile stare from across the table. She should not be raising the subject of another woman's beauty, even a dead woman. Christina was the blushing—almost—bride in this scenario. But Margaret couldn't stop doubt from seeping through her. She tried to come up with an excuse to get away from The Raven's hall and out into the community where she might learn more about the dead girl.

"I've heard there's a large religious community nearby," she ventured. "Might we go visit them?"

"I'm not sure you'd want to," said Fingal. "They're an odd lot."

"Are they followers of Saint Columba?"

"We here in these rugged and water-girded lands all walk in the footsteps of Saint Columba," said Fingal. He turned and shone his imperious countenance on Christina again. "Perhaps we could make a pilgrimage by boat to the holy island of Iona, where he lived and preached."

Margaret was about to enthusiastically agree, then she realized that would be a bad idea. She knew the famed Iona was an island off the far western coasts of The Raven's lands and would involve a lengthy journey which would be a distraction from her main purpose here of retrieving Oswin.

"I'd rather stay here if you don't mind," said Christina sensibly. "Is this your usual seat?" No doubt Christina was trying to discover if this visit would serve as a window into her future life.

"I have halls up and down my lands, my lady," he said, taking her hand. "From the isles of Man and Islay to this fine hall, I travel and dine and ride and sometimes I fight." He kissed her fingers softly and Christina's color heightened.

Margaret wanted to roll her eyes. He'd recently inherited the lands from his father, not conquered them himself. Also, he'd basically just admitted that they'd be traveling all the time. Even great men had to keep their nobles loyal and exert their authority throughout their lands, and Fingal was still trying to prove he could fill his father's big boots.

Margaret didn't mind travel. Or at least she hadn't until she had her baby. Her chest ached with longing as she thought of little Edward, his tiny fists curled tight and his sweet soft cheeks. She'd have to make sure that provisions were made for him to come along with her and Malcolm on any future journeys.

The sooner a betrothal is agreed, the sooner I can get home to my baby. The sooner we can retrieve Oswin from his captivity and take him with us.

But then her sister would be bound to her fate. Bound to this man.

Whom she didn't trust.

CHAPTER 8

*M*argaret struggled to stay awake during another long evening of eating and drinking and entertainments. As the others sank deeper into their cups she sipped at hers just enough not to draw attention.

Finally, when she'd reached the point where she could barely keep her eyes open, the company broke apart and The Raven wished Christina a night of sweet and peaceful sleep. Again Margaret was grateful that Christina shared a bed with Agatha, so their host couldn't put in a surprise appearance behind her bed curtains. She thought him quite capable of it.

Grizel unbraided her hair and helped her out of her gown behind the privacy screens that separated their bed from the hall. Malcolm always undressed himself and threw his garments down carelessly—though Grizel rushed in to hang them neatly.

In bed she curled up close to her husband, grateful for the safety of his embrace after a long and worrisome day. "What do you really think of our host?" she asked, keeping her voice as low as she could.

"I like him."

She stiffened. "Don't you think he seems rather…false?"

"He's laying it on thick with your sister, to be sure, but I find that to be entirely appropriate under the circumstances. I'd look dimly on him doing anything less."

She tried to relax. "That's an interesting perspective. He's trying to woo her and it's working, so I can hardly fault him for that."

"Christina likes him."

"She does. In fact I haven't seen her this cheerful in years. It makes me anxious, in fact. What if he disappoints her and breaks her heart?"

Her husband squeezed her and whispered. "Then I shall have his heart on a stake and roast it."

"It's not a joke!" she found her voice rising and hushed it again. "She's been through so much sadness that she'd quite given up on any happiness for herself."

"Let her worry about her own life and keep your eyes on your book," whispered Malcolm. "That's what my tutor used to tell me when I was a lad amidst all the intrigue in Westminster. A small Scots boy in a foreign land like a fish in a pot of soup. But all's well that ends well."

She squeezed him back. "I shall endeavor to remind myself of that."

Still.…

"I can't get that poor dead woman's face out of my mind. So young! And her nursemaid saw distinct marks of strangulation on her neck, so someone killed her." She put a finger on his lips to stop him telling her to keep her eyes on her own prayerbook. "I know we're here to retrieve Oswin, and to get Christina married, but I couldn't live with myself knowing that poor girl's murderer will go free."

Malcolm kissed her finger. "This isn't my kingdom. I can't appoint you as justice to determine guilt or innocence."

"So justice must be swept into the hearth along with yesterday's scraps?"

"No, but we—you—cannot determine its course, either."

Margaret's heart rebelled against this idea. "If our host is found to have anything—anything at all—to do with the girl's death, do you agree that the marriage must be called off?"

Now Malcolm paused. "You think our host a murderer?"

"All I know is that the girl accused him of breaking a promise, and now she's been found strangled. A man like him wouldn't do the deed himself, but sending a proxy wouldn't absolve him of guilt in my eyes."

Her lips were so close to his ear that her breath must be tickling the small hairs there. She didn't want any servants hovering nearby—even Grizel—to overhear. "If he didn't want to marry my sister I might be able to look away. But the idea that my dearest Christina could be betrothed to a cold-blooded killer—"

"From a heartbreaker to a murderer—" breathed Malcolm in her ear. "Your opinion of him continues to plumb new lows." He squeezed her gently. "But your concerns aren't falling on deaf ears. We must bide our time and take the measure of him."

"For how long?"

"However long it takes."

Malcolm's sturdy embrace soothed her into a fitful sleep. But she awoke in the dark from a disturbing dream where everyone she cared about—her mother, her husband, Christina and worst of all little Edward, were being kept away from her for reasons she didn't know and couldn't seem to find out.

She awoke panting, and soon found herself in floods of

tears at the prospect of losing her baby. He was so tiny! A babe could sicken and die at that age with little warning. What if her fond goodbye would be the last time she ever saw him?

"What's amiss?" Malcolm's voice was foggy with sleep.

"Nothing."

"Then why are your sobs shaking the bed?"

"I miss Edward so much I feel like my heart is breaking," she admitted. "The thought that we must stay here for weeks —perhaps even months—feels like torture. But if we don't, then I might be pushing Christina into a life of horrors." She'd pulled the covers over her head to absorb her ragged whispers. "I can't bear it!"

More sobbing racked her chest. What kind of a queen was she? Her husband needed her at his side—a steady head and a steady hand—to help him manage his kingdom. His bed should be a sanctuary, and here she was raining arrows of chaotic emotion upon him. "I'm sorry!"

Malcolm wrapped his strong arms around her and held her tight. "Edward shall join us here."

"How? If we couldn't bring him safely then how will the servants manage it? And I don't want to leave Christina and my mother here. They seem too easily smitten by our host's charms and may fall into a trap."

Malcolm rubbed her back. "You shall stay here, and I shall return to Dunfermline and retrieve little Edward, his wet-nurse, and anyone else you fancy. I shall ride with the babe strapped to my body, and shall guard his life with my own."

This sounded like a terrible idea. "Won't his body be forcibly shaken by the horse's movements?"

"Not if I ride your new black palfrey. She rides smooth as the surface of a lake." This wasn't the worst idea Margaret had ever heard. Maud was a good size, and Malcolm's easy and quiet riding kept almost any horse steady, she'd noticed. "Would you feel safe staying here with my men?"

"My brother Edgar would be here," she said, as if this was supposed to be reassuring. It wasn't really. But Malcolm didn't need to know that.

"Indeed he will! And I shall take every care with Edward. We will rest for him to nurse and he'll be sheltered from the weather."

Margaret hated the idea of her baby traveling overland without her. But then she hated the idea of spending the next month—or more—separated from him.

"Will Fingal be offended at your leaving? Surely you won't tell him the true reason."

Malcolm's chest shook with silent laughter. "You're right, I probably shouldn't. I'll tell him an urgent missive from William forces my temporary return, or some nonsense like that."

"Don't say such things. You'll speak it into being." Margaret lived in silent terror of William the Bastard's long arms reaching into her life and plucking away her newfound happiness.

"Don't you worry. I'll come up with something. Fingal knows I have messengers coming and going with news. I'll leave this morning and be back before you notice I'm gone."

"Hardly." She shivered. She hated the idea of sleeping alone here, in this strange bed, in this strange hall, surrounded by all these strange people. Which she supposed must mean that Dunfermline now felt like her home. And if the Scots knew their king was traveling from one side of the country to another—and back again—on a nursemaid's errand they'd probably stage a revolt. "I'm not sure it's a good idea."

"I miss Edward too. Those first weeks and months are

gone by so quickly and before you know it their head is at your shoulder and they're begging to train a kestrel."

She sighed. Malcolm's two sons from his first marriage had all the interests and habits of young noblemen, despite still being years from becoming belted knights. "I keep thinking about his tiny fists."

"And how they grab onto a finger and don't let go," said Malcolm softly. "Don't fret, my love. You'll feel those little baby fingers around yours soon enough." He kissed her forehead. "Get some rest. I'll leave tomorrow morning."

She nestled her face against his neck. She wasn't sure she'd even be able to sleep without him here, but at least no one would notice if she spent the night on her knees praying.

"One good thing about me being away—" he added. "Is that you can ask all kinds of questions about the missing girl and it won't be perceived as an insult from me since I won't be here." She could feel his smile lean against her cheek.

"You wouldn't mind?"

"Would it help if I did?"

"It's only because I'm so concerned about Christina's future."

"Of course it is. You otherwise wouldn't give a fig for justice for the downtrodden and forgotten," he teased.

"Agnhilda wasn't downtrodden. She was a local noblewoman. And why is no one looking for her gold that was stolen? Doesn't that strike you as odd?"

"It does indeed, and I trust that you'll find some answers while I'm gone. Not that I could stop you if I wanted to. Though I will tell Aidan to keep a close eye on you and make sure you don't get yourself into trouble."

Margaret hesitated for a moment. A new worry had occurred to her since her last mention of Edgar. "You might want to take my brother with you."

"So he doesn't drag our host into a war against William?"

"Something like that."

Malcolm laughed. "That's not the worst idea in the world."

"Do bring him back, though. In case there's a wedding to celebrate." The idea caused a ripple of unease in the pit of her stomach…still, she wouldn't want Christina to take her vows without Edgar present.

"Oh, aye. And best not to leave Edgar there with my brother Donald Ban hovering about unattended. They might find new mischief to get up to." He gave her a playful squeeze. "Brothers…can't live with them, can't live without them."

THE NEXT MORNING Malcolm left early with little fanfare. He took Edgar and six other men. Margaret wasn't even sure what excuse he'd given to their host, but The Raven seemed quite satisfied with it.

Their host was now applying his considerable charms to Agatha, having discerned that she wasn't a deaf-mute and even spoke, or at least understood, considerable amounts of Gaelic as well as English.

Aidan Mac Donal approached Margaret before Malcolm had even crested the nearby hill. "Anything you need, my lady. I'm at your service." The lad was probably only her age but he'd been in her husband's service for eight years. The younger son of a thane from somewhere just south of the Firth of Forth, he'd been sent to Malcolm's household to finish his education and earn his keep. He'd since proven himself invaluable. With his wavy chestnut hair, wide hazel eyes and snub nose, he looked like a simple peasant lad dressed up as a knight. His mind was subtle and sharp, however, and his reflexes as quick as his muscles were strong.

"I appreciate that, Aidan." She leaned in close. "And I'd also be grateful for any intelligence you can provide me about our hosts and the surrounding communities. I intend to learn as much as I can about the recent death."

"Aye, the king said as much." He didn't smile or look amused, the way Malcolm might have. He didn't look doubtful either, to his credit.

"I'm sure I can count on your discretion."

"You can indeed."

She dismissed him and he returned to the other twelve or so men her husband had left behind to guard their party.

Malcolm had assured her that they'd be as safe here in The Raven's fiefdom as if they were in the palm of his own hand. Their host knew that if even a hair on their heads was disturbed or discomfited, every armed man in the Kingdom of the Scots would descend on this place like a swarm of locusts. Since Malcolm was always looking for an opportunity to engage his loyal thanes and mormaers in acts of war and pillage—for both training and reward purposes—Margaret knew this was not an exaggeration.

The Raven knew it too.

Margaret approached Fingal where he stood talking to Agatha and Christina. "I'd like to visit the local communities. Perhaps we could offer alms to the needy."

"My sister's obsessed with washing poor people's feet," said Christina.

"What?" The Raven looked like he wanted to laugh.

"I'm serious!" continued Christina. "She gets upset that

the abbey almoner can't find enough paupers who want their toes toweled off by royalty."

Margaret listened with cool shock cascading through her. While everything that Christina said was true, she could hardly believe her sister was mocking her acts of charity and self-abasement, especially in front of this character. "I'm surprised you feel that way. I thought you were grateful for the opportunity to serve Christ in the form of these paupers." She felt like adding that Christina had talked of little else but becoming a nun for at least a year, but decided that might be going too far.

"I'm glad to give sustenance and comfort to the poor, but I'm not sure we need to wash and anoint their feet as well. It's not like we're in a hot Mediterranean climate, after all."

That was certainly true. A light mist of rain blew into their faces and a chill west wind was picking up.

"I'm not sure my people would want their feet handled," said The Raven with a wry look. "But I dare say they'd be up for some cakes and ale."

"My sister holds a feast for them every Sunday right in her husband's hall."

"Every Sunday?" said The Raven, looking both shocked and amused.

"Not every Sunday," said Margaret, through tight lips. "For example not this last Sunday since we're away. But an opportunity to serve your subjects would be most welcome." Visiting the locals would give her an excellent opportunity to observe them and perhaps ask some probing questions. "Perhaps when you show us about your local area we could bring alms to distribute?"

"I shall send instructions to the kitchens to prepare something suitable." Fingal now regarded Margaret with a curious look. A look you might give to a rare and exotic animal that unexpectedly bounded across your path. Perhaps he was wondering what King Malcolm had gotten himself into with this English princess of his.

Perhaps he was wondering what he might be getting himself into by wedding her sister.

"Does the prospect of this alms-giving expedition please you?" he asked Christina and Agatha.

"If it's not too much trouble," said Christina. She didn't look overly thrilled but probably didn't want to appear to be lacking in charitable impulses. Agatha had returned to her previous deaf-mute act, an odd little smile fixed to her mouth. "I should like to meet more of your people."

So it was arranged that the cook would prepare fresh buns and other portable delicacies. Folding tables would be transported and—weather permitting—set up outside in a place where the people might be summoned to gather, starting the following morning.

THAT EVENING The Raven made an effort to thaw the somewhat frosty sentiments that Margaret had developed toward him. He recited Latin verse and sang a stirring rendition of one of the psalms in Gaelic.

"How does one receive an excellent education here in—" She tried to think of a polite way to say the-back-of-beyond.

"Most of the nobles benefit from tutors educated in the monasteries. I had the good fortune to spend several years at the king's court in Dublin."

"That explains a lot," she admitted. "My husband and I were both lucky enough to receive our educations at the court of the Confessor."

"Exile can sharpen the mind as well as the senses," he said with a penetrating stare. "Do you feel yourself to be in exile now, in your husband's kingdom?"

"Oh no," she said quickly. "It's fast become my home. Of course I'm still learning the language and have to reach into my mind—or even ask my husband—for the right words to use, but I've improved a lot in the last year."

"Your Gaelic is excellent, and so is your sister's."

"Queen Edith insisted that we study the language."

"I'm surprised to learn that the Irish culture was celebrated at Westminster."

"The King was keen to know the language and culture of all the surrounding kingdoms. We learned French as well, which has come in perhaps more useful than I might have hoped."

The Raven laughed. "Perhaps King Edward wisely sought insight into the mindset of his erstwhile enemies through studying their culture."

"He didn't see the French as enemies. William insists that King Edward promised the crown to him."

"Do you believe him?" The Raven looked curious.

"No." Margaret didn't see any reason to keep this view a secret. "He'd intended for my father to be his successor. After my father's death he let the Witan choose the king, as they eventually did."

"Was your brother upset that they didn't choose him?"

Margaret felt awkward being put on the spot, but saw no reason to lie. "Of course he was. But he was a youth and hardly ready to defend the nation from all comers, as he would clearly have had to do if history is our guide."

"Indeed. Tis a shame your brother's efforts to reconquer the kingdom have not met with success."

"Yes," was all she would commit to that. "Perhaps one day." *But not soon, God willing. Could they please have some time to breathe and live?*

She wondered if The Raven had any ambition to expand his territories. Might he lay claim to her husband's lands that bordered his? Or did his ambitions lie in the direction of Ireland, where the great Kingdom of Dál Riata once extended. "Have you met with William yourself?"

"I've not had the pleasure," he said slowly. "If indeed it is a pleasure, which I doubt." He laughed at his own joke. Christina laughed with him and he seemed to suddenly remember that she was there. He turned to refill her wine cup and flatter her with pleasantries.

He's intelligent and well taught. He talks to women as people, not as servants. He's passably handsome and with a noble enough countenance. He'd already showed her sister more kindness and consideration than any man since her father's death.

So why did her spirit, her gut and even her heart seem to reject him as a suitable husband for her sister?

CHAPTER 9

Margaret spent a somewhat fitful night without Malcolm. She wasn't used to sleeping alone, having always shared a room and often a bed with her sister before her marriage. She contemplated asking Grizel to join her under the covers, but thought better of it. She was a queen now.

Even though the curtained bed she slept in lay under the roof of The Raven's great hall where probably fifty people slept, she felt as alone as if she slept out on the cold moor.

She wondered where Malcolm was sleeping. Or was he riding through the night? He and his men sometimes took hunting parties out under the moon—when it showed its face—for the sheer sport of it. Or perhaps to practice leading a raiding party under cover of night.

She hated the idea of him riding over the uneven and unpredictable terrain of this rugged and roadless land in the dark. He wouldn't do that with the baby. Would he? Did she trust him to bring tiny Edward, with his soft milk-scented cheeks, safely back to her across this windswept and rainy country?

She mouthed repetitive prayers to calm her mind and finally drifted into a dreamless sleep.

~

GRIZEL HELPED her dress and arranged her veil, adding a few extra pins against any gusty winds they might encounter on their travels.

Christina looked radiant at breakfast, in a gorgeous gown with an unusual mix of pinks and rust colors that brought out the pink in her cheeks. Margaret kissed her cheek before sitting. "You look glorious, sister."

"Is it too much? I rather think it is." She stroked her gown. The pattern had some silver or gold thread in it—not too much—and glittered a little.

"You're a princess," said Agatha, breaking open a fresh oatcake.

"A princess of England or a princess of Scotland?" mused Christina.

"Both," said Agatha firmly. "And perhaps soon a princess of…whatever this place is called." She smiled encouragingly.

"The Isles, mother," said Christina, with a touch of approbation in her voice.

"What kind of a name is that? What Isles? How many Isles?" She spoke low, in a teasing voice.

"All the isles he sees fit to conquer, I'd imagine," said Margaret quietly. There were servants all around and nothing was private. "His realm includes Iona, monastic seat of the great St. Columba."

"And the Isle of Man," said Christina. "Which is halfway to Ireland."

The Raven joined them and they set out on foot. "It's not so far to the place where I've arranged the almsgiving. Just across the river and over a hill. An easy walk."

They crossed the river in groups, the boatman ferrying the royals and their host, then the remaining guards and servants. As they passed over the water, Margaret couldn't help but think of the dead girl: her pale face with its open, staring eyes filled her mind.

On the far side of the river, they followed a track around the side of a gentle hill and emerged into a plain on the other side. Servants had gone ahead and set up the trestle tables, now laden with plates of baked goods and flagons and cups of ale.

Word had spread and people were arriving from at least four different directions. The weather proved surprisingly accommodating, with even a hint of blue sky peeking through the clouds. People had shed their cloaks and approached in just their tunics. Nearly everyone was barefoot and Margaret wondered what the prickly-looking turf felt like underfoot.

"We must serve them," said Margaret. She noticed people were staring at them like a tapestry hanging on a wall. As well they might! Three women in extravagant patterned dresses, they stuck out amidst the scenery like exotic birds that had flown off course.

They hurried forward and Margaret picked up a flagon and began pouring cups of ale and handing them to people with warm Gaelic greetings. Christina took up a platter of fruity buns and Agatha just stood there, hands clasped at her waist, with her favorite deaf-mute smile.

The Raven surveyed the scene with a bemused look on his face. Margaret knew better than to suggest that he might pour some of the ale himself. That was the noble lady's work even at the highest of high tables. She couldn't picture him washing anyone's feet, either.

Her work of pouring ale without splashing it on the table or her gown took up most of her attention. She noticed a variety of people approaching The Raven to engage him in conversation. When she finished one flagon and put it down for the servants to refill, she noticed that a tall woman now engaged him in rapid conversation.

Margaret strained her ears to hear. From what she could gather the conversation was about calves and bulls, which struck her as odd. The woman was young and pretty, but in a different way than poor dead Agnhilda. She had chiseled features and thick dark brown hair that hung loose over her shoulders instead of being neatly braided.

Fingal said something she couldn't catch and the woman's uttered a bell-like laugh. This attracted Christina's attention, and Margaret soon noticed her frowning as her intended continued the pointless-seeming discussion of livestock.

Not wanting Christina to embarrass herself by seeming jealous, Margaret distracted her. "Quite a good turnout at such short notice!"

"Yes indeed," said Christina, her voice quite flat. She snuck another glance at The Raven, who now noticed her and bid adieu to the girl. He strode toward them.

"I'm surprised your arms haven't grown tired from lifting those heavy flagons," he said to Margaret. Then he shone a winning smile at Christina. "Your generosity of spirit matches your beauty."

Margaret was tempted to point out that it was her generosity of spirit that brought them here—but in truth it was her desire to nose around the local area and dig up dirt on their host. She put her flagon down on the table. "I shall go for a quick walk around, if you don't mind."

Leaving Christina with him, she beckoned to Aidan to attend her. He'd been hovering nearby the whole time, scanning the crowds in his pleasant manner. Now he hurried to her side without a word.

"I wish to speak with the people. Please stay close and help with translation if needed."

"Yes, my lady."

Fixing a beatific smile to her lips, Margaret marched up to a group of ladies standing nearby. They hadn't approached the table for alms, but seemed to be watching the proceedings like an entertainment. From their clothes—neat and new but not extravagant—they appeared to be of a respectable class: perhaps the wives of prosperous farmers or the miller or the blacksmith. "Good morning, ladies. Do you live nearby?"

Two of them stared at her blankly but one responded in a confident tone. "Yes, my lady. We live in the valley over yonder." They pointed to one of many hills nearby. Presumably the valley lay behind it.

Margaret decided to get to the point. "Is there any news in the death of Agnhilda Finnsdottir?"

"Such a tragedy," said the same woman. She was forty or so, her hair covered with a wrap. "They're saying she missed her footing in the dark and fell in the river."

"I saw her earlier in the evening," said Margaret. "And she was wearing a gold band around her head, and gold rings as well. They weren't found on her body. Has anyone asked what happened to them?"

The women looked at each other and spoke in rapid Gaelic. Margaret understood that this was news to them and none of them had heard anything about missing gold.

"She lived with her brother and his wife, if I'm not mistaken," said Margaret. "Are they here today?" So many people had arrived that it seemed like everyone in the surrounding area must be there.

The women looked about, then pointed to where Fingal stood engaged in quiet conversation with a man and a woman.

Margaret's heart leaped. "That's them?"

"Yes."

She realized later that she'd left without a word of good-bye, but she didn't want to miss hearing what the dead woman's relatives asked of him. Did they also suspect that he might be involved in her death?

Margaret hurried toward them, trying to keep her expression neutral and pleasant. The Raven looked unmistakably irritated when she entered their little huddle, with Aidan lurking at a discreet distance. She was hoping they'd keep talking but they stopped and stared at her, so she introduced herself to the couple.

The man said they were Drostan Finnson and his wife Gyda. The Raven introduced her as Margaret Queen of the Scots. She offered her condolences on the sad death of Drostan's sister and revealed that she was one of the first to see her body. She told them that the dead girl's face haunted her and she felt called to seek justice for her death.

She then asked if they knew of anyone who would have reason to want Agnhilda dead. Fingal was standing right there so they could hardly accuse him. Still, she wanted to see their reaction, and his.

Drostan and Gyda did immediately look uncomfortable and muttered that they couldn't imagine why anyone would want to hurt a hair on Agnhilda's head. Margaret asked about her missing gold, saying that they'd seen her not long before her death.

Again they said they didn't know anything about it.

"Don't you want to find the gold?" asked Margaret, perplexed. "Surely these are heirloom pieces that have been handed down through your family?"

"Sometimes it's better not to delve too deeply into these matters," said Fingal in sonorous tones.

"Why not?" said Margaret, her voice revealing her shock at this answer.

"Because it will stir up things that are better left asleep."

"What do you mean?" Surely the whole point was to stir up information so the killer could be accused.

"There's a dark spirit that's been known to take young girls," said Gyda softly. "They're usually found drowned in water just like Agnhilda." She crossed herself.

Margaret crossed herself reflexively. "How many young girls have died?"

"Countless," said The Raven, sounding rather bored. "Over a long period of time."

"Every year?" asked Margaret, now incredulous.

"Not every year," said Gyda. "The intervals are longer, Sometimes much longer. But sometimes two or three are taken in one year if the spirit is stirred by too much poking and probing."

Margaret blinked. "When was the last time this happened?"

The couple and Fingal looked at each other, almost like conspirators. "A few years, I think," said Fingal.

"I'm relieved that it's that long but I think it far more likely that her death is the work of a mortal man than of a mystical water spirit."

"The people of this country cling tenaciously to their ancient beliefs," said Fingal. "Wood sprites and water sprites and dark shadows slithering out of the forest."

"I would hope the bright light of God's teachings would have caused such shadows to shrivel into nonexistence."

"Things change slowly in this quiet corner of the world."

Margaret got an impression that Fingal liked it that way. Perhaps a simple-minded and unquestioning people, bedeviled by suspicion, were easier to dominate and rule than a more civilized populace.

"You think this spirit took the gold?" This part Margaret couldn't get past. "Is this a normal feature of such deaths?"

"I don't know. But since we can't get dear Agnhilda back what is the loss of some trinkets?"

Something is off here, thought Margaret. These "trinkets," could likely be traded for two or three head of fine cattle or a whole flock of sheep. Their careless dismissal of them seemed disingenuous. She would love to get a moment with the couple away from the peering gaze of The Raven.

Margaret excused herself and went looking for Christina. When she saw her standing off to one side, she approached and whispered in her ear. "Could you please engage our host in conversation? I wish to speak privately to the people standing with him."

After considerable convincing, complete with pleas and promises, Christina stirred into action. She asked Fingal to take her on a walk around the village and thus left Drostan and Gyda free for Margaret to approach them. She apologized for intruding and asked whether Agnhilda had ever been betrothed to anyone.

They looked at each other, as wondering whether to say something. Not wanting to miss the moment, Margaret took a bold step. "I just wondered if she'd been promised to Fingal Mac Gofraid, because when she entered the hall she said something to him about broken promises."

They both looked rather sheepish, which was not what Margaret had expected at all. "I sent her," admitted Drostan after an awkward pause. "There was no betrothal—not a formal one, anyway—but we did have hopes for a union." This was the opposite of what the old nursemaid said, but as a servant she might not have been privy to her master's thoughts.

"You heard that The Raven was courting my sister?" Margaret asked it softly, not wanting to sound accusatory.

"Word did reach us that there was some preliminary discussion," said Drostan stiffly. "Of course if we'd known that his guests were of such very high status…" he trailed off.

Margaret suspected that he knew exactly who the guests were. It would hardly be a secret in a place where everyone knew everyone else and likely had for five generations. "I'm surprised you would send her alone, and at night. Surely it's your duty as her brother to arrange and defend her marriage prospects."

Again he looked chastened. As well he might. "The Raven is not a man to argue with. A heartbroken girl alone seemed more likely to touch his feelings."

"And to get murdered in the night." She felt considerable resentment against this man. "Surely you don't think she was killed by a water spirit?"

"I saw the body," protested Gyda. "Found as it always is… and found in water."

"Her old nursemaid, Maeve, came to visit me and said there were strangulation marks around her neck," said Margaret. Drostan and Gyda looked at each other, clearly shocked. "She was sure she'd been murdered. She didn't know that you'd sent her here. She thought she was going out to the chapel to pray or something like that."

"That old woman pokes her nose where it doesn't belong," said Drostan. "She means well but she should not have come here. It could make trouble for us."

With The Raven? Margaret really wanted to ask outright if they thought that Fingal might have had anything to do with it. Was Agnhilda —and any promises he'd made her—an inconvenience who might interfere with his ability to marry Christina? But she couldn't ask. She was his guest and her sister might soon become his wife.

She drew in a steadying breath. "I don't think a spirit took her life. I think a man did, and stole her gold. If her gold can be found it will point the finger at the guilty party. That would be a good reason to demand a full investigation."

"But what if the spirit is angered and comes to claim another life?" said Gyda, brow creased. "We have two young daughters, only nine and eleven. And nothing can bring Agnhilda back."

"Has that happened before? That this….spirit comes back to claim another family member?" Margaret was trying to get a sense of the types of crimes being committed in this place. That would be one way for the killer to stop the family poking and prodding into a suspicious death.

Gyda nodded. Her eyes clenched shut and tears appeared around her eyelashes. Her husband held her close.

"I shall pray for the soul of your sister and that the true perpetrator of this terrible crime is soon in custody."

She turned to Aidan as they walked away. "I wish I could ask them to report back to me if they learn anything. It's frustrating being outside my husband's jurisdiction. Is it common for people to blame shadows and spirits for acts of man?"

"Common enough," said Aidan. "And the wind and water in these parts can be forceful enough to make people believe there's more to them than just weather." Lively gusts had picked up and now a prickle of rain rode in on them. Margaret pulled the hood of her cloak up over her head.

"Sometimes even I could believe the wind is alive, the way it whistles through the trees around the tower back in Dunfermline," she said. She didn't remember the weather being so…spirited….at Westminster or Wilton, or back in Hungary.

The repast they'd brought had been eaten and drunk and servants were gathering up the platters and drinking vessels. She wondered where Christina and The Raven had gone to. She couldn't see them among the local villagers and shepherds who still milled about the almost empty table.

Margaret spoke low to Aidan. "Their superstition disturbs me. Men and women with true faith in Christ would not fear some mysterious shadow from a darker time when ignorance reigned. I wonder what their holy men think of such foolish fables? Are they doing the work to combat them, or do they humor and tolerate such pagan foolishness?"

Aidan didn't respond since it was clearly a rhetorical question. How would he know what the men in these far western lands believed?

Not wanting to miss the opportunity to question more villagers about the girl's death, she approached a group of girls, all under twenty but likely not by much, and asked them if they knew Agnhilda.

They all nodded. "Everyone in these parts knew her," said one, a pretty girl with long red braids. "We don't know what she was thinking traveling by herself in the dark."

"The ferryman told me that it's common for women to travel in the dark, especially in the winter when there are few hours of daylight."

"The ferryman perhaps sees and knows more than most men since he's privy to people's secret comings and goings. But any sensible girl knows not to leave home late at night by herself."

The ferryman. Margaret tried not to frown. Could he be a suspect in the girl's death? He eked out a living braving wind and water in all weathers. Surely the gold from her headband and rings could give him comfort he'd never find in years of plying his trade.

"Do you know the ferryman well?"

"Old Cormac?" said the girl. "As well as we might from going back and forth over the stream. He rarely leaves his post. Pays a lad to bring him food there."

"Why must he remain there? Surely anyone needing to cross the river would have to wait for him to come back anyway, so he'd hardly miss out on custom."

"There are other crossings," said a dark haired girl with pale green eyes. "Over that hill yonder there's a gravel patch that can be forded. That's where they bring the horses back and forth. Sometimes when the water's low you can walk right across it and barely wet your feet. It's just more of a hike to get up there and back and impractical with a load of goods."

"I see. Has Cormac ever been married?"

The girls looked at each other. "Not that I can remember. But he's been here long before we were born so you'd have to ask someone older to know for sure."

The dead girl was found only a short distance from the crossing. He'd barely have had to leave home to take her life —and her gold. On the other hand surely that pointed the finger of suspicion at him a little too easily.

Except that no one did seem to suspect him.

"Is the boatman well liked?"

"Well enough, I'd say," said the redhead, looking at the others. "If he wasn't he'd soon be out of business." They all nodded.

"Do any of you have an idea who might have killed Agnhilda?"

A sudden spray of rain made them all tug their cloaks about them. "They say it was a kelpie," whispered the blonde girl. Shorter and younger than the others, she'd been holding back. "He enchanted her and pulled her under."

"A what?"

"Margaret!" Christina's voice rose above the wind. What was she thinking calling out like a fishwife above the crowd?

"Aidan, tell her I'm here," she said. But before he could take a step Christina came running up to her, long skirt gathered in her hands. "We need to get going. Fingal says it's about to pour and he knows the weather like a farmer knows his sheep."

The three girls were already scattering and Margaret regretted losing the opportunity to learn more about their strange and primitive beliefs. Beliefs that poor dead Agnhilda had likely shared.

"Ladies, hurry now, before sheets of rain blind us." The Raven's voice boomed out.

"This is so uncivilized," hissed Margaret, as they hurried back toward the river crossing, gathering up their dresses like peasant women. "If you live here you must have at least enough of a road put in to use a carriage. And a decent bridge over this trickle of a river." She'd been saying the same in Dunfermline, and there were now the beginnings of neat cobbled streets between important places such as the tower and the new cathedral.

Christina startled her by grabbing her arm with force. "I could never live here."

CHAPTER 10

They were drenched and chilled by the time they arrived back at The Raven's hall. "How is it like this in June?" hissed Christina, as they peeled off their wet outer layers.

"The wind blows in off the sea," said one of the servants, who hadn't been asked.

"But we're not even that near the sea!" protested Christina.

"One is never very far from the sea here in the north," reasoned Margaret. "And the deep lochs and firths must affect the weather too. You've surely noticed how fog gathers over a lake." There were too many people around to ask Christina what she'd meant when she said she could never live here.

But as soon as the rain cleared and the wind lulled, she invited her sister to join her for a breath of air so she could get to the bottom of her ominous statement. Leaving their maids and guards behind, they strolled away from the hall and toward a clump of woodland, just far enough away to be out of earshot.

"Did something happen? I thought you'd warmed to the idea of moving here."

"Our host tried to lay his hands on me," said Christina quietly.

"He hit you?" Margaret could scarcely believe it. Surely even The Raven knew he'd risk the wrath of Malcolm's armies with such an affront.

"No, I mean that he tried to draw me into an embrace! I think he wanted to kiss me." Christina drew her wool wrap about her. Her cloak was inside drying by the fire and there was a nip in the air. "It was all I could do not to scream."

Margaret frowned. "But he's been flirting with you non-stop and from what I could see you'd been enjoying his advances."

"That doesn't mean he can paw me!"

"I see what you're saying but I don't think such advances, when gently made during a formal wooing process, are quite as outrageous as you think."

"Did Malcolm kiss you before your wedding day?"

"He did." Margaret recalled her shock at his first attempt. "And it startled me, to be sure, but the kiss—and the ones that followed it—helped warm my heart toward the prospect of what until then had been a purely practical courtship."

"So you don't think he was taking liberties?" Christina looked confused. "I'm a princess of England."

"I do think he was taking liberties, but I suspect that such liberties are part of courtship. Fingal is a great man here, with the sense of entitlement that such men have. Though you're a princess of England, he's the ruler of his realm and no doubt sees himself as your equal, or perhaps even your better. It hardly endangers your reputation to exchange a kiss with the man you'll soon be wed to."

"I can hardly believe you're defending his actions," said Christina, now looking more confused than ever. "I thought you'd be shocked. I confess I had no idea Malcolm kissed you before your wedding. Did he do anything else with you?"

"You mean did we lie together?" Margaret looked back toward the settlement, as if she feared someone might overhear. "Not that, but he did caress me. It sounds strange but his touches and kisses reassured me that we would be a good match. His kisses tasted like sweet wine and his caresses were gentle and encouraging. If his kisses had been wet and sloppy and his fondling clumsy or discomfiting, I might have had cause to call off the marriage."

Christina blinked. "So I should let him kiss me?"

Margaret now had a dilemma. Should she encourage Christina in pursuing this marriage that would be a benefit to Malcolm and the kingdom of Scotland in securing an important ally? Or should she follow her heart and remind Christina that The Raven was a flirt at best and, at worst, a scoundrel and murderer?

She wanted to know more of her sister's feelings and instincts about him. "Did you secretly want to let him kiss you? To see how he tasted?"

"You mean like trying a strange new sweetmeat at a banquet?"

"Exactly."

Christina shivered slightly. "What if I tasted him...or rather let him taste me...and he wouldn't stop but then forced himself upon me?"

Margaret felt herself frown. "Do you feel like he might?"

"I don't know." Christina hugged herself. "When he talks sweetly to me and tells me I'm pretty and regales me with stories and songs, I fall under his spell. Then when I'm in bed at night my heart and mind are filled with misgivings and worries."

"So you're torn."

"I am. What do you make of him?"

Margaret hesitated. "I feel much as you do. I can see that the match makes good sense in many ways. He's an important enough man to be worthy of your hand. He's handsome enough and perhaps more charming even than a man should be. But there is something of…." Of what? She wasn't even sure what put her on edge. "Of the gambler about him. Or perhaps of those foreign diplomats we'd meet at Westminster, there to grease palms and form allegiances that might not be in anyone's best interests but their own."

"I suppose that's his duty as the ruler of his people," said Christina quietly. "Marrying me is an act of diplomacy."

"There's nothing wrong with that, in itself. My marriage to Malcolm was just that, but he's already proven to be a caring and thoughtful husband."

"Then why has Malcolm abandoned us here?"

"He has good reason. And he'll be back soon." She hadn't told anyone, even her mother, that he'd ridden back across Scotland to retrieve their baby. That was a secret they'd keep between them. "And it gives me a chance to ask more questions about the dead girl."

"Why are you obsessed with this girl? It truly isn't our business what happened to her." Christina looked behind them into the dark wood as if shadows might reach out for them.

"Surely you don't want a killer to go unpunished?"

"No, but we're strangers here, so it's awkward when you keep asking about her. I'm sure they're looking into it."

"Are they? Her nursemaid came begging for help in finding the killer, but everyone else seems to think that some mysterious shadow came and stole her breath or something. They don't even want to talk about it. That's un-Christian, for one thing."

"Is it? Christianity has its dark creatures." Christina pulled her wrap tighter again.

"The best way to combat evil is to shine the light of truth on it. And I find myself wondering about the ferryman. He was the last person to see her alive. He's old and been here for years, and they say girls have been disappearing for as long as anyone can remember."

"What?" Christina looked appalled.

"Not all the time, just every few years. Sometimes more than one in a single year. Don't you think our host needs to take the matter seriously? He hasn't been the ruler here all that long, but now that the deaths are in his jurisdiction he must find the culprit."

"Let's go back." Christina looked behind her into the woods again. Margaret didn't find them spooky at all. The trees were coppiced and pollarded so it was obviously a busy place of wood production, not a mysterious realm of evil fairies. "But I do agree with you that this mystery needs to be solved."

THAT NIGHT at dinner Margaret coaxed Christina to raise the disturbing topic of local girls being found dead over a long period of time. Margaret's ears pricked for how Fingal would explain this to his newly beloved, but instead he muttered a few words to one of his bards, and sat back in his chair.

This bard, one of three they'd heard so far during this visit, was a youngish man with a wistful air and a rather high haunting voice. He launched into a story-song about a beautiful young girl who found a majestic horse in a forest glen.

The girl approached the horse and found it friendly, so decided to climb on its back from a nearby tree stump. But as soon as her legs were wrapped around its sides, the horse stormed through the trees and galloped headlong into the nearby river. The girl tried to jump off but found that her body was now firmly fixed to the horse's back and her screams rent the air as the horse carried her deep into the river and drowned her.

When the harp notes accompanying the poem died down, Christina wanted to know why the horse had killed her.

"To eat her," said Fingal, taking a bite from a tiny roasted bird that he held pinched between his fingers. "He's a kelpie."

"That doesn't make sense. Horses don't eat meat," said Christina sensibly.

"Well, he's not a horse, is he? He's a water spirit. He transforms into a horse to trick a human into getting on his back."

At a signal from The Raven, the bard then launched into another story, very similar to the first but this time with a young warrior in need of a mount to escape his enemies. Once again, he ended up carried under the water. This story had more stirring and horrific descriptions of the horse turning into a monster once the man was aboard it.

"Your bard tells a very vivid story," said Agatha, fanning herself. "I'm half afraid of this kelpie charging in here to eat us right now!"

"If these kelpies were real, someone would have seen one," said Margaret, herself rather shaken by the bard's haunting voice. "And let me guess, they haven't?" She spoke to Fingal.

"Well, anyone who's had the misfortune to meet one of these kelpies has been enchanted by them, climbed on their back, and been cruelly drowned." From his expression she could see that he found this idea amusing rather than horrifying.

"So you think a mysterious horse lured poor Agnhilda Finnsdottir to a watery grave?" asked Christina, one eyebrow lightly lifted. "You surely don't believe this creature is real."

"Who am I to argue with centuries of tradition?" asked

Fingal, lifting his cup of ale. "Do I know better than my fore-fathers and their forefathers?'

"Probably, yes," said Margaret. "After all you're likely more educated and well traveled than they were."

"Don't be so sure," he said. "The kings and clerics of old traveled widely to conquer fresh land and bring the Word of God."

"The earth is the Lord's and everything in it," quoted Margaret defiantly. "How could anyone who believes in the teachings of the Bible think that a sea spirit is going to rise from the depths of a river and drown someone?

"I'm not sure why you see them as contradictory," said Fingal, looking mildly amused. "Surely both things can exist at the same time."

"Like the monsters in Queen Edith's *Beatus*," said Christina, suddenly agreeing with him. "Remember? It used to give us both nightmares."

"How could I forget it," said Margaret with a shiver. The lavishly illustrated manuscript told the stories in the Book of Revelation complete with bone-chilling and vivid pictures of multi-headed monsters and man-eating beasts.

For some reason there was a fashion for kings and queens to commission themselves copies of this work, origi-nally created by a man called Beatus of Liebana in some far-flung region of Iberia more than three hundred years ago. Queen Edith had commissioned hers from a monastery in France.

Christina turned to Fingal. "Queen Edith told me that at the time of creating the book, Beatus of Liebana was a monk living in one of the only parts of Spain not dominated by Muslim control. As one of the last Christian strongholds in the region they must have felt that the world was surely about to end, and the Day of Judgement would soon be at hand."

"And here we all are three hundred years later, drinking ale to the sound of music."

"While most of Spain is still governed by the Moors," mused Margaret. "Though I believe the Moorish lands have shrunk somewhat since the time of Beatus."

"I suppose the Christian people of Spain must have felt much as we did when the England of our forefathers was overrun by the Normans," said Christina.

"God forbid that the Normans should rule our grandfather's kingdom for three hundred more years," said Margaret softly. "Though I suppose at least they are Christians." She looked right at Fingal, with a question that had just occurred to her. "Perhaps the old kings of England were ancient enemies to you? Always within reach for a skirmish over land and the shifting of a border. Did you tremble or celebrate when William and his men ran over the land of England?"

"A little of both, I suppose," he said. She had to admire his honesty. "My father was still alive at the time and he thought it bode ill. The Normans took the whole country with such speed and force that they almost did seem to have supernatural aid."

"Do you mean that you thought God rode with them?" asked Christina.

"God, or the other one," said The Raven with a wry smile. "Does God turn innocent women and children from their homes and burn their barns and slaughter and eat their cattle without a penny of payment?"

"No, indeed he does not," said Margaret. She appreciated this show of compassion for the suffering the invasion had inflicted. "My husband's kingdom has been overrun by refugees driven into exile."

"Aye, and your husband's countrymen are driving them like cattle to sell as slaves in our markets."

Margaret snuck a glance at Aelgith and Osgifu who'd once been among their number. "Such cruel and inhuman behavior is below any man who calls himself a Christian. And William forbade the sale of slaves out of England, so they're breaking his laws as well."

"I doubt many of us here in the north care much for the laws of William," said Fingal. "As you've no doubt noticed we have our own culture, with laws and songs and stories dating back a thousand years or more. Our kelpies may well be older than the Gospels."

"What a thought," said Christina, as if truly struck by the idea. "But surely the light of Christ must vanquish the darkness of these old terrors."

"One might hope," said Fingal, not looking as if he particularly cared one way or another. "Would you like to hear a legend about another one of our mythical creatures?"

Margaret and Christina looked at each other doubtfully.

"Have you ever heard of the Nucklavee or the Selkies?"

They agreed that they hadn't.

The bard now regaled them with horrifying stories of a skinless creature, all bone and sinew, with a horse's body but a man's head emerging from its back. Its appearance from the seas could herald crop failure, famine and death.

The story left them shivering and Margaret even found herself taking extra sips of sweet wine to calm her nerves. She'd barely rallied when The Raven asked for another song. The bard lifted his harp and sung a tale of a strange seal-like creature who could shed her seagoing skin and transform into a beautiful woman who came ashore to seduce a mate.

Utterly in love with the sea-creature, who kept vanishing back to the sea and leaving him filled with longing, the man stole her seal skin so she couldn't escape him. The seal-woman was then trapped into marriage with the man she'd charmed, all the while longing for her home in the sea and unhappy on land.

Margaret thought this last legend sounded like a stern warning against marrying outside your own people. It might have alarmed her if she hadn't been so lucky in the husband that fate had chosen for her. "No wonder everyone's terrified of these mythical creatures. Your bards are very gifted at bringing them to life." She forced a smile at the young man, who looked pleased.

"Our people do have a gift for storytelling," Fingal said with a smile. "I'm delighted that you ladies have learned our language well enough to enjoy them. Some foreign brides live and die without learning more than a few sentences in their new tongue."

"We were raised speaking English and Hungarian fluently, and reading Latin," said Christina proudly. "And once we arrived at Westminster, Queen Edith insisted that we study Norse and French as well as Gaelic. She hailed them as literary languages but perhaps she had our marriage prospects in mind all along."

"A toast to Queen Edith!" called The Raven.

He's changed the subject, thought Margaret. Still, she knew better than to belabor it now that everyone was sliding into their cups. Besides, her nerves were rattled by the eerie legends. It would be hard to sleep alone in her cold, dark bed tonight.

When Malcolm came back she intended to make sure that the bright light of Christianity shone into the dark corners where these creepy and disturbing myths persisted. An amusing and hair-raising story could be dismissed as harmless fun, but not if it frightened people out of discovering who killed Agnhilda Finnsdottir.

Tomorrow she wanted a chance to take another look at the ferryman, who'd punted people back and forth across the same stretch of river for decades. She wanted to ask him who had crossed both before and after Agnhilda.

And she wanted to lay eyes on the local holy men who allowed strange tales from another time to linger in the hearts and minds of Christian men and women. "I'd like to go visit the local Culdees tomorrow," she said to Fingal. This time she intended to insist.

"I think you'll find their monastic settlement quite primitive compared to what you're used to."

"Don't be so sure. I've seen some quite unorthodox arrangements since I arrived in my husband's kingdom. I've long since given up expecting grand abbeys with neatly swept cloisters. It would mean a lot to me to meet the holy men here. I've heard they're a very ancient community."

Doubt persisted on his face. "If you wish to visit them, we shall go." He turned to Christina and looked at her hand where it rested on the table next to her cup. For a moment Margaret thought he was going to reach down and caress it and she braced for Christina's reaction. But he didn't. "Would that please you, Princess Christina?"

"I think so." Christina was soft and almost shy, apparently recovered from her shock of earlier. Fingal would be wise to move very slowly in wooing her, which perhaps he'd learned the hard way. It was certainly inappropriate for him to take liberties with her while Malcolm was away.

Margaret's heart ached for her husband as well as her baby. Truly no one had warned her of the fear that strikes the heart of one who cares too much for those they love. And since her father's sudden and totally unexpected death, she knew that disaster could strike with no warning at all. "I look forward to praying with them, if they'll permit it."

"They'd better, if I have anything to say about it," said Fingal with a grin. Margaret glanced at Christina, to see what she made of this arrogance. But Christina was staring off into the darkness, as if her mind was miles away.

The bard now strummed on his harp, playing a haunting, wordless tune that wrapped around them like a fur cloak. On this relatively warm evening in early summer, only a small fire burned. The table still groaned with uneaten delicacies and jugs of wine and ale.

Margaret could see that living here, in The Raven's hall—this or one of several others—could be quite a pleasant and even moderately luxurious life for Christina. Her qualms about his realm being a savage and primitive place had been somewhat soothed by their visit so far.

It was Fingal Mac Gofraid himself she had questions about. And each day, instead of answering questions and feeling reassured, she found herself with more questions tugging at her mind.

CHAPTER 11

In the morning, Margaret discovered that the servants were already preparing food and comforts for the journey to visit the holy men. The Raven—who slept late, it seemed—must have given the orders for it the night before.

"Can we see Oswin today?" whispered Aelgith, when they were away from listening ears for a moment.

"We're going to the local religious settlement, so probably not." She didn't want Aelgith to get a flea in her ear about it. Aelgith could be quite singleminded when she wanted something, and had got herself and Osgifu into terrible danger by taking matters into her own hands last year.

"But he's right there on the other side of the river. They brought the horses across it."

"If we happen to stumble across him, we shall greet him. But please don't go looking for him." She spoke softly and took Aelgith's hand in hers. "I know how desperately you crave to have him back with you again."

"I wish to greet him," said Aelgith, a pitiful look in her eyes. "I'm not even sure he recognized Osgifu and me. She's not the little girl he left behind, but a young lady with long braids, and I'm much changed as well and was hiding behind my veil."

"He knows you're alive and that we plan to take him with us, but we don't want to put everyone here on alert that his family has come to retrieve him. As I've said before they could decide to move him far away or hide him, or ask a king's ransom to release him to us."

"Our host already promised to release him on your sister's marriage," said Aelgith, as if this removed all those obstacles.

Margaret glanced behind her to make sure they weren't overheard. "My sister's marriage is not a *fait accompli*, not by any means."

Aelgith's eyes widened. "You mean she might not marry him?"

"She's still making up her mind. Nothing has been agreed upon. And naturally the decision rests with my husband. Please, don't push things too fast. This is a delicate situation."

Aelgith pressed her lips together as if holding back words she knew she shouldn't utter.

"We came here to find him, and we found him," said Margaret, trying to reassure her. "Believe me, I understand the anguish you feel in wanting him by your side, especially after the long absence." She ached for her baby, and—truth be told—for her husband as well.

"I thought he was dead!" rasped Aelgith. "And now he's come back to life. I'm so afraid to lose him again."

"Have faith. Let my husband manage the situation. He knows these people and how to handle them." She glanced over her shoulder again. "When the time is right, we will leave with him."

~

MARGARET'S HEAD hummed with questions as they approached the ferry crossing. They'd walked from the settlement, a long procession due to all the guards and servants. She'd brought Aelgith and Osgifu as well as her mother. Christina strolled next to Fingal, who was politely listening to her tell stories about their life at Wilton Abbey.

The boatman came out of his little hut as they approached and unwound the rope holding his boat to a post at the shoreline. "A few trips this morning, I see." Margaret had no choice but to get on the first group. She would have made a spectacle of herself insisting on waiting on the bank to observe him.

She looked the ferryman in his eyes, pale blue with the beginnings of a cataract visible in the left, as he took her hand and helped her onto the boat. The wooden boat had crude benches built against the sides and she took up a place right next to him, so she could talk while he punted across.

"I keep thinking about that poor drowned girl," she said softly, watching his expression.

"Aye, a terrible thing."

"Did you know her well?"

"Well enough."

Margaret didn't find this enigmatic answer very satisfying. "Did she ride in your boat often?"

"She would come over with her family to dine at the hall or partake in some kind of festivity. Other than that, I don't remember."

"But you knew her name?"

He hesitated. "I'm not sure if I did or didn't. I know it now, since people have spoken of little else since she died."

"Who was the last person to travel across this stream before she died?"

He'd now helped her mother and Christina on board, and Fingal gestured for Aelgith and Osgifu to climb up next. The ferryman screwed up his face. "She was the last person that night, to be sure. Both ways. But before her I think it might have been Olaf the cloth merchant. He was traveling back to the village after delivering a plaid to the hall."

"Does he live locally?"

"Aye, he makes the cloth. Or I should say his family does. His father raises the sheep, along with the bairns who tend them. His mother and daughter spin, dye and weave the wool. His brother is the fuller—when one is needed that is. He has cows as well. I dare say it's their piss he uses to—" He seemed to suddenly realize he was talking to a queen. "Begging your pardon, my lady."

"No need. I appreciate your information." Though it did seem rather irrelevant and rambling. Almost like someone wanting to change the subject. But perhaps she'd see if there was an opportunity to seek out Olaf the cloth merchant on the pretext of needing some fine wool. "And who was the next person to cross after Agnhilda?"

"No one, my lady. It was the dead of night by then, wasn't it? I'm not sure I came out of my hut until after dawn when the two girls come over to milk the cows." There were cows on any patch of decent grazing near The Raven's settlement, and a great quantity of excellent butter and cheese had been served at his table, so this was hardly surprising.

"Do you have a wife?" she asked, wondering if anyone monitored his midnight activities.

"No, my lady. Sadly I've never enjoyed the blessings of a wife."

He wasn't a handsome man, with thin lips and a bulbous nose, though he might have looked quite different as a young man. She still found it odd that he'd never married. Any man who could support himself and a family usually found himself a prospect for one girl or another.

"I'm surprised at that," she said. Was he lonely and

resentful that a lovely young woman should be dashing about in the night without an escort? "Do you not find it a very solitary life here by the river?"

"Oh no. As you can see I'm quite busy during the day. Even when the lord is away at one of his other halls, they're fussing over his flocks and herds and the goings to and fro keep me quite busy. And I've the company of the birds and the wild creatures."

He shone a little smile at her as he pushed his pole against the riverbank. Everyone was now seated except three servants carrying baskets who stood in the middle of the boat, legs braced in a practiced manner as the boat lurched away from the shore.

He seems like a nice enough man, she thought. She tried to imagine him seizing Agnhilda and tightening his grip around her neck or holding her face under the water to drown her, and couldn't picture it. Still, he was in the right place at the right time, with no one else there to observe his comings and goings.

On the far bank she asked the servants if they'd heard any further news about Agnhilda's death. They said that everyone was buzzing about it and very afraid that a kelpie had been awakened and would come for more victims.

"Surely they don't really believe in such a creature of children's stories?" asked Margaret, exasperated.

"Oh yes, my lady," said one servant girl, young and with a serious face. "We'd be rash not to. My mam always said to cross yourself twice and spin around if you're near anywhere known to harbor fairies. It keeps them at bay."

"What do the fairies have to do with the kelpies?" asked Margaret, humoring her. "Do they ride on their backs to go to the fairy market?"

"Ah, now you're pulling my leg." The girl looked embarrassed. "But maybe they do."

"Do you feel scared walking around the countryside by yourself?" Margaret had always had a penchant for slipping off alone, even as a young girl in Hungary. She knew it sometimes drove Malcolm mad when he awoke in the morning and she was missing and no one knew where she'd gone. She'd found a hidden cave—in between the tower and the town—where she loved to go pray, away from the bustle of the royal court. Thus far, she felt entirely safe in the woods and fields around Dunfermline. "Is this area safe? Or do young girls usually walk with someone else?"

"It's safe for the most part, my lady. Every once in a long while a girl dies or disappears. But those are years apart, long enough for people to forget the danger."

Margaret glanced at the ferryman again. He'd know if a girl was traveling alone late at night or early in the morning. His hut sat on a little knoll above the bank of the river and might have a commanding enough view of the countryside that he'd likely know if there was anyone nearby.

The river wasn't that wide so they were already at the other bank, and the ferryman jumped out to tie the boat. "How long have you punted this boat back and forth across the river?" asked Margaret of him.

"My whole life. I grew up in that hut and my father did it before me."

"I suppose it would be rude of me to ask your age," she said with a smile. His hair was white but that didn't always mean much. With his weatherbeaten skin and powerful callused hands he could be anywhere between forty and eighty.

"I admit I lost track of my age some years ago."

Margaret turned to Fingal. "How old would you guess your ferryman is?"

"He could be a hundred for all I know. He's been old as

long as I can remember," he said with a good humored glance at the man.

The ferryman had probably been here long enough to have been quietly killing girls for two or three generations. She stole another glance at his wide, placid face with its crinkled blue eyes. His arms, which had propelled them across the river, were powerful and his back broad and strong. He'd have no trouble overcoming or smothering a young girl, especially if he caught her by surprise.

With the boat tied, he now held out his hand for her to alight. As queen she was expected to go first. She wondered if the old boatman had any inkling of the dark suspicions that lurked in her brain.

After they'd all stepped ashore he punted back to pick up more passengers, and Fingal suggested that they forge ahead.

"I wonder why you haven't built a bridge," said Margaret to Fingal, once they were all dismounted and walking. "That way we could be riding horses instead of doing all this walking."

"A few times a year the river swells so much that any bridge would be washed away. And why would we want to put the old man out of work?"

Margaret wondered who would ferry people across if the old man was clapped in irons. He was a solitary man, perhaps with no love for woman, who'd been the last person to lay eyes on the dead girl. She'd be a fool not to take those snippets of information seriously, since they made quite colorful cloth when woven together.

MARGARET WASN'T QUITE sure what to expect from the monastic settlement. Her visit to the shrine to St. Andrew at Kilrymont last Advent had shown her that they could be as large and elaborate—and as ancient—as any in England. She'd visited other monastic communities that were more rustic than their English equivalents, built of wood and thatch, but still arranged in a familiar manner with a chapel, a dormitory and sometimes a hospital for guests.

But she'd heard of holy men living in huts and dripping caves and was prepared for almost anything as they walked the trodden path around the side of a hill that hid the monastic settlement from view.

At first glance it looked much like any settlement, a hall surrounded by smaller cottages. She gradually realized that the large, rectangular building was the church, distinguished by a carved wooden cross—painted in vivid colors—that stood in front of the doorway so that everyone entering must walk around it.

The huts, unlike those in Dunfermline or other settlements she'd seen, were tiny and round, with round thatched roofs. There were a few larger ones, but most were very small. And so many! "Are there men and women?" she asked Fingal as they drew closer.

"Just men."

"But there must be women to manage some aspects of their lives. Otherwise who would clean and cook?"

"I'd not advise dining here if I were you," said Fingal.

Christina giggled. "You're so funny. But seriously, what do they eat if they cook for themselves?"

"Do you really think men incapable of roasting a fish?" asked Fingal, clearly amused. "Or brewing a keg of ale?"

"I'm sure they manage fine with the ale," said Christina. "Men always seem to find the means and time for that. But do they grind their own flour and bake their own bread?"

"Surely you've seen a male miller or baker," said Margaret. She didn't want Fingal to think Christina was as naive as she pretended. "Men are hardly excluded from those professions."

"With their wives and families at their sides," said Christina. "But I suppose a religious community is a family of sorts and they divide the tasks among those with more affinity or ability for them."

Smoke rose above the settlement into a blue sky with fluffy clouds, making a picturesque and rustic image. Sheep and cows grazed around the settlement, and Margaret spotted a few shaggy ponies among them.

The Raven had clearly sent advance warning of their arrival, so the abbot emerged to greet them and seemed to know who they all were when The Raven introduced them.

"May we visit your chapel first?" asked Margaret eagerly. The chapel near The Raven's hall was small and mean and this one looked relatively large and grand from the outside.

His doubtful look gave her pause. "We don't usually allow women over the threshold."

"These are honored guests of royal blood," said Fingal loudly. His tone made it clear that there was to be no argument.

The abbot bowed his head and gestured for a young monk to open the door. Margaret glanced at Christina. "They're ignorant rustics," whispered Christina. "Don't take it personally."

The great wooden doors opened to reveal—as promised —a very large, long nave with a high timbered ceiling. Tiny windows high in the walls let in diffused light, giving the space an eerie glow. The sweet smell of incense wafted toward them from censers that hung from iron hooks by the altar.

The stone floor felt hard underfoot. The walls were wood, and wooden pillars carved with elaborate chevron designs lined the nave, holding up the high thatched roof.

Margaret crossed herself at the top of the nave, and walked slowly toward the altar. The party followed behind her in silence, perhaps awed by the strikingly spiritual atmosphere of the remote abbey.

The altar was made of elaborately carved wood and looked considerably older than the rest of the abbey. Perhaps it had been brought here from a more ancient structure. The chalice and paten and two silver candlesticks sat upon a simple linen cloth.

Margaret wanted to kneel and pray but kneeling on the hard, dark floor in her gown didn't seem sensible. "Do you have cushions to kneel on?"

The abbot looked confused. Grizel rushed forward and wadded her cloak into a bundle and laid it down for Margaret. Another servant did the same for Christina and Grizel found another for Agatha, so they were all three able to kneel and pray before the altar. Fingal and the other men and the servants knelt on the floor.

The abbot seized the moment to usher some holy brothers up to the front of the nave and cued them into song. Margaret recognized the words of one of her favorite psalms, hauntingly beautiful in Gaelic, though naturally she would have preferred the more familiar Latin version.

Margaret prayed for the safe delivery of her baby and husband back to them as soon as possible. She also prayed that the wisest possible decision should be made with regard to Christina's marriage. She prayed that they'd be able to take Oswin home with them without having to drive too hard a bargain—certainly not one involving Christina's future.

And she prayed that they'd find out who'd killed Agnhilda, and possibly countless other girls, and that the killer might be safely dispatched to meet his maker, rather than hiding in the shadows of ancient terrors that had no place in this Christian country.

CHAPTER 12

After their sojourn in the church the abbot took Margaret, Christina and Agatha on a tour of the settlement. The Raven wandered off in conversation with one of the clerics, and the rest of the party went to set up food for a midday meal.

"The community itself is very ancient," the abbot explained. "But our abbey is quite new as the old one was rotted beyond repair."

"Has the community been here since the time of St. Columba?" asked Christina.

"It's said to have been founded by one of his disciples. Despite all the war and upheaval in the region it's remained here in some form ever since."

"Why are there so many little huts?" asked Margaret. "Do the men live in solitary cells?"

"Indeed they do, my lady. The better for prayerful contemplation, though most of them gather to celebrate the Hours, and for meals."

"It seems rather inefficient to have so many different buildings when they could all be housed in one large dormitory," said Margaret, perplexed by the odd arrangement. Though it wasn't even that cold, there was still smoke rising from some of the roofs. "So many different little fires burning to heat many spaces."

"Some of the oldest brothers do live together in a dormitory where they can be cared for. And we burn turf that's easily harvested over yonder." He pointed off into the distance. Margaret had long since ceased to be amazed that people burned the ground they walked on—and built houses out of it as well. It seemed an inexhaustible resource.

"Solitude can be a great luxury," she admitted. As a princess, let alone a queen, it could be hard to come by. "It seems a rather enviable existence."

"Some still find living within the settlement too busy. They live out in the hills and woods."

"I've heard of men living in caves, like the early Christians," said Christina. "Is that true?"

"Indeed it is. There are caves that have been inhabited by holy men for hundreds of years."

"I should like to see one," said Margaret, truly curious to see how one lived in such a space. She loved to pray alone in her own dark cave, but she couldn't imagine sleeping in there on a cold winter's night.

The abbot looked doubtful again. "The men who seek such solitude don't like to be disturbed."

"I should like to ask a holy man what he thinks of the people clinging on to old fashioned ideas of evil like the kelpies and the nucklavee."

"The what?" the abbot looked confused.

"We've learned that people are blaming a cursed water spirit for killing a young woman by the ferry crossing a few days ago. Surely such woeful ignorance is a danger to the villagers' immortal souls," said Margaret quietly.

"How extraordinary. I'm not from these parts myself so I

haven't encountered such nonsense. As to your first question, there are only three holy brothers who currently live in naturally occurring caves. Brother Aidh is one. I believe he knows the legends associated with the holy wells in these parts, but he's now so profoundly deaf it can be difficult to communicate with him. Brother Sechnall is another. People have long visited him for marital blessings for some reason and he seems to humor them well enough, though I've never heard him mention any legends. He's not from here but from somewhere in Ireland originally. Brother Lugaid is local to this area and travels among the people still, as part of his ministry, so he may be more familiar with the stories. He lives in a funny little cave almost like a badger hole, burrowed into a hillside. Perhaps we could pay him a visit?"

"I'd like that very much," said Margaret enthusiastically.

The abbot's expression still looked doubtful, but they set off across the countryside. Aidan, sword hanging on his belt, wanted to come with them, but the Abbot insisted that men of war would not be welcome and that the women would be safe in his—and God's—care. Aidan handed his sword to one of the other guards for safekeeping, and insisted that he was there at the king's orders to attend the queen, and nothing more.

They took a path through a small and well-maintained wood. "Much of this area used to be a forest, once upon a time, if legends are to be believed," he murmured, as they stepped over a fallen log. "These last copses are all that's left of it."

"What happened to the forest?" asked Christina.

"Burned for fuel and used for building, I suppose," said the Abbot. "We still have need of wood for rafters and tools and tables and the like so we're careful to preserve what's left."

The abbot announced their arrival when they were still

some distance from the hermit's abode. In fact they couldn't see his dwelling at all until they almost stumbled across it, an odd slanted arched doorway buried in the hillside. It didn't look large enough for a man to pass through.

There were no signs of the cave's occupant, so the abbot rapped on the door with his rough wooden staff. "Queen Margaret of Scotland and her family wish to call on you, Brother Lugaid."

Margaret wasn't at all sure what kind of apparition might greet them at the door, so she was surprised when a stout middle aged man with rosy cheeks and a neat tonsure opened the door—with some difficulty due to its odd construction—and stepped outside.

The abbot made introductions and Margaret greeted him and asked for his blessings for her and her party. After his brief benediction, she boldly asked if she might peep into his home, since it was so strange and unusual to her. He apologized for its mean and meagre state but did let them poke their heads inside, where it was far too dark to see anything at all, especially after the stark bright light outside.

As she peered into the darkness, Margaret heard Brother Lugaid ask Christina if she was the woman promised to The Raven. She almost bumped her head on the low door frame coming back out. How had this remote hermit heard of Fingal's marriage plans all the way out here? Were they common knowledge when a betrothal agreement was not even drawn up?

Christina seemed equally surprised and muttered pleasantries about the rugged beauty of the landscape that didn't answer his question at all. He listened with a pleasant expression on his face, then stared at her in silence for such a long time that Margaret began racking her brain for something to break it with.

"You will need many blessings and much prayer for the marriage to succeed," said Brother Lugaid.

"I think one could say the same of most marriages," said Margaret into the awkward silence. "But is there any particular reason why you say that?"

"Being married to a powerful man brings many challenges," said Brother Lugaid slowly, with a pleasant expression.

"Like what?" said Christina.

"Conflict, war, the murderous intent of others," said Brother Lugaid. "Much prayer is needed to protect him."

"I have spent the last years preparing to enter a convent, so I am well prepared for a life of prayer," said Christina, with some indignation.

"That will serve you well," said Brother Lugaid with a tiny smile. He pressed his hands together and nodded his head.

"What makes you say this?" asked Margaret, finding his oddly prophetic tone unsettling. "Do you claim some mystical foreknowledge?" If so, she'd throw that in an old trunk along with the kelpies and the fairies.

"Only such glimpses as the great Lord allows me."

Margaret was tempted to retort that the great lord around these parts was The Raven himself, and that he'd better hope his odd pronouncements didn't get back to him. But she managed to mind her tongue. She'd come here to ask him about the local legends. "Have you heard people speak of the kelpies?"

"The water spirits?"

"Don't tell me you believe in them," said Margaret.

"My faith in the Lord has happily supplanted any of the native superstitions I was raised with."

"But you were brought up to believe such spirits are real?"

"They're part of the fabric of life in our lands, as real as the clouds and the rain for many people."

"The local people really believe that water spirits assume the form of a horse and drag unsuspecting victims under the water…and eat them?"

He now tucked his chin and laughed a little. "It does sound foolish, but yes, the belief persists."

"But horses don't live in water. Why not a giant fish?" asked Christina curiously.

"How would a fish walk on the land and tempt a maiden onto his back?" asked Brother Lugaid, as if quite serious. "And who can resist a fine steed?" He was joking, clearly.

"Do you not feel a duty to dispel these superstitions?" asked Margaret. "To better focus the minds of the people on God?"

"I see no harm in them entertaining themselves with the ancient stories."

"But a girl has been recently murdered—surely news of it has reached you, if you know of my sister's future prospects —and the people are blaming her death on a water spirit!" She heard her voice rise. "She's been killed by a mortal man, not a watery demon."

"Calm yourself, my lady," said Brother Lugaid. "Perhaps it soothes their spirits to think of the death as a mystical event rather than a simple crime."

"It may soothe them but it also may prevent them seeking justice for poor murdered Agnhilda. It seems too easy to blame the crime on a creature of the mist when they should be aggressively pursuing whatever evil creature of flesh and blood had done this cruel deed."

"No doubt you're right, my lady," he said calmly. "I shall pray that her killer is discovered and punished."

"I hear that other women have been killed and their deaths blamed on these mystical kelpies. How is such a thing tolerated?"

"People here live a simple life, close to nature and

accepting of the will of God. A true believer will simply accept that God has called the women to his bosom. Do you not agree?"

Margaret struggled with feelings of anger and confusion. He'd made an argument that was hard to dispute, if indeed you accepted that any events on God's earth were simply his will.

Was it God's will for William of Normandy to conquer fair England and slay the flower of her nobility? She felt her heart pound faster.

"Perhaps we should leave, sister," said Christina, taking hold of her arm. "They're probably growing impatient for our return."

"Yes, I suspect so," said Margaret, trying to get her temper back under control. "Thank you for your time, Brother Lugaid."

As they walked back through the wood, Margaret muttered about silly superstitions perverting the course of justice.

The abbot nodded in agreement, then muttered, "Holy men live apart from the world of men and do not concern themselves with matters of earthly justice. God is our final judge and all men shall meet the fate that he has prepared for them. Our work as men of God is to pray for the living and the dead, that their souls may find eternal rest."

"I suppose great men do need someone who can pray for them day and night," mused Christina, as they walked back through the small wood. "You pray for Malcolm, don't you?"

"Indeed I do," said Margaret truthfully.

"I'm sure The Raven would benefit greatly from a wife with a heart for prayer."

"Any man would," said Margaret.

~

GRIZEL and the other servants had set up a table borrowed from the Culdees inside the low wattle enclosure that surrounded the huts, presumably to keep animals out. A light repast was now spread upon it and indeed everyone stood around, impatiently swatting flies from the food and drink.

Agatha, relaxing in a borrowed chair, greeted them with relief. "Darlings, we thought you'd rowed to Iona by now. I hope it was worth the trek to see a funny little man in a cave."

"We were barely gone at all," said Margaret. "Where's Fingal?" he wasn't at the table and she didn't see him standing nearby.

"He wandered off a while ago," said Agatha. "Please, eat something!"

Grizel brought Margaret a small platter with meat wrapped in pastry. She took a bite, even though she felt far from hungry and wondered how many flies had sat upon it. "I rather despair of dispelling superstition among the people here since the local holy men clearly tolerate it and see little wrong with it." The abbot had excused himself and hurried back to his quiet world of men.

"I'm sure people can believe in God and kelpies at the same time, much as we're able to speak two languages," said Agatha, holding a morsel of pastry in her dainty fingers.

"Where are Aelgith and Osgifu?" asked Margaret, suddenly noticing their absence.

Everyone looked around. No one answered.

"Grizel, when did you last see them?"

"They were on the boat behind us."

"Mother, were they here setting up the meal?"

"I don't think so, no," said Agatha.

Margaret's pastry curdled in her stomach. The last time they'd stolen away together, in a bid for freedom, they'd wound up drenched in blood and in prison accused of murder. She rose from her chair. "We must find them at once. Aidan, can you look into where they might have gone?"

He hesitated. "Your husband warned me not to leave your side on pain of death."

"Aelgith must have gone to see Oswin. She'll be there for sure if she hasn't foolishly tried to run away with him."

Aidan gave orders for two guards to hurry to the horse enclosures and not to come back without Aelgith and Osgifu. Margaret attended to her meal with considerable reluctance. "Aelgith seems so quiet but she has a fiery core. I suppose that's how she survived her years of captivity and privation. What if they can't find her?"

Aidan did not answer. Perhaps he was pondering that Aelgith was an adult with free will. Or perhaps he thought Margaret foolish for sheltering someone who'd already proved to be rash and unthinking. Either way, he had the wisdom to remain silent.

Fingal returned and no one mentioned the two missing women, so Margaret hoped he hadn't noticed their disappearance. He now seemed intent on making Christina laugh and blush. Margaret reflected that if she truly believed he'd keep this smile on Christina's face for the rest of her life, she'd be fully in favor of the marriage. But something told her he wouldn't.

After they'd finished eating, there was still no sign of the two guards or the missing women, so Margaret asked Grizel to accompany her on a walk around the settlement. Aidan stuck close behind. She could feel the holy brothers sneaking glances at them as if they were strange creatures of legend themselves, wandering about their remote settlement like will-o-the-wisps.

"I'm glad to have seen this place," said Margaret softly. "It's rather demystified the famous Culdees for me. Here a thousand years and can't banish the local belief in fairies."

Grizel said nothing. Her job was to agree silently and brush out her mistress's hair and pin her veil and keep her opinions to herself. Sometimes Margaret became so frustrated that the group of people who might dare to contradict her could be counted on one hand. "Am I a fool to keep Aelgith in my household?"

"No, my lady," said Grizel quickly.

"Are you just saying that to humor me?"

"Not at all. Aelgith is kind and caring and sings your praises day and night."

"I'm not sure how valuable that last merit is." They walked past an enclosure of beautiful white cattle. "And what do you make of Osgifu?" Unless prompted, the girl was quiet almost to muteness.

"She's still recovering from being taken captive, but she's coming out of her shell," said Grizel. "She can be quite funny sometimes. And she's very sweet with the baby."

Margaret had been trying to keep her mind off her baby. Babies were so tiny and delicate, so fragile and vulnerable to the evils of the world. And even being royal gave a baby little protection from the childhood sicknesses that could extinguish a precious life in days.

"My husband went home to fetch Edward," she finally admitted. "I wonder if I made a mistake sending him. What if they run into foul weather on the way back? Perhaps I should have gone home myself and left Christina here with him and my mother." Doubts gnawed at her.

"He's a strong and bonny babe, my lady. He'll be fine. I can't wait to hold him again."

"Me either!" exclaimed Margaret. "I hadn't expected to have such strong feelings for him. Which sounds ridiculous, I know! But I don't know how my mother has managed all the worry she must have endured for myself and my siblings over the years. Being a mother makes you prey to such awful fears."

"You've nothing to worry about, my lady. He'll never go hungry, or cold, or find himself friendless and alone. He's a prince of Scotland and will one day be king."

Grizel's words were no doubt intended to reassure and cheer her, but they had the opposite effect. Born into a comfortable existence as an English noble, Aelgith had surely never expected her husband to die by the sword and herself and her children to be sold into slavery.

Fate could bring some very cruel twists and turns to a human life. "I pray that you're right. Sometimes I—"

"Someone's coming this way, my lady," said Aidan suddenly. The rhythmic thudding of hooves in the distance heralded the arrival of horses before she could see them. Suddenly the riders appeared around the side of the hill. Margaret saw three men mounted, and Aelgith and Osgifu riding behind two of them.

They look almost like an invading army, she thought with alarm. Aidan held up his arm to attract their attention and the horses slowed and stopped near them. Margaret saw that Aelgith was riding behind her son, who sat atop a powerful gray horse. "Please dismount," she said to Oswin. "I wish to speak with you."

He helped his mother slide off the horse, then jumped down and tied up the reins and left his horse to graze. Aelgith didn't look particularly apologetic, but took Osgifu's hand and stood as if waiting to be scolded.

Margaret left Grizel with the other woman and summoned Oswin to come with her a little distance away. Aidan shadowed her at a discreet distance. The young man showed no emotion, which was surprising considering that he'd clearly reunited with his long-lost mother.

"You can see I didn't lie about your mother and sister being here."

His lip now trembled, but he got control of it quickly. "Yes, my lady. My mother apologized for slipping away to find me, but she said her life has shown her that any moment might be your last chance to…" He trailed off. "It was rash of her. I hope you won't hold it against her."

"I'm not sure her absence was much remarked upon except by me. But I wonder what you make of this place and its ruler? My sister may be coming to live here." She glanced back to make sure that no one but Aidan was in earshot.

She had few opportunities to ask a stranger their opinion of Fingal Mac Gofraid. Anyone in his household or even a local inhabitant would be well motivated to sing his praises. This seemed a rare chance to hear an unvarnished opinion. "Tell me anything you know that might make her wish to return home with me."

The lad hesitated. "The Raven is well liked by his people."

Margaret tried not to look doubtful. "He has no enemies?"

"He has enemies in Ireland. I've heard that, to be sure. Someone who craves his realm for himself."

"Who?" She could ask her husband if this might present a serious threat that could endanger Christina's future here.

"I don't know."

She wasn't sure she believed him. "Is there fighting going on?"

"I've been living here quite isolated so I'm not sure. But there's a brisk market in well-trained war horses," said Oswin. "Which isn't something you'd necessarily expect in times of peace."

Margaret wasn't sure that they'd ever know peace again, with William and his men galloping all over England crushing any hint of rebellion. "Continue your duties and don't reveal anything about our plans. I'll reassure your mother that we'll bring you home with us."

Oswin showed little emotion. She wasn't sure he believed her. Not that he thought she was lying, but perhaps he'd learned not to harbor too much hope since he had little to no agency in his own life.

She turned to Aidan and told him to dismiss the horsemen, who then rode away at a canter. She startled when she realized that Fingal and Christina had followed them and seen, though not heard, some of her exchange with Oswin.

"You had a lot to say to the horseman," said Fingal, after she rejoined them.

"I look forward to him working for us in Dunfermline." This was no secret. "We're in need of a good horse trainer."

"I shall be sad to part with him, but will be more than delighted with my side of the bargain." He turned to Christina and for a tense moment she thought he was going to kiss her sister. Christina stiffened as if the same panic surged through her as well.

"I am worth no more than a horseman?" asked Christina, clearly only half joking. The prospect that one was a good bargain for the other was insulting on many levels.

"You are worth so much more, my angel. I shall cherish you for the rest of my days." Christina softened a little, but didn't show that simpering smile she'd been exhibiting lately.

Would the rest of The Raven's days be a long time? Or did he have enemies seeking to shorten his time here on earth? That would be something for her husband to examine with his advisers before Christina's life and safety were delivered into the hands of this man.

CHAPTER 13

alcolm returned sooner than Margaret expected. Longer summer days meant that light now stretched into the evening. Still, it was almost dusk —and quite late—when a troop of horsemen approached the camp at a slow and steady pace.

Margaret was sitting outside with the ladies, enjoying the fair evening and enough light for stitching before yet another night in Fingal's dark and smoky hall. When she saw the large group of men she sprang to her feet, hope and panic surging in her heart.

Grizel picked up her dropped embroidery, a cap she was making for the baby, and Margaret hurried forward to meet the group, searching for little Edward. "Where is he?" she cried. Had he died while they were gone? Or on the long journey? He was so small and delicate, just a few weeks old—

"He's right here, strapped to my chest," said Malcolm. His broad fingers fiddled with some buckles and released the bundled form of her son. Startled awake, the boy let out a wail. "He's been good as gold for most of the journey, though we had to stop many times for the wet nurse to feed him."

Margaret looked behind him and saw the long procession of horses and people on foot, a larger group than they'd originally come with. She held out her arms. "May I hold him?"

"Yes, you can hold me," said Malcolm, with a grin. "But here, take the baby first so I can dismount."

Margaret was so excited about holding her baby that she missed his joke until her son was in her hands, already heavier than when she'd left. "Oh, my precious one! How I've missed you." She rained kisses on little Edward's cheeks and forehead, then gathered him close and gave him a gentle squeeze.

He was wrapped in many layers, and now wriggled as if desperate to be free of them. Grizel and Aelgith hurried forward and together unwound his wrappings while Margaret sank into her husband's embrace.

"I've missed you so much," she breathed against his chest.

"I've missed you more." He kissed her gently on the lips. "The journey was smooth with good weather."

"Thank God for your safe passage, and Edward's. I never want to be parted from him again." Now unwrapped, little Edward was flailing his arms and fussy. "He's probably hungry." Margaret could feel her breasts, which had quieted down considerably during this sojourn away from him, starting to ache as if milk might spurt forth. "Where's the wet nurse?"

Mairi hurried forward, limping slightly as her legs adjusted to being back on the ground after riding all day. "Here, my lady! He's been eating well. He'll grow up to be a strong warrior like his papa." The ladies hurried Mairi to a seat in their midst and settled her comfortably with the baby at her breast.

Servants brought refreshments outside, offering them first to Malcolm and his men, and then to the rest of the company.

Fingal accosted Malcolm with effusive greetings and the two men spoke too fast for Margaret to follow the conversation. Or perhaps her mind was addled by the joy of having little Edward back again. Her chest still ached with panic and longing, which made no sense since he was safe! Perhaps those hallmarks of new motherhood would be slower to fade than aching breasts...if they ever did.

"Aelgith, why are you crying?" Her friend was now sobbing into her hands.

"I don't know my lady," she gasped, between sobs. "I'm sorry."

"Calm yourself," she said softly. She stroked Aelgith's shoulder. "Everything is fine. Edward is back with us." *And soon Oswin will be too.* She said the last part in her mind, hoping that Aelgith heard it. "All will be well."

Was she trying to convince Aelgith or herself? Christina was smiling and cooing at little Edward while he sucked fiercely at the wet nurse. "I can't wait until I have a baby of my own," she said with a sigh.

Margaret glanced at Fingal, who was mercifully out of earshot, still jawing with Malcolm. "There's no rush. You're young and could marry in five years time and still have ten babies."

"Why would you not want me to enjoy the same happiness that you do?" asked Christina suddenly. "Do you prefer to have me as your lady-in-waiting?"

"No! I just want to make sure...." She trailed off. *I just want to make sure you're not marrying into a nightmare.* There were far too many people around for such frankness.

"Edgar!" she called to her brother who had arrived and dismounted and was now looking around for a welcome. "Thank you for helping to bring little Edward here."

"Your husband made us ride so slowly I thought we'd grow roots," said Edgar with a grin. "He took very good care of his son but I had to leave him behind any time I wanted a good gallop. It's good to be back here." He looked around enthusiastically. "I found myself missing The Raven. A capital fellow! I was talking to Malcolm about how we could all join forces and perhaps lead a—"

The Raven looked up then strode toward him and clapped him on the arm. "Now that you're back we shall go for a hunt."

"I was telling my sister that we might form a united front against the Normans. They wouldn't stand a chance if we—"

"Come inside and have some ale," said Fingal, interrupting him. "Settle down and listen to some music. I have a new bard here just arrived from Kilkenny."

"Oh, does he have news?" said Edgar, giving a mysterious look. "I'd be most interested in learning what the king of—" Fingal ushered him inside, rattling on about a stag in some nearby woods.

"Dear Edgar, always trying to start an intrigue," said Christina.

"He'll start a war if we're not careful," muttered Margaret. "Haven't we had enough of war?"

"Fingal at least doesn't humor his nonsense," whispered Christina. "You see how he deflects him."

"He probably hasn't realized how single-minded our brother is." Margaret's lips were right against her sister's ear. "Poor Edgar still feels like the crown was snatched from his head when it was never his to begin with."

"And if he had it, he'd probably think of nothing but hunting and feasting. We need to get him married. The right woman would settle him down."

"Now you're all in favor of marriage," said Margaret with a smile. "After swearing up and down it was nothing but bondage and servitude to this earthly realm."

"Let's just say I'm able to see the advantages now."

Margaret swallowed. "Are you falling in love with Fingal?"

"Girls! What are you whispering about?" called Agatha. "Let's go inside before the evening air chills us to the bone."

"It's summer, Mama!" cried Christina. "And the air is lovely."

"That west wind goes right through me," said Agatha, with an imaginary shiver. "It's my old bones."

Margaret and Christina laughed at their youthful and beautiful mother, who could easily marry again if she had half a mind to. But who would be a suitable husband for the widow of the almost-king of England?

MARGARET COULD BARELY LET GO of Edward now that he was back within reach. If she'd had maternal feelings before, they'd been strengthened tenfold by her tiny son's absence. Each little coo and cry tugged at her heartstrings and made her want to hold his small body close.

"He's grown even since we've been gone!"

"He'll be sitting up soon," said Agatha. "And next thing you know he'll be running around pulling the dogs' tails."

"No, he won't!" protested Margaret. "He's going to be gentle and kind to animals and people."

"He's going to be a king, not a saint," said Malcolm. They sat around Fingal's table. Wine, ale and a good meal created an atmosphere of relaxed conviviality.

"A man can be a kind and gentle king. You're one yourself," said Margaret.

Both Malcolm and Fingal laughed loudly.

"Why are you laughing?"

"Your husband is soft and gentle with you but his enemies quake in their boots when they hear his name," said Fingal.

"Do yours as well?" asked Margaret.

"I certainly hope so." He and Malcolm laughed again.

"Do you have enemies?" continued Margaret brightly. She wanted to get to the bottom of this.

"If a man doesn't have enemies, is he even a man?" asked Fingal, looking to Malcolm for backup. Malcolm nodded and they both chuckled.

Margaret sighed.

"I'll side with both of you against your enemies if you'll side with me against mine," chimed in Edgar.

Both Malcolm and Fingal made agreeable but noncommittal noises.

"If we could gather a force of allies from among the kings of Ireland, and join together and assault England from the western side, we can take them by surprise—"

"Calm down, lad, you'll give us indigestion," said Malcolm with gruff cheer. "That's a subject for another day."

"Are the kings of Ireland friends or enemies?" asked Margaret. As far as she knew, Malcolm saw them as allies but didn't maintain much contact with them. He was far more concerned with the thanes and mormaers in his own kingdom, and beyond that the earls of Orkney and the always simmering Danes and Norsemen. The seas of The Raven's territory, by contrast, lapped right up against Ireland's shores —or was it the reverse?

"It's a complicated matter best saved for another day," said Fingal breezily. "Bard, a tune!" The bard struck up a melody on his harp.

Enemies, thought Margaret. She would have to ask Malcolm to look into this. Christina's safety and happiness would depend on peace and what prosperity could be wrung from this windswept and rugged land.

～

MARGARET AND MALCOLM left the table before all the others, at Malcolm's suggestion. Fingal jovially wished him a happy night in his wife's loving arms, and turned to flirt with Christina.

Margaret was relieved to get some distance from the incessant strumming and piping of the bard and musician. The wet nurse had already taken little Edward to sleep in a quiet corner. She'd watch over him during the night and feed him if he became fussy.

Grizel undressed her and unbraided her hair, then went away to sleep near the wet nurse. Margaret climbed into bed and under the covers, where Malcolm already waited for her. "I've missed you so much," she breathed into his neck.

"I've only been gone a few days, but I'm glad to be missed."

"It felt like an eternity, but I'm eternally grateful that you brought our son back with you, safe and happy and healthy."

Malcolm kissed her gently. "I struggled to make myself ride slowly and steadily for the baby, when I wanted to gallop back toward you. What did I miss while I was gone?"

Margaret sighed. "I haven't found out who killed poor Agnhilda, but it seems that girls have been disappearing for years. Because they're usually found in or near water, the locals think it's a legendary water spirit."

Malcolm laughed. "Oh dear."

"The old ferryman is a possibility, for that reason, but there's nothing sinister about him. And why would he kill them?"

Malcolm kissed her again. "I can't imagine. And how is your sister's romance with our host progressing?"

"She seems quite enamored of him and has warmed to the prospect of married life, though he scared her off a couple of days ago when he tried to kiss her."

"He wouldn't have done that if I'd been here," said Malcolm, his voice dropping an octave.

"I know. And I'm sure she did, too. He tried to take advantage of the rapport he's built with her. I worry that he's a man who enjoys women's company a little too much. I think he's seduced women before and I suspect that Agnhilda was one of them. Her brother and his wife admitted that there had been some kind of informal presumption—at least on their part—about a marriage between her and Fingal and that her brother sent her to his hall."

"He sent her alone in the night?"

"He said he wanted it to seem like the whim of a love-struck young woman rather than a formal challenge that could spark a conflict between the families. Then when we had our almsgiving feast I saw our host laughing and smiling with a dark-haired woman."

"A man can laugh and smile with a woman without it being bawdy."

"Yes, but something about it struck me as...oh, I don't know. At the very least he's a practiced flirt."

"You'd hardly expect him to be a virgin." Malcolm seemed amused by this idea.

"I suppose not. But then why shouldn't he be? I'm pretty sure my brother Edgar is still a virgin. A Christian nobleman should save himself for marriage and his wedded wife."

Malcolm was silent for a moment. Did he know something about Edgar that she didn't? She did tend to leave the table for prayer and bed before the men dove too deep into their cups. Did Edgar tell stories of exploits that were unknown to her? Anyway, that was not important right now.

She stroked his face. "I know you were married before and you're now a wonderful husband to me. But I worry that he'll still want to enjoy other women after they're married, which would be awful." She trusted Malcolm not to cheat on her. He knew she wouldn't take it lightly. "My father never stepped out on my mother. I'm sure of it. He loved her like they were newlyweds until the day he died."

"I feel like a newlywed every day with you," said Malcolm softly. He kissed her lips.

"We are newlyweds," she said, a smile crossing her mouth. "Not even two years. Do you think our passion for each other will fade?"

"Never."

THE NEXT MORNING, Margaret rose to attend early morning mass in the chapel. She'd formed a sort of routine, with Grizel always ready to dress her and accompany her. Aidan too waited inside the hall to attend her and stay with her throughout the service.

She'd grown used to the modest chapel behind the hall, a rather ancient wooden building on a stone foundation, where The Raven's forbears had likely said their prayers for centuries. After the mass she waited to make confession with the priest—another daily habit.

But today she had another purpose. Her most grievous sin was doubting the wisdom of her sister's marriage to Fingal. Confessing it was a risky gamble, since the priest lived and worked in the service of The Raven. The cleric was an older man, though, probably almost three times the age of his young master.

She'd also formed the impression that he was—as one would hope—a man of true faith. He'd have heard The Raven's confessions. While she would never ask a man of the cloth to betray the secrets of the confessional, she might ask him to give his own informed opinion of the matter of her sister's impending marriage.

There was no separate area for confession as one might find in a larger abbey. Instead Grizel and Aidan retired outside while she approached the right side of the altar where a cushion now awaited her daily use.

"Bless me, Father, for I have sinned," she whispered, kneeling on the cushion. "I confess that I have doubts about my husband's wisdom in wishing for my sister to marry here and spend her life in this place—" She hesitated. "Perhaps you could soothe my doubts if you could reassure me that this is indeed a holy and peaceful realm."

There was a pause. Margaret wondered if her words would get back to Fingal, even though they should be protected as secrets of the confessional. Surely the priest couldn't blame her for wanting to ensure that her sister wasn't marrying into danger or depravity?

"You are right to see such doubt as a sin, my lady. Your husband's wisdom is your best guide in life. Your penance is to abstain from questioning his decisions for yourself and your family."

Margaret's heart sank. "I shall fast for five days," she said. "And wash the feet of thirty paupers as further penance."

"The Lord does not ask that of you, but for you to submit to your husband as a good and dutiful wife must do."

"Yes, Father," she whispered, bile rising in her throat. Why did her spirit rise up against this injunction? She stood up, uncomfortable emotions roiling inside her. He hadn't answered her question about whether Fingal would be a suitable husband for her sister, which was at least somewhat impertinent considering that she was Queen of the Scots.

Still, she had presented her doubtful attitude as a sin because she knew that it was, at least in the minds of many. And he had responded in kind.

But the question still burned in her heart. "Now that we've risen and you're not my confessor, please reassure me that my beloved sister will be marrying into a holy atmosphere."

Despite the priest's great age, for all she knew he had a concubine in the nearby village. Or three mistresses and eight children and thirty grandchildren among them. Such a thing was not even unusual. Would she trust his answer if he gave it?

"Do you not hear the bells that mark the hours?" he asked. He stood a head taller than her, with wispy white hair and cold gray eyes that peered down into hers with disapproval.

She wanted to say that she rarely did hear the bells, which seemed quieter than most, as if to avoid disturbing sleep. But she held her tongue.

He continued. "You yourself have attended mass daily during your time here. Do you find it unholy?"

"Of course not! I'm impressed by the solemnity of the services, hence my trusting you with my anxious questions."

His expression softened somewhat. "Your sister would do well to trust in the Lord and his plans for her. And you would as well."

Margaret blinked. "Well said." The priest had now effectively shut her up with an entirely appropriate response. What had made her distrust the Lord's plan for her sister? Or even her lord's plan for them all. "We've just been so buffeted by fate...."

"We are all passengers on a ship through this weary world," he said slowly. "If God blows storms at us, it is our destiny and our duty to weather them with faith."

"Yes, Father. Thank you for your wise counsel." She pressed her hands together in gratitude, then turned and walked slowly out of the chapel. The door opened as soon as she pressed on it, since Aidan waited outside for her, with Grizel at his side.

"Are you well, my lady?" asked her maid. "You look pale."

"I'm very well, thank you," she said. "I shall spend today in fasting and prayer."

Grizel looked like she wanted to protest, but held her tongue. They walked back to the hall. It was a bright day, with patches of blue in the white sky. The hilly and rocky landscape looked picturesque rather than forbidding.

The priest's image of them being on a ship was an interesting one. A ship had brought her family north to Scotland. She'd boarded that ship wracked with doubts and recriminations, having begged to stay safely in the convent at Wilton but finally succumbing to her mother's worries that they needed to secure a home for Edgar, who might not be safe if William saw him as a threat.

High winds and rough seas had disabled their vessel and they'd narrowly avoided being wrecked on the rocky coast. Yet here she was, happily married to a good man and mother of the sweetest baby on earth. Perhaps the Lord had such happiness in store for Christina as well.

Back in the hall, she was surprised to see both Malcolm and Fingal sitting at the main table, breaking their fast bright and early and wreathed in smiles.

"Such good cheer!" she exclaimed. "And a beautiful morning it is."

"A beautiful morning indeed," said Fingal. "For your husband and I have agreed to the terms of my marriage to your dear sister." He lifted his cup. "To her good health."

Margaret stood in stunned silence. "Where is my sister?" she managed, when she finally found her voice. "She must be overjoyed."

"I believe she's with the cook making arrangements for the wedding feast," said Fingal.

"When will it be?" Margaret heard the tremor in her voice.

"As soon as the requisite delicacies can be secured," said Fingal with a smile. "And all the guests invited."

Margaret took a seat at the table. The wet nurse appeared with little Edward, and Margaret took him in her arms, grateful for the sweet distraction. His plump hand gripped playfully around her wrist and his sudden smile filled her heart with joy.

"I look forward to meeting the nobles of your kingdom," she said, when she remembered to look up. "Will you be inviting men from Ireland as well?"

A shadow passed across his face. "I don't wish to delay our happy union by waiting for people to make too great of a journey. The attendance of those nearest to us will be more than sufficient to celebrate our marriage."

Margaret looked at Malcolm, whose face betrayed nothing of his thoughts. *He arranged this without consulting me. I wanted more time to learn what my sister is getting into.* The priest's words clawed at her conscience.

This is a test from the Lord. He wishes to humble me. I must submit to His will, and to my husband's. Surely with age and the seasoning of life she'd eventually be wise and steady enough to do that without having to question everything first. But then why did her mind fill with questions and worries?

Surely the Lord had put them there.

CHAPTER 14

After sitting for a while with Edward nestled in her lap, Margaret handed the babe to the wet nurse and went to look for Christina. She found her speaking with the cook, a woman of forty or so with a red face, and the steward, a tall, thin man with a long nose, about what would need to be ordered for the feast. The cook nodded with a panicked look on her face while probably making mental calculations involving hundreds of duck eggs. The steward was frantically taking illegible notes on a much reused scrap of parchment with a scratchy quill that he kept dipping into a pot of ink sat on the prep table next to a pile of plucked feathers.

"Sister! What wine should we order for the feast? How long will it take a ship to get here from the coast of France?"

"I don't know," said Margaret. "Perhaps it would be best to buy from a wine merchant who already has wine stored nearby." Over the last year, she'd gradually arranged for Malcolm to have a steady stream of luxury goods arriving from the continent, avoiding England and King William altogether. But the prospect of carrying heavy casks of wine overland from Dunfermline or Edinburgh seemed daunting and she had no idea if the straits between England and Ireland were sailed by pirates—such a thing wouldn't surprise her in the least. "Why don't we discuss and plan it together and then give the steward a list?

"All right, but do go ahead and secure the beef and lamb and ducks and geese," she said gaily to the steward. Those can be found locally, I'm sure!" Christina practically skipped out of the kitchen. "It's happening! I'm getting married. Oh, I'm so happy."

"I'm happy for you," said Margaret, trying to sound cheerful. "How did this come about? Did The Raven say something last night to convince you?

"He promised that I should spend as much time with you and the family as I'd like every year," she said with a smile.

"That's certainly wonderful. And it's not that far at all if you think about it." On the other hand, Christina's absences might give her husband ample leisure time to enjoy the company of other women.

"To think, I shall be sharing my bed with him every night, just as you do with Malcolm. The look on your husband's face as he ushered you away from the table last night gave me quite a pang of jealousy." Christina laughed. She did seem quite overjoyed by this turn of events. "And soon my husband will have that same silly expression on his face."

Margaret didn't remember Malcolm looking foolish in any way, but she had found it sweet that he wanted to leave the company so they could be alone in bed. He was a romantic man, very tender despite his gruff manner. "I only hope he shall be as kind and loving as Malcolm," she said warmly.

"You sound doubtful. Like you don't think he will." Christina's voice rose. "Do you think my attractions are so inferior to yours?"

"No! You're beautiful and clever." *I just worry that your*

husband will be more like....most men. "I'm sure you'll be very happy together." She was glad she'd already confessed her qualms about this union to the priest. Perhaps that made her continued doubts less egregious in the eyes of the Lord.

"Mama was so happy with Papa. He loved her so much. And Malcolm adores you. Surely the Lord will grant me the same blessings," said her sister hopefully.

"That does only seem fair," said Margaret, trying to sound optimistic. "When do you think the ceremony will take place?" She still wanted to leave here as soon as possible with Aelgith's precious son Oswin in their party. She just hadn't planned to leave her beloved sister behind in his place.

"I wonder how quickly I shall get pregnant?" Christina's eyes widened. "Perhaps I could have a baby by Christmas."

"Christmas is barely six months away. A baby takes nine months to cook," said Margaret with a smile. "Perhaps by Easter, though. I wonder if you could come spend Christmas with us this year. The prospect of losing you weighs so heavily on my heart."

She found herself suddenly clutching her sister in her arms. Christina patted her back gently then pulled away. Margaret became conscious of the people watching them. They stood outside the kitchen and Grizel and Aidan hovered nearby. Aidan was apparently still "on duty" even though Malcolm had returned. "I'm sorry," she murmured. "I just—" she wiped away a sudden tear that rolled down her cheek. "I love you so much, sister."

"I know," said Christina, looking suddenly more solemn. "The separation will be hard for me as well. But I can't spend my whole life as a handmaid in my sister's court. Even if I wasn't marrying, I'd be leaving soon to take the veil."

I wish you could stay in my court. She had a sudden flash of panic that their mother might leave with Christina. Agatha might think that as Margaret was now so well settled with

Malcolm, her younger daughter would need her more. "I shall so look forward to your visits and I pray that they will be long ones!"

"If my husband will let me out of his sight. Or perhaps he'll come too?"

Margaret thought it unlikely that Fingal would leave his own lands and people for more than a few days at a time. If a leader was absent then the other nobles might start to get ideas about how much more effectively they would lead the people. Her husband had seized the throne for himself and held it with an iron grip.

"I can visit you here as well," said Margaret. "It already feels like a second home. And Malcolm says that Fingal's realm is vast and varied, with natural wonders and holy places that rival the Kingdom of the Scots."

"I shall strive to do good works for the people, as you do," said Christina softly. "I wish to go visit the Culdee who's known for blessing marriages. They say he gives advice as well as benedictions to couples. I'd like to gain any wisdom that he might offer me on how to start my wedded journey."

"What would a man of God know of married life? Surely a celibate monk is the very last person to know any useful advice to give you. You'd learn more from talking to our dear mother. Let's walk a little." Margaret wanted to get away from the crowd of people hovering nearby. They strolled away from the hall, and Grizel and Aidan took the hint and hung back.

"Mother only knows of her own marriage to our father, who was a very different man than Fingal," said Christina. "Papa was mild-mannered and gentle and—" She tailed off. "I miss him so."

"I miss him every day," said Margaret. "But do you not hope that your husband may be a gentle man as well? He has a taste for drink and music but I've heard no clamoring for battle. Our brother has tried several times to coax him into fantasies of violence against William and he's brushed him off with pleasantries. I see this as a promising sign that he's a peacemaker, not a man of war."

"That is a good observation, sister," said Christina cheerfully. "And naturally I shall encourage him in this."

"My concerns about your future husband," Margaret chose her words carefully. "Are not that he's warlike but that he—perhaps—enjoys the company of women too much."

"He shall have my company," said Christina with a smile.

Margaret's heart sank. Was her sister really so naive? "I just wonder...when that girl burst into the hall, I got the impression that she'd been encouraged then jilted by him. I spoke with her brother and his wife at the almsgiving and they all but confirmed it."

"They were betrothed?" Christina did have a hint of alarm in her voice.

"Not in a formal way. But I got the impression that he might have...had relations of some sort with her."

"Like a kiss?"

"Quite possibly." Margaret bit her lip. "You resisted such an attempt as being inappropriate before marriage, but a girl of less—character—might have been tempted to encourage his affections instead."

Christina was silent for a moment. "I suppose I'd be a fool to think that a man like Fingal has never kissed or caressed a woman. But surely he'll forsake other women for his wedded wife?"

"I would certainly hope so."

"But?"

"But many men succumb to temptation even after marriage. Especially if they engaged in such behavior before it."

Christina inhaled slowly. They were still walking, and

Margaret glanced back to make sure no one was near them. "I'm not saying this to be cruel or even to discourage you from the marriage, but just to warn you. A husband's infidelity is something that many wives must manage with grace."

"And silence," said Christina. "Since it's a wife's duty to uphold her husband's reputation."

"You'd accept that?" asked Margaret, surprised. "I don't think I could manage to maintain decorum if I suspected that my husband had spent even one second in another woman's embrace since our marriage."

"I don't know," said Christina suddenly turning to look at her. "I hate the idea."

"Do you hate me for bringing it up?" She took her sister's hand and squeezed it.

"No, sister, I don't. I thank you for putting this worrisome thought in my head that I may mull it over." She stopped suddenly, jerking Margaret to a halt as they were still holding hands. "Such behavior by my husband might turn me into an angry shrew."

"I have no evidence that he's…taken advantage of any woman in particular, but it's a suspicion. And we still don't know who killed poor Agnhilda. I do know that it wasn't a water spirit shaped like a horse."

Christina frowned. "Surely you don't really think that he killed her?"

"Not with his own hands. But it's possible that he might have arranged for someone else to do the deed if he thought her a serious impediment to his betrothal to you."

"That would be murder, even if done by proxy," said Christina, with surprising calmness. "I could never marry a murderer."

"I have no proof, or even the slightest suggestion by anyone, that he is a murderer. However, I would very much like to find out who did kill Agnhilda, as it would soothe my nerves greatly to discover that it was someone else."

Christina blinked. "How can we find out who killed her?"

"I've been turning this subject over in my mind." She turned and they looked back toward the settlement. Smoke rose over the thatched roof of the kitchen, but not over the hall, since the June day was comfortable without a fire. A girl leading a donkey loaded with sacks approached from the direction of the river. She wondered if the donkey had ridden in the boat to cross it. "People say that several women have been killed over the years, and they're usually found near water."

"Water is hardly in short supply in these parts. There are lakes and rivers and pools and waterfalls in almost every direction. I'm not sure that means anything."

"It may be a deliberate attempt to have people dismiss the deaths as the work of a mystical beast. And by a long time I mean decades, since before your intended was even born."

"Which would absolve him of the crimes," said Christina, looking her in the eye hopefully.

"It would, if indeed all the killings were by the same person. But they may not be. If a man, for example, wished to rid himself of his wife to pursue another, he could choose to dispose of her in a manner that would easily blame her death on the same source—mythical or otherwise—as the previous killings. It's possible that every woman was killed by a different person, for a different reason, but arranged to look like a similar circumstance."

"These people cannot be so simple as to blame every murder on a fairy of some kind," said Christina.

"If the deaths were coming thick and fast I'm sure they wouldn't. But typically there are years between each one. Which made me wonder if it was someone older...." She drew in a breath. "Like the ferryman, who knows everyone in the area and would have occasion to be alone with anyone who crossed the river unaccompanied. Which seems quite common. Look at this girl arriving with her donkey."

The girl was about fourteen, from all appearances, and the donkey followed placidly behind her on the end of a rope as if both had made this journey many times. Christina shivered.

"Are you all right?" asked Margaret.

"I'm fine. And it's a good sign that girls and women feel free to travel alone without male protection. I shall be happy to live in such a place. Let's go back to the hall."

As they walked back to the hall, Margaret noticed the guards arguing with a small group of people. A woman and two men. The visitors seemed to be trying to gain access to the hall and four of Fingal's men were refusing them.

The woman looked vaguely familiar, and Margaret stared at her trying to remember where she'd seen her. It suddenly dawned on her that this was the tall woman she'd seen at the almsgiving, talking to Fingal about livestock. Her long dark hair had been loose then, but now hung in two braids under a veil. The men were different ages and might be her father and brother.

Overwhelmed by curiosity, Margaret turned and hurried toward them. "What's going on here?"

Fingal's men looked at her in astonishment. None of them replied. She directed the same question to the group of visitors.

"We seek an audience with Fingal Mac Gofraid, said the older man. "On a matter of great importance." The speaker looked her up and down, clearly not recognizing her—why would he?—and trying to puzzle out who she might be in her finely trimmed dress. "Are you the woman we hear is betrothed to him?"

"No, but I am her sister," said Margaret. How had word

spread so quickly? Perhaps those delivering food and supplies to Fingal's hall carried the news to the surrounding communities. "I am Margaret of Scotland, queen to King Malcolm. Were you coming to offer your congratulations?"

The younger man let out a snort of laughter. "Instead I should demand payment for what he took from my sister!"

"What did he take?" asked Margaret. The girl looked panicked. "Nothing," she hissed. She grabbed the older man's sleeve. "Father, we must leave."

"Aye, I suppose we must." Her father gave Margaret an odd look. "For there's nothing to be done about it now."

They turned and left, leaving Margaret feeling slighted and uneasy. They were obviously angry. Margaret wanted to ask the guards why but knew that as a guest of Fingal, and as his almost-sister-in-law, that would be utterly inappropriate.

"What's going on?" called Christina from behind her. She'd been standing a short distance away."

Margaret hurried to her and whispered in her ear. "This family wanted to see Fingal. I have a feeling that the girl's a jilted would-be bride of some sort."

Christina sighed and tossed her veil over her shoulder. "I'd imagine there will be several of those. Likely every noble within two hundred miles wishes to have one of his daughters married to The Raven."

I should demand payment for what he took.

What had he taken? Did he enjoy intimacies with the girl after promising her the security of marriage? How did her family know of such a shameful thing happening? Had she told them? Or worse, had they coaxed her into allowing the seduction, hoping it would trap him into a betrothal?

"Your husband was married before and has children," said Christina. "Did that bother you?"

"It's not like I had a choice in the matter," said Margaret.

"Whether it bothered me or not, it was my clear duty to marry him to save our family."

"That doesn't answer my question. Knowing him now, do you mind that you're not his first and only?"

"No."

"Then I shall be equally accepting. The Raven has been very attentive to me."

"Indeed he has," said Margaret. " But don't lie with him, or even kiss him, until you're wedded by the priest."

"You know I wouldn't!" said Christina, in a shocked tone.

"Good."

CHAPTER 15

That night they ate an extravagant feast to celebrate Christina's betrothal. The Raven seemed triumphant, grinning like a fiend, and wine and ale and mead flowed in excess.

"These northmen love their music so much," said Christina, as she and Margaret listened to yet another bard rambling on about some ancient battle, accompanied by chirping pipes, harp and a thudding hand drum.

"I know. It's possibly my least favorite thing about them," said Margaret, attempting a smile. "I used to think I loved music and song, but in truth I prefer dawn birdsong to anything uttered by humans."

"Me too," said Christina into her ear. They weren't even whispering as their words were drowned out by the musical cacophony and the sound of men clapping and stamping their feet in rhythm. "But I suppose I shall get used to it. Do you think it's too early for us to slip away to bed?"

"I think we should stay a little longer. We are celebrating your betrothal, after all. Sitting through these feasts and even looking happy about it is our duty." She nudged her sister. "Are you sure you don't want to be a nun?"

"It's a bit too late now, isn't it?" said Christina with an wry smile.

The evening wore on and the men became increasingly loud and boisterous. Christina stayed away from Fingal, likely for fear of him wanting to grope or fondle his newly betrothed sweetheart.

Malcolm was leading the company in an old song about his ancestors arriving from somewhere called Scythia and being turned away from Ireland and sent to populate Scotland, when two guards approached the table and whispered in Fingal's ear.

His expression hardened and he said something sharp to them, then sent them away and joined back into song. Margaret watched the two guards retreat into the darkness. When Fingal was next distracted by conversation, Margaret caught Aidan's eye and beckoned for him to approach her.

"I'd like to know what that guard said to our host," she whispered in his ear. "Please find out."

Aidan slipped away. The high table where they sat glowed with candlelight, throwing the rest of the hall into shadow, so she couldn't see where he went. Margaret watched Fingal's expression. Underneath his practiced gaiety she detected a note of something more serious.

"Let's rise from the table," she whispered to Christina. "I think it's late enough for us to take our leave." They smiled and thanked Fingal for another wonderful feast. He called for Christina to come sit with him but she wisely begged fatigue. They walked away from the table, in the direction Aidan had gone. Where was he?

Rush lights glowed in a few dim corners, where servants hunched against the walls, no doubt exhausted and waiting for their master to bed down for the night so they could do the same. "Let's go outside." She hoped they could speak with Aidan out there where there were less listening ears.

A rare clear night sparkled with stars. The chilly nip in the air felt wonderful on her skin after the thick, smoky atmosphere of the hall. Cows snoozed in a pen nearby. "I think I shall suggest that the animals are moved further from the hall," said Christina crinkling her nose. "The way things are arranged at Dunfermline."

"I like the smell of horses," said Margaret, "so I don't mind them being stabled nearby. But cows are a whole different matter." She looked anxiously around for Aidan. "I wonder if he knows where we are?" Just as she was about to suggest they go back inside, Aidan approached.

"I learned what they told him," he said quietly, leaning toward them. "Another girl has been found dead."

"Murdered?" asked Margaret.

"They said there are no signs of violence on her."

"Was she found near water?" asked Christina.

"Yes, face down in a small stream, they say."

"Ah, the famous kelpies," said Margaret darkly. It suddenly occurred to her that the dead girl could be the same one who came to plead her marital case earlier and was turned away without seeing Fingal. "Did you learn her name?"

"The guards said they didn't know it."

"We must go view her body tomorrow," said Margaret to Christina.

"Why?" She wrapped her arms around herself. "You're giving me the shivers."

"To find out who killed her. You don't really believe it was a water spirit in the form of a horse, do you?"

"I mean....I don't know. Maybe it was such a thing."

"Aidan, please tell me you don't believe in murderous water spirits."

"Ah, I've lived my whole life in Scotland and I'd be lying if I said I hadn't been raised to tread quietly around the sprites of the woods and waters." He appeared to be deadly serious. "But I dare say a thorough investigation is called for."

"It's not really any of our business, though," protested Christina. "How would you feel if Fingal came to Dunfermline and wanted to stick his oar into local matters? You'd find it rude that he didn't trust you to handle them yourself."

This was true. Still, if yet another girl who had reason to feel jilted by Fingal had been murdered, then the finger of accusation would point quite squarely at their host.

"Aidan, can you be my ears among the male company?" said Margaret. "And tell me if you hear anything related to the death. Anything at all."

"Yes, my lady, though I suspect your husband's ears are as good as mine."

"His ears are sharp enough, but he's the king, so lips lock up when he enters the room. I shall draw him away to bed with me and I'd like you to learn as much as you can while he's absent. You can tell me what you find out in the morning."

"I wish you'd leave it alone," protested Christina. "We're going to be busy preparing for my wedding, and don't have time to run around the countryside peering into other people's business."

Margaret's foremost concern was finding an opportunity to do just that. It wasn't easy to come up with a convincing excuse to leave the hall. "Perhaps we could go visit the holy men again. We might ask to meet with the hermit who blesses people's marriages."

"Perhaps The Raven and I could visit him together."

"Yes," said Margaret flatly. She was hoping to get away from their host so she could ask more probing questions, but if she didn't have a good pretext she might end up stuck in the hall all day embroidering Christina's wedding attire.

~

MARGARET RE-ENTERED the loud and smoky hall and approached the long table, where she whispered in Malcolm's ear that she'd like him to come to bed with her. He grinned appreciatively, said good night to the assembled company, and rose to follow her.

She sent Grizel away to sleep near little Edward and undressed Malcolm herself, grateful to be alone with him. Inside the bed curtains, he peeled off her clothing and she left her gown folded at the end of the bed.

"I've missed you so much," he growled, taking her in his arms. "When we get back to Dunfermline we shall stay in bed for a week straight and my men can manage the affairs of the country."

Margaret laughed. "If only. I'd like to spend a week with your arms around me. It's the only place I feel truly safe." She wasn't joking. The stone tower he'd built for her gave a level of practical protection from the elements and enemies, but Malcolm's embrace made her feel supported and sustained in a way she'd never known before.

"I found out what the guard whispered to Fingal."

"So did I," said Malcolm. "Since I was sure you'd want to know." She couldn't see his eyes sparkle in the dark, but she was sure they did.

"I wonder if we learned the same information. What did he tell you?"

"He said a girl was found dead. I knew you'd be interested in that so I asked her name."

"What was it?"

"Catriona Maclean. She's a local girl."

Margaret inhaled. Was this the girl who'd come with her brother and father? "I don't suppose you asked if she had dark hair?"

"I should have, but I didn't." Malcolm's chest rose and fell against hers. "What did you learn?"

"That she was found in water, like the last girl. So if someone killed her, they wanted it to look like a water spirit did the crime." She put her lips right into his ear, in case anyone was listening outside the curtains. "Which makes me think it's the same person who killed Agnhilda."

Which makes me think it's The Raven. She didn't dare say that part out loud. Partly because someone might be listening, but partly because she didn't have any solid evidence. Just a hunch. But she did want Malcolm's opinion on the matter. "Is a man in this society under any legal obligation to women he might have….led on?"

"An idle flirtation, probably not. If he's taken her maidenhead, then absolutely. Her family could force him to marry her."

"And what if he didn't want to?"

"They could take it to the local lord or the Brehons to seek satisfaction."

"What if the man who'd—taken advantage—was the local lord?"

"Well, then they wouldn't have much recourse."

"So he wouldn't have any reason to…dispose of her."

Malcolm tensed. "What are you getting at? Are you saying what I think you're saying?"

"I'm just wondering, that's all." She sighed in his ear. "I don't want my dear sister to marry someone who…" There was no need to finish the sentence.

"Nor do I, but he's hardly had the opportunity."

"You know as well as I do that he'd use a loyal man to do the dirty work."

"If I thought he were capable of such a thing, we wouldn't be under his roof," whispered Malcolm.

"Do his people seem to be...afraid of him?"

Malcom stroked her back. "He's young yet, but with my support his arrogance can transform into authority. An element of fear is an essential part of holding power."

"Surely you hold power—or they allow you to hold power —because they trust in your ability to defend their safety from outsiders."

"Indeed they do." He nuzzled her. "It's a complicated relationship. Made more complicated by you wanting me to wash their feet every Sunday." His chest shook.

Margaret felt herself relax. He had that effect on her. He made even the most difficult things—like managing a kingdom bristling with bloodthirsty warlords—seem like child's play. "You trust that he's a good man?"

"I hope that he is one." He stroked her back again. "And if he proves not to be he'll have me to answer to."

"I must find out who killed those girls. Until I do, I'll always have a nagging suspicion in the back of my mind."

"And I was ready with my questions to help you."

"You're the very best of husbands." She stroked his rough cheek. "And I want nothing less for my dear sister."

"As do I."

IN THE MORNING Margaret was able to arrange for another visit to the Culdees. Her main purpose was to view the body of the dead girl and make inquiries. She did, however, have a lot of unanswered questions about the local holy men and their beliefs and practices, so the trip had a two-fold purpose.

Christina had convinced Fingal that they must visit the

holy hermit known to have sage advice for young romantics. Margaret suspected that the man was likely a charlatan of some sort, but it served her purpose of getting out of The Raven's hall and into the outside world again.

Malcolm seemed amused by this expedition and content to tag along. Margaret left Aelgith and her daughter under the watchful eye of Agatha, with strict instructions that her mother should not let them out of her sight. She didn't want Aelgith sneaking off to speak with Oswin again, or—God forbid—attempting to run away with him.

Baby Edward slept quietly in the arms of the wet nurse as they donned their light cloaks and headed out into the morning air. Blessed with another dry day, they headed straight for the ferry crossing.

Margaret seated herself on the bench right next to where the ferryman stood to punt, and as soon as he'd pushed away from shore, she addressed him. "What have you heard about the murder that took place last night?"

She watched his expression closely and saw that her question did startle him. "Why, nothing, my lady."

"Nothing at all? Am I the first to inform you of a death?" She didn't believe that, since he'd likely been ferrying people back and forth since dawn, if not before.

"All I know is that a young woman was found dead."

"Did they say how she died?"

He looked nervous. "Not that I recall."

"How would I get to the location where she was found?" She didn't need to ask the ferryman this, as Fingal's guards already knew, but she wanted to see if he knew.

"It's to the left of that loaf-shaped hill, my lady. There's a stream that runs around it in a loop. I think that's where they found her."

"Did you know the girl?"

"I dare say I know everyone around here." He glanced at

Fingal, who sat on a bench on the opposite side of the boat, looking over the prow and talking to Christina about something in a low voice. This piqued Margaret's interest. Was the boatman afraid to speak frankly in front of The Raven?

"What do you know of her?"

"Nothing in particular, my lady," he said politely. At this moment the prow grounded on the opposite bank and he scurried up the center of the boat and leaped ashore to tie the boat for them to climb off. His relief at arriving was palpable.

Was the ferryman still a possible suspect? Or did his wariness in front of their host suggest that Fingal was a more likely candidate?

Margaret was almost sure the dead girl would be the same one who came to his settlement with her family the previous day—until that girl appeared, running toward them.

The whole party stopped in astonishment at the sight of her—dark hair flying, long skirts clutched in her hands—pelting across the ground. Margaret glanced at Fingal, who looked utterly unperturbed by the sight.

Margaret was ushered off the boat first, helped by the boatman, just as the girl arrived. Two of Fingal's guards stepped off next and grabbed the girl. Margaret hadn't heard Fingal give any orders but they immediately started walking her away from the boat.

"I will speak my piece!" said the girl.

Christina now stepped off, and Fingal right behind her. Malcolm followed.

"What does this girl want?" asked Margaret to Fingal, curiosity overcoming her trained politeness.

"I can't imagine," he said casually, offering his arm to Christina.

"I should like to find out," said Margaret calmly. Her main concern was to protect Christina's interests. If this woman had a grievance with her sister's betrothed, she wanted to know the details.

The girl struggled with the guards, who didn't seem to know what to do with her. They stood in a small open area between hills and there was nowhere for any of them to go other than to follow one of the established trails toward one nearby settlement or another. In that sense, they'd either have to abandon their lord or bring the girl along with them.

"I'll speak with her," said The Raven, voice lower than usual, and he walked away from their group to where the guards now held the struggling girl. Margaret tried to follow him, but Christina grabbed her hand and hissed at her. "What are you thinking! Are you trying to embarrass our host?" Her whisper rang with mortification. "Please," she said to Malcolm. "Stop her."

"I simply want to know how he has offended this woman," whispered Margaret. "Don't you think that's important information?"

"No! It's none of our business."

The rest of the party had disembarked and they now stood around in awkward silence. Malcolm seemed to be fascinated by watching the boatman gather up his rope and punt back to the other side to fetch the servants bringing supplies for their midday repast.

Margaret strained her ears to listen to The Raven's conversation with the woman, but a low wind blowing from the west, combined with their rapid Gaelic speech, meant that she couldn't catch more than the occasional word.

Now alone with him, and getting the audience she wanted, the girl looked somewhat chastened. The Raven even laid a hand on her shoulder as if reassuring her. After a short exchange he turned away from her and muttered something to the guards. The guards then led the woman away on a beaten path going to their right, while Margaret knew that they would be taking the path to the left toward the settlement of the Culdees.

"Where are they going?" she asked, when The Raven returned to them.

"They're escorting her home to her family."

Margaret could feel Christina's nails digging into her arm, a warning to her not to ask any more probing questions. How could Christina not want to know anything—everything—about her intended spouse? "What did she want?"

The Raven sighed. "She seems to have become possessed of a delusion that I was going to marry her." He shot Margaret a wry smile. "I'm sure you know how it is."

"No, I don't," said Margaret. "What do you mean?"

"Well, when you're blessed with power or wealth, every family in the district is wondering how they can ally their family to yours."

"That is true," said Christina brightly.

"Naturally that was my purpose in approaching your dear husband about obtaining the hand of your sister in marriage." He spoke directly to Margaret, who was somewhat disarmed by his frankness. Christina seemed to shrink before her eyes.

Then he turned to Christina. "I could hardly believe my good fortune when the lady in question was even more beautiful and charming than rumor had suggested." He picked up Christina's hand and kissed it, and a silly smile crossed Christina's lips.

Margaret glanced at Malcolm, who still seemed to be riveted by the sight of the ferry punting back across the stream.

"So what did you say to her?" asked Christina. "Was she devastated that you're now betrothed to another?"

Fingal tilted his head, gaze resting on Christina. "I cannot speak for her innermost feelings, but she was certainly disappointed that I now have eyes and mind for only one dear woman."

Margaret fought the urge to roll her eyes. This man acted as if he was God's gift to women. He wasn't even that handsome with his long horse face and beaky nose! Her brother and even the odious Donald Ban could run circles around him in that department.

But now the girl and her escorts had disappeared from view behind a copse of trees and their party was in motion toward the Culdee settlement—and the scene of the dead girl's murder.

CHAPTER 16

As they approached the Culdee settlement, Margaret found herself most interested in visiting a "holy well" she'd heard mentioned several times. She strongly suspected that such places were sites of pagan worship that had been embraced by the Christian brothers in the distant past as a way to draw the local people into accepting the Word of God.

In this new age, did it still make sense to talk of them as holy? Margaret pondered this discreetly with Malcolm while they walked up the path toward the settlement. Christina and Fingal walked ahead. Margaret couldn't hear what her sister was saying but she babbled animatedly in a way that seemed unusual for her.

She really is falling in love with him. Why did this fill her heart with dread? Is he such a bad man? Why did her gut warn her against trusting him with her sister's future? She asked the Lord to give her some answers today in this remote outpost of His church.

Still walking, Christina turned to her. "You and Malcolm must visit the hermit too, and get your marriage blessed."

"Our marriage is already blessed," said Malcolm. He put his hand on Margaret's back. "I have more blessings than I can count." Margaret could tell that he also found the prospect silly.

"Well, it can't hurt, can it?" said Christina. "Can a person ever have too many blessings?"

Both Margaret and Malcolm muttered that they probably couldn't. "I imagine he expects a generous donation in exchange for his benedictions," she whispered.

"I dare say you're right," said Malcolm.

Smoke rose in the air as they approached the Culdee settlement. Young boys ran about, chasing the sheep into or out of pens. Holy brothers with bent backs carried stacks of peat from a nearby bog and chickens flapped about.

While Christina and Fingal went off toward the cave of the marriage-blesser, Margaret asked a young cleric to take her and Malcolm to the most famous local holy well and explain its mysteries.

He led them on a walk to a place where a spring bubbled out of the side of the hill and the water fell into a small stone-lined pool below it. "It's a spring, not a well," observed Margaret. No one challenged her. "How is it holy?" She looked at the Culdee.

"It has healing powers, my lady." He was a young man with a wide, pale face and honest hazel eyes.

"Have you seen it heal someone?"

"Oh yes, it heals people all the time," he said cheerfully. "They come from miles around."

"Who discovered that it has such powers?" she asked, genuinely curious.

"I don't know, my lady. It's of ancient knowledge. They say that Saint Columba himself visited it." The landscape all around was littered with stone circles and dolmens erected in pre-Christian times, now tilting and leaning in their old age. She could easily imagine that people had been visiting this well for thousands of years. It confused her that the well could serve both the mistaken superstitions of pagan people and the faith of true believers.

They'd walked into the shadowy enclosure and Margaret now reached out her fingers and let the cold water run over them. "God created the earth," she mused. "He created the land and the water and all the beasts. If water has healing properties then they flow from the works of God." She turned to Malcolm. "It's not a pagan well, it's God's creation."

A smile played around Malcolm's mouth. "Was there ever any doubt about that?"

Margaret thanked God for opening her eyes to his mysteries, which were all around them. "Could we bring some back to Dunfermline with us, to heal the sick? Some of the refugees that pass through are suffering awful maladies caused by their privations."

"Water is heavy to carry, my love," said Malcolm softly. "And we have holy wells close to home."

"We do?"

"Indeed."

"With healing properties?"

"The very same."

"How has no one mentioned them to me?"

Malcolm shrugged. "Perhaps you'd have thought them relics of local superstition rather than the work of God," he said mildly.

Margaret felt chastened by his words, mostly because she knew they were true. "I've been brought up to be wary of the delusions of the heathens who walked these lands before us. I suppose that blinded my eyes to the fact that they walked God's earth and drank His water exactly as we do. Just because they didn't know such mysteries were the work of

God, doesn't mean that the well itself was contaminated by their ignorance."

Malcolm looked at her for a moment. "My wife's reasoning is sometimes too complicated for my own," he said to the young cleric.

"Hardly," said Margaret. "I must apologize for being so slow-witted. Sometimes the common people are wiser than those of us who spent years with our heads in old books."

Malcolm now guffawed.

They left the spring and walked through the Culdee settlement, this odd little village of men, many of them quite aged. Margaret stopped to speak with some of them, asking questions about where they came from and how long they'd lived there.

"Am I imagining it, or are they rather rude?" she asked Malcolm after the third such encounter.

"I suspect their conversational skills are rusty after years of living amongst other hairy-headed hermits."

She spied Christina walking back toward them. Christina waved and beckoned. "I think she wants us to follow them," said Margaret. They set off toward her.

Christina's face as all aglow. "You simply must meet with him. His blessings and insight are such an inspiration."

Margaret felt doubtful. What could a hermit know of love and marriage? "What did he say to you?"

"Well, that would be telling, now, wouldn't it!" She shot a glance at Fingal, who smiled back indulgently. Margaret felt secondhand embarrassment for her sister's blushing infatuation. She felt fairly sure it wasn't shared by her swain, whose interests in her were far more practical than romantic.

"I don't think Malcolm and I need to visit him. We're already married."

"He can bless your marriage that it may be long and fruitful," said Christina enthusiastically. "What's the harm?"

Margaret looked at Malcolm with considerable skepticism. "Is this something that a king would consider?"

"Why not?" he said cheerfully. "I hardly think the blessings of a holy man could tarnish my crown."

They set off back to his cave in the nearby hills. Christina clutched Margaret's hand with such enthusiasm that she almost dragged her along the narrow path. "Whatever did he say to you?" she asked quietly, once they were a little distance from the men.

"He said that our marriage was ordained by God and blessed by all his angels!" breathed Christina. "Can you imagine?"

Did this old man have angels whispering in his ear? "What if he says mine isn't and that my husband must immediately put me on a boat and shove it away from the shore?"

"It's not a joke, sister! This man is known and respected for many miles around. Women go to him to get advice on who they should marry, and they say that the couples that he blesses always have a long and happy marriage."

"Always?"

"Why are you such a doubting Thomas?" said Christina, with a pout. "Do you really think it so ridiculous and unlikely that I could have a long and happy marriage with many children? Are those blessings reserved only for you?"

"Of course not, sister. Nothing would delight my heart more than to see you happily married with a babe in arms."

"And soon I shall be," said Christina. "Though I do suspect there are some things that would make you happier. No more poverty and suffering, no more war, all men living in peace."

"I would gladly sacrifice my own happiness if all those wonders could be achieved," admitted Margaret. "And I shall be grateful for this holy brother's blessings."

THE ENTRANCE to the hermit's cave, though fairly narrow, had been filled in—possibly with turf, it was hard to tell—and a low wooden door in a wood frame inserted into the middle of it.

Malcolm knocked.

A thin voice called for them to enter.

"He can't get up," said Christina. "He's crippled. You two go in and we'll wait here." The Raven had wandered off somewhere but Christina was still accompanied by two of his guards and Grizel.

Malcolm opened the door. The dark interior had a strong and slightly unpleasant smell. Margaret stepped over the threshold into the dim space, hoping her eyes would adjust. She could hear a faint trickle of water.

"Welcome, my lady," rasped the old man. He sounded ancient. Christina had warned them that he didn't see very well.

"I am Malcolm, King of the Scots, and this is my fair wife, Queen Margaret. We come to seek your blessing."

Margaret credited him for playing along. At the very least they could give this poor old man alms that might keep him warm in this miserable damp cave. She shivered in her thin summer cloak as the air inside the cave was a good deal colder than the air outside.

She could barely made out the shriveled shape of a man, wrapped in sackcloth and hunched into a corner.

"Forgive me for not getting up, but my limbs no longer obey my will," he said, in his croaking voice. "I praise God that people still come to visit me that I might keep body and soul together."

"You're much respected by the local people," said

Margaret, finding him rather modest. "Pray, how do you gain your insight into matters of love and marriage?"

"The Good Lord puts his blessings into my heart that I may spread them among his beloved. Your union will be long and fruitful and your heirs shall rule Scotland for twenty generations."

"Twenty generations," said Malcolm cheerfully. "I don't mind the sound of that. I'd reckon that's about five hundred years, give or take."

"Will my brother sit on the throne of England?" asked Margaret suddenly. She wasn't sure if it was curiosity for her brother's future that pressed her or doubt about this mystical hermit's prognostications. Maybe he earned his keep by telling everyone what they wanted to hear.

"The fate of the throne of England is far outside my purview, blessed queen. But I fear that your brother shall die childless."

"Oh!" She couldn't hide her shock at this bleak pronouncement.

"Though his death shall not be soon."

Margaret blinked. Her eyes adjusted to the dim light as daylight poured in through the door and pooled on the earth floor. She could now see that the trickling sound came from a stone font carved into the cave wall, which seemed to be constantly filling with water trickling down the damp and oozing wall.

The old man's eyes were closed—perhaps he was fully blind?—and his fingers curled onto each other like gnarled branches.

Perhaps he wasn't just a flatterer. His portents about her brother certainly weren't what a loving sister would want to hear. "What of King William," she asked, curiosity overcoming her. "Will he live a long life?"

The old man shifted in his seat. The cave was so dark she

couldn't even make out what he was sitting on. "Not much longer." He spoke the words very slowly. Margaret hung on them, wanting more detail, but his mouth settled into a wide line.

She glanced at Malcolm.

"The local people certainly credit your visions," said Malcolm. "Time must have proven them true for you to have so much respect among them."

The old man mumbled some generic blessings, then croaked, "You may anoint yourselves with water from the holy font."

Margaret wondered if this was how he dismissed people.

"Is it a holy well?" she asked, still trying to understand the concept. "Does the water have healing properties?"

"Perhaps you'd best be the judge of that, my queen." His gruff reply silenced her. Malcolm had already dipped a cupped hand into the water and now wet a finger and lifted it as if to make a cross on Margaret's forehead. She held herself still while he completed the gesture. She wondered if she should do the same for him, but he thumbed a quick splash of water onto his own forehead.

"God's peace be with you," said Margaret slowly, as she backed away from the old man. He raised his gnarled hand and made a cross, though the cross had a very awkward shape given that his shoulder, wrist and elbow seemed as crooked as his hands.

Back out in daylight, Margaret blinked and gulped air in relief as they closed the door behind them. "The atmosphere was quite oppressive in there," she murmured quietly.

"I doubt he's using the holy water to wash himself with," said Malcolm. "Though I shall seize this excuse to boast that my children shall rule Scotland for five hundred years."

Christina and Grizel had climbed to the top of a nearby

hillock, perhaps to admire the view. They saw Margaret and Malcolm emerge from the cave and started back down.

"Do you suppose he's just making it all up?"

"I dare say we shall find out. I wouldn't mind finding out that he's right about William's life being short. I'd far rather deal with one of his feckless sons than the man himself who is all tempered steel and raw cunning."

"Is God really whispering prognostications in the ears of his clerics?" asked Margaret, as they walked away.

"Would you prefer a burning bush? I suspect the rain in Scotland might extinguish it."

"Do you find everything funny?"

"Not everything, but it does help. You have him in the same basket with the kelpies, don't you?"

"I don't know. I really don't. I'm confused about how ancient myths and the foretelling of soothsayers and the Holy Church of Rome might intersect. Where does the sacred end and the sin of idolatry begin?"

"Why is she grumbling about idolatry?" asked Christina, as she walked up to them.

"My dear wife wonders if the old man is bearing false witness," said Malcolm cheerfully.

"Why would he do that?" asked Christina, looking confused. "What does he have to gain? He didn't even ask for money."

"Did you give him any?" asked Margaret. She'd seen Malcolm leave some coins at his feet.

"Yes, but he must eat, must he not?"

"Indeed he must, being a mortal man and not a mystical being," said Margaret, as if this proved some kind of point.

"A man can be both mortal and mystical," said Christina indignantly. "And so can a woman. You've spent enough time reading the Lives of the Saints to know that."

"I think she's got you," said Malcolm to Margaret. "Perhaps the man is a living saint whose miracles will be immortalized after his death. I shall certainly recommend him for it if my scions rule Scotland for half a millennium. I shall even write a proclamation suggesting that he be raised to sainthood when that milestone is passed." He laughed at his own joke.

Christina looked annoyed.

"I'm not saying he's a fraud," said Margaret, touching her sister's arm. "Not at all! He said we'd have a long and fruitful marriage, just like yourself."

"That's good news," said Christina evenly. "And since you've a babe he's already half right. Shall we head home and rain more kisses upon little Edward's sweet forehead?" Her face brightened at the prospect.

Margaret started to smile, then remembered her main purpose in venturing out today. "While I long to do that, I fear we must gaze upon the face of the poor dead girl first."

CHAPTER 17

They ate a repast in a pleasant spot with a view over the main settlement of the Culdees. After they'd eaten, a local man took them to the stream where the dead girl had been discovered.

The Raven stayed behind at the resting place with Christina and the rest of the party. He didn't even send guards along to investigate and report back. Margaret found Fingal's lack of interest rather strange, considering that one of his subjects had been killed. On the other hand, if he were guilty surely he'd be hovering close and trying to control the narrative.

The stream was a small one, almost a trickle of water running over smooth round pebbles. Its graveled edges suggested that it could swell significantly, and also concealed the outlines of any nearby footprints. If someone approached by walking in the stream itself, they could travel some distance—even dragging a body—without leaving a discernible footprint. Nearby the damp earth was much trampled by the feet of those who came upon the corpse and removed it.

"Please take us to see her body," said Margaret boldly. She knew they'd taken it to a nearby chapel.

There was some hemming and hawing amongst the guards, then they led her along a well trodden path to a tiny local chapel built of peat and thatch that served the hamlet around it. Behind it lay a small annex room that must be the vestry. She saw a stack of candles on a shelf and priests' vestments hanging from a hook. "Where is she?" asked Margaret. There was surely no space to hide a full grown woman in here.

"She's in the nave, my lady," said an older man with a wispy gray tonsure around his rather red face. "I'm the priest here. I'm afraid the altar table was the only surface large and long enough to lay her out. We didn't want to leave the poor thing on the floor."

"Goodness." Margaret crossed herself. "Please lead the way."

The chapel itself was barely bigger than the vestry and the altar a crude wooden table. Its usual covering had been removed and the girl laid out on the wood surface, then covered in a large plaid.

"Please show me her face," said Margaret softly. She held her breath as he lifted the fabric.

This girl's hair, still damp, splayed out around her face, curly and almost gold in color. Her face was deathly white, eyes closed, and with smudges of river silt still visible around her ears. Someone must have cleaned her and missed that spot. A dark bruise spread over her temple.

A crushing sadness came over Margaret at the thought of this young girl's life being cut short so cruelly. She didn't even look to be twenty.

"How is she thought to have died?" she asked the elderly cleric. She braced herself to hear that the girl had been drowned by the kelpies.

"She seems to have hit her head, my lady," said the priest, pointing to the bruise. "And there are some marks on her neck. He pulled the plaid down further to reveal dark bruises against the white skin.

"She's been strangled from behind," said Malcolm in a low voice, startling Margaret. "Those are fingers on the front of her neck. I'd wager that the back shows thumb marks. Can you turn her over for us?"

The priest looked rather shocked by the request, but summoned two young holy brothers, in somewhat ragged robes, who awkwardly and rather clumsily managed to turn the girl over so she was face down on the altar. Margaret crossed herself again. Everything about this situation, including the sight of the dead girl being laid on the altar like a sacrifice from pagan times, struck horror into her heart.

"There, you see!" Malcolm pointed out the large dark bruises caused by two brutal thumbs. "Someone with big strong hands, to be sure."

"I wonder about the bruise on her forehead. Perhaps after she was strangled she fell and hit her head on something hard." She frowned. "There were no big rocks by the stream where she was found, only small pebbles."

"She might have been carried there from somewhere else," said Malcolm. "It's a shame there are so many footsteps going hither and yon or we might have traced them back."

"We might still try. It must have been a large man to carry her body in his arms over any distance."

Malcolm sighed. "She's just a slip of a girl." He shook his head and signaled for them to gently place her on her back and cover her again.

"Who is she?" asked Margaret of the priest.

"Her name is Catriona Maclean."

This confirmed what Malcolm had learned earlier.

"What's her status in the village?" Her clothing was plain but neat and well made.

"She's the tanner's daughter," answered the priest. "Her father's well respected here."

"Unmarried?" Margaret suspected he'd have mentioned her husband before her father if she had one.

"Betrothed, they say, though she never spoke to me of it."

"To whom?" asked Margaret, wondering if it was The Raven.

"A local lad whose father is a wool merchant and has been training him in the business."

Margaret froze. Hadn't the boatman said that an Olaf the cloth merchant was the last person to travel before Agnilda's death? She'd quite forgotten about him. Could he be the same person and a link between the two killings?

"Could he have killed her?" asked Margaret quietly. Malcolm had told her that in his long experience of presiding over crimes, most women were killed by their husbands.

"He seems a nice enough lad, but I suppose you never know."

"What's his name?"

"Padraig Neeson. The family lives in a croft just past the old mill."

"Can you think of anyone else in the village or nearby who might have reason to kill her?" asked Margaret.

The priest shook his head. "They're saying it's the kelpies again. Her parents want me to bless the stream to rid it of the foul beasts."

"This stream is hardly deep enough to harbor an otter, let alone a horse." Margaret peered at him. "Do you believe in such mysterious and demonic forces?"

"I know there are forces of evil in the world," he said, in a low voice. "Terrible things happen that are beyond our understanding. I once saw nigh on eighty men massacred on the battlefield in one day and a night when I was but a lad of twelve and it was on that day that I swore to devote my life to Christ." He crossed himself. "Evil stalks the earth as sure as mortal man does."

Margaret reflected that the near-demonic forces of William of Normandy had wreaked havoc beyond her imagining. But this woman had not been killed by a mystical demon. "The bruises on her neck tell tales of a man's hands."

"Indeed they do, my lady."

"What man would risk his immortal soul to snuff out such a young and innocent life?"

The priest shook his head. Margaret snuck a glance at his hands. Long, slender fingers that had never wielded a sword or pushed a plow, but spent their hours lighting candles or perhaps turning the pages of old books. Should she insist on examining the hands of every man in the local area?

"I wonder if the girl had a jealous lover," said Malcolm suddenly. He'd been standing so quietly behind her that Margaret almost forgot he was there. "Who'd rather deprive the world of her than lose her to a rival."

The priest held up his hands and said he had no knowledge. He didn't know the girl well. She'd simply had the misfortune to be found dead near to this church.

"Do you know where we can find her parents?" asked Margaret.

"They should be here soon. They came this morning and identified her but didn't have the means to remove her. I think they went home to fetch a donkey."

MARGARET ASKED Malcolm to send his men to find the parents with their donkey and escort them back. They didn't wait long before the sorry family group arrived. Margaret's heart broke for this weeping mother, a relatively young and beautiful woman still herself, and the stoic father trying to keep his emotions from his rugged face.

"Your loss is a terrible one to bear," she said, after she'd introduced herself. "I want nothing more than to discover who killed your dear daughter and to bring that fiend to justice."

The mother's lip quivered. "Who would do such a cruel thing to destroy all our hopes?"

Margaret shook her head. At least her parents didn't seem convinced that their daughter's life had been stolen by a sea spirit. "What of her betrothed? Where is he?"

The mother looked surprised. "Who told you she was betrothed?"

"The priest inside the church. At least I think he did. Was he wrong?"

"She was being courted but had not yet pledged herself to a man," said her mother.

"Was there more than one who sought her hand? The priest mentioned a wool-merchant's son."

"Aye, that was one," said the girl's father, who'd been silent up to now. "Though he was not our first choice."

"Why's that?" asked Margaret.

"A nice enough lad, but feckless. You can't eat sheep's wool in a hard winter."

Margaret wanted to point out that you couldn't eat tanned leather in a hard winter, either, but for all she knew this man had a thriving garden and his wife a well-stocked larder. "Who would you have had her marry?"

"With a face like hers she could marry almost anyone. Even a noble," said her father, lifting his chin.

Margaret froze. "You had such high aspirations for her?"

What nobles were in the district other than the one now betrothed to her sister? "Who did you have in mind?"

"I don't like to say and it's a moot point now she's been cruelly murdered."

Had this girl spent time with Fingal Mac Gofraid? She couldn't think of how to ask the question without seeming to cast aspersions upon her sister's intended husband. She looked at Malcolm, hoping his mind was working faster than hers.

"When did you last see her alive?" he asked.

"She went out in the late afternoon to deliver some eggs to my husband's mother," said her mother. "We expected her back long before dark but she never arrived."

"We went out to search for her after dark," said her father. "All the way to my mother's house but she'd left the eggs there and set off out again hours before."

"And she didn't mention any errand she intended to go on?"

They shook their heads.

"I wonder if she went off to meet someone," said Margaret quietly, glancing at Malcolm. "Who did she want to marry?"

"That feckless Padraig Neeson I suppose," said her father.

"We should speak to him," said Margaret to Malcolm.

Before they left she turned to ask one last question that nagged at her mind. "Was she wearing anything of value, like gold jewelry?"

"Nothing, my lady. We're simple people. All she took with her was the basket of eggs, and he didn't rob her for those as she left them with her gran as she intended." The man's face crumpled. "Whoever killed her stole the best treasure a man could have wanted."

"And I shall do my best to find the thief of your joy," said Margaret solemnly. "May God give you solace in your grief."

THE WOOL MERCHANT'S son was found at home in his family's modest turf and thatch house, a short walk into the hills. The boy's father—who they quickly established was not named Olaf—greeted them in the doorway of the house, where the family immediately stopped what they were doing and stared as if struck by lightning.

Margaret had pictured a large barn piled high with neat bales of wool such as she'd seen in the tithe barn at Wilton, but this wool was piled loose in a corner of their smoky farmhouse.

From what she could see, the wool itself looked to be of rough quality and the wife and daughter sat carding and spinning it right next to a cooking pot bubbling with a stew that smelled like root vegetables and not much else. Balls of spun wool filled several baskets pushed up against a wall.

Padraig himself sat in a corner whittling something with a knife, but stopped when they entered. At first Margaret wondered if he was carving a drop spindle for his mother or sister, but as her eyes adjusted to the dim light she could see it was actually a crude musical instrument.

Padraig's father summoned him outside to speak to Margaret and Malcolm, then stood there with them, rambling on about the terrible loss their family had suffered, the weather, the quality of wool that year…

"We'd like to speak to your son alone," said Malcolm kindly. The father blustered a bit, but retreated inside.

"Were you betrothed to Catriona Maclean?" asked Margaret softly.

"My father seemed to think so," he responded. He still had the crude half-carved pipe in his hand.

"Did you want to marry her?"

"She's a nice enough girl, but her family didn't think I

was good enough for her and neither did she." He spoke plainly, but without obvious hostility. But was he a jilted lover?

"So you weren't betrothed to her?"

"No."

Margaret glanced at Malcolm. "The village priest seemed to think that you were."

"Ah, that's my father trying to turn rumor into reality. He'd like to be allied with the tanner's family as he has good trade connections."

"I see," said Margaret. "Was there ever any… understanding between you and Catriona?"

"Nay. She was kind enough to me, like she was to anyone I suppose, but she never gave myself or my father any reason to think she'd like to be my wife."

"Was there a boy—or a man—who did hold her interest?"

"She had eyes for that horse trainer! The English lad. They say he's from a grand family, not that it means anything since he's a slave now."

Margaret's heart almost stopped. The dead girl and Aelgith's son Oswin? "How would they have met?"

"There's few enough people in these parts that it's hard not to rub elbows with everyone here at some point. And the outsiders attract attention due to being new and exciting, I suppose." Padraig fidgeted with his half-carved flute.

"Were you jealous of him?" asked Margaret.

"No." He looked at her for a moment. "Are you wondering if I killed her? Because I didn't."

"Seems odd that you'd deny something you're not accused of," said Malcolm gruffly.

"I'm wondering why else you'd come here," said the lad. He moved his half-carved pipe from one hand to the other.

"We came because the priest said you were betrothed to her. We wanted to see if you could give us any information about her, and you have." Margaret frowned. Was he trying to put them off course with the news about Oswin?

"You haven't asked me anything about the horse lad," he observed.

Margaret didn't really want to. Her whole purpose in coming here was to help Aelgith retrieve her son to safety with a minimum of fuss. Identifying him as a possible lover of a newly-murdered girl would hardly help that cause.

Still.… "What do you know of him?"

"He thinks highly of himself. You can see it in the way he rides. More like one of King William's knights than a lowly slave."

Margaret wanted to correct him and observe that King William's knights had killed the lad's father and were likely the very last people he'd wish to identify with, but she restrained herself. "He seems to have found a place for himself here, using his skill with horses to earn money for his master."

"Indeed he has." Padraig Neeson's pudding-like face revealed little emotion. "And turned Catriona's head I reckon. But that didn't mean anything to me since she never noticed me before or after."

"You don't seem very sad that she's dead," said Margaret.

"I'm sad enough," he said. "I don't have an unkind word to say about her and I wish she hadn't been killed. But she wasn't mine to fret over."

A few more questions only confirmed that Padraig Neeson was a rather dull young man with few aspirations and no apparent passion for Catriona Maclean or anything else. She also asked him about Olaf the cloth merchant. He said that his family worked closely with Olaf, who was a cousin of some sort, and that he was away delivering a load of woven cloth to the islands and had been gone for a week— which removed him as a suspect at least in this latest killing.

As they and the guards walked back to where they'd left Christina and the others, Malcolm muttered that it would be unfortunate if it became known that the girl had eyes for Oswin.

"Indeed. Though I'd imagine if that rather dull lad noticed, probably others did as well. I do hope he won't become a focus of attention."

"What if he killed her?"

"And all the other girls found strangled in water over the years? I'd believe it was a kelpie before I'd point the finger of blame at Oswin."

"You may soon be trying to convince them it's a kelpie," said Malcolm, with a wry look.

"I suppose we should ask Oswin about the girl—if he ever spoke to her or has any idea who might have wanted to end her life."

"That should be easy enough since I've already bargained to have him return home with us when the time comes."

"By offering to barter my only sister in exchange for him."

Malcolm grimaced. "I do drive a pretty irresistible bargain."

CHAPTER 18

ack in The Raven's hall, preparations were well underway for Christina's wedding. Kegs of ale, brewed by the most reputed alewives, arrived strapped to donkeys. Already, they were being tapped and enjoyed by Fingal and his men, along with roasted fowl and venison and seafood of all kinds.

Aelgith and Osgifu were bent over embroidery to decorate Christina's wedding attire. They'd brought the materials with them and their beautiful stitches unfurled across ribbons and trim like flowers growing in the forest.

Margaret had decided not to tell Aelgith that the dead girl had feelings for her son. For now it was just hearsay and she wanted to hear Oswin's side of the story. She could easily imagine a young girl admiring the horsemanship and athleticism of a clever young man—even a foreign slave—but that didn't mean they'd ever exchanged even a single word, let alone a kiss or a promise that might entangle their fates.

Margaret asked Malcolm to keep Fingal busy and for her mother to keep a close eye on Aelgith and Osgifu, and not let them out of her sight. Then she gathered Grizel and Aidan and headed out across the stream to where the horses grazed.

As they boarded the ferry yet again, Margaret couldn't resist asking the ferryman if he'd ever seen any of the horsemen in the company of a girl.

"Never," he said, without hesitation.

"Did you see Catriona Maclean in the company of any man at all, that wasn't her own family?"

"I don't recall. I see people go back and forth across this river all day long."

"How can you be so sure of one and unsure of the other?"

The boatman shrugged awkwardly, and Margaret was reminded that the girls all died in water—the substance he traveled on day and night and that made him his living. But what reason would he have to take the lives of the victims?

"Do you think it's safe for young girls to move about without the protection of a man?"

"Yes," he said. "Oftentimes they're with their mother or aunt or sisters. What kind of a world would this be if women needed armed men at their side to go about their business?" Margaret couldn't be sure but she thought that he glanced sideways at Aidan's sword.

"How safe can this world be if two young girls are found dead and no one knows who killed them or why?" she asked honestly. "And I firmly believe their lives were taken by a mortal man and not a kelpie."

"Aye, I do as well." He frowned. They'd reached the other side and he jumped out to tie up the boat. "Some men have evil in their hearts and take a life for the twisted thrill of it."

His words struck Margaret just as she tried to stand and the boat lurched in the current. "Who would do such a thing?" Was he speaking about himself? She studied the boatman's weathered face and big callused hands as he tied to boat to the post at the shore.

Aidan leaped off and held his hand out as she alighted carefully. "I've heard of such a thing, my lady. Some men have a sickness in their hearts that makes them want to take a life."

"I understand men wanting to kill their enemies or even to seize property by force out of greed. But these were young girls—no one's enemy. The first girl might have been killed for her gold but the second one wore nothing of value, according to her family."

"Some men hate women," said Aidan quietly.

"Why?"

"I don't know. Maybe their heart was broken by one, or the women in their family disdained them. You see such men in fighting forces, wanting to take out their frustrations on whatever enemy is close at hand. It pains me to say that women are often the victims of their rage."

Margaret's gut clenched. "I've heard of such. Violence against women is an abomination in the eyes of God and man." She gathered her skirts and walked up the bank. A light mist of rain dusted her face.

Could Oswin feel such bitterness, deprived as he was of property and power or even the means to govern his own life from day to day? Could he have felt…lust or attraction to the girl and been frustrated to the point of rage by his inability to possess her or even court her?

The thought chilled her as they followed a well-trodden path through the scrubby countryside.

The horses now stood inside a fenced enclosure with their backsides to the weather. Smoke rose from a thatched hut next to it. Margaret gestured for Aidan to approach the hut and bring Oswin outside.

What would she tell Aelgith if she discovered that her son was a cruel and callous murderer? She doubted that Aelgith's heart would survive the blow. For her son to miraculously come back from the dead only to be hanged for murder would be a punishment so cruel that few mothers would survive it.

Margaret thought suddenly of little Edward, her own dear son, so tiny and helpless, in need of the gathering arms of those who loved and cared for him. Oswin had been that tiny, pink-cheeked baby in Aelgith's arms back in happier times. One day her own son would be a warrior, taking his father's side in battle.

She could hardly imagine it. The work of nurturing a child from infancy to adulthood was a long and complex endeavor. Building his confidence, fostering his skills, encouraging him to read and think and also surrounding him with men who could train him to fight and kill.

What if something went wrong along the way?

Aidan emerged with the boy, who blinked in the bright daylight. The rain had stopped. Oswin bowed his head to her. Margaret beckoned for him to walk away from the enclosure with her. Once they were out of earshot she stopped and turned to face him.

"A girl was killed last night." She watched his face closely. His features barely moved and he said nothing. Was he controlling his emotions or did he feel nothing?

"Catriona Maclean. Did you know her?"

He shook his head.

"You've never heard that name before?"

"No, my lady."

Margaret's heart clenched. Was he lying to her? "I just had a conversation with a young man whose father was trying to arrange a betrothal of his son to her and that lad told me that Catriona Maclean had eyes for you."

Now he looked startled. "I know nothing of that."

"A very pretty girl with curly golden hair."

"I have no business looking at women or girls. I could be beaten or even sold for such a thing."

Margaret drew in a steadying breath. Even if he did know the girl—even if he'd kissed her in secret—he could hardly admit it in public. "I'm your mother's dear friend. I want nothing more than for you to leave this place and return with us to live in peace and freedom. But I must know what happened to this girl."

A flicker of something passed over his face. "If this girl ever spoke to me it was not because I wished it."

"You do know which girl I mean."

"I think I might. She would come and watch us train the horses. She may even have spoken to me and I returned some polite words. But in no way did I encourage her attentions and I never spent even one moment alone with her."

Margaret nodded. She was inclined to believe him. And his words didn't make Padraig Neeson a liar, either, if the girl had been seen to gaze upon Oswin. Foolish of her, under the circumstances, but young girls often had their heads turned by men they had no business admiring.

She swallowed. "Did you ever see her with your master, Fingal Mac Gofraid?"

He blinked rapidly. "Yes."

Margaret's heart beat faster. "Did he show an interest in her?"

He looked at the ground. Then looked up and past her shoulder. She found herself turning her head to see what he was looking at behind her. She saw only the hills.

"You're afraid to speak plainly."

"I am because he holds my fate in his hands."

"I am the Queen of Scotland and have arranged for you to return to Dunfermline with me so I would argue that I hold your fate in my hands."

He hesitated. "Will my words get back to him?"

"I seek only to protect my sister's interests. I want to know if her intended husband is a—" Is a what? A philanderer? A killer? In her heart the two were almost equally horrific, even though she knew the former was almost the norm among noblemen. Truth be told, she was terrified to leave her sister here with this man. "Did your master flirt with the girl or speak intimately with her that you saw?"

He pressed his lips together. "I think I did see that." He spoke very low.

"And how did she respond to his advances?"

"She seemed enchanted by him."

No wonder her parents had started to nurture hopes of a noble marriage for her. Margaret knew that a man like The Raven would no sooner marry a local peasant girl than he would take a local hind or pheasant for his bride. He'd enjoy her, drink the sweet juices of her ripe youth, and toss her away like a bitten plum.

Margaret felt fury rise with in her—for both his toying with a girl he'd never marry and for playing with her sister's emotions. He'd put an impressive effort into sweet-talking and charming her sister; far more effort than a man of his standing really needed to expend. Clearly he wanted this marriage to happen.

Had he seen this girl—like the angry girl who came to his hall—as an impediment to his royal marriage? A fly in the ointment of his bright future that needed to be plucked out and disposed of?

"Did you see them alone together?"

"I didn't, but then I keep my eyes on my work with the horses. No good could come of me peering into another man's business." He looked right at her while he said this, and she believed him. "What he did with her in private, I don't know."

Margaret wondered if she could ask the servants for

more information about The Raven's private movements, but realized that they had everything to lose and nothing to gain from telling tales on their master. Perhaps Grizel could loosen lips, though even that seemed unlikely. Everyone knew Grizel as a member of the king's household and if they had any sense they'd keep their own counsel.

"I thank you for your candor. I'm sorry to have frightened you with this inquisition. I truly just want to find out who killed this poor girl, Catriona Maclean, and who killed Agnhilda Finnsdottir who was found a week ago."

"The local people say that this has happened before," he said softly, glancing over her shoulder again. "That there's something, or someone, evil, living among them who snuffs out the lives of young women."

"I've heard the stories about a sea-horse. I'm surprised they haven't asked you to train it."

A tiny smile tugged at the side of his tense mouth. "I don't think they really believe those tales. They think it's someone local, but no one knows who."

Like The Raven. Except that he wasn't old enough to have been killing women for decades, which suggested someone more aged, like the ferryman.

"Please, listen for any information you might glean about the two deaths, or any of the earlier ones. In the meantime go about your business as usual. I hope that we shall soon be riding away together, with you and your mother and sister reunited again."

He held her gaze. "It seems too much to hope for but I shall keep that hope burning in my heart."

"Am I imagining things or are they drunker than usual?" asked Christina of Margaret after a long evening feast followed by music and a primitive form of dancing. Two of Fingal's guards had started the dance, putting their swords on the floor and leaping over them in an impressive display of athleticism.

Soon more of the men joined in and they were hopping about, sweating and shouting. Malcolm cheered and clapped and soon two women were twirling around among them, lifting their skirts over the swords.

"Who are these women?" asked Margaret. She hadn't seen them before this meal. Both young and beautiful, they wore the clothing you'd expect of a minor noble, or a wealthy merchant's daughter—but girls from a good background wouldn't jump around with drunken men.

"I don't know." Christina was noticeably upset. Solicitous to a fault with her all day, The Raven now seemed to have forgotten her amidst the drunken merriment.

Are they whores? Margaret knew there were women whose work—if it could be called such—was pleasuring men, but she'd never seen them in the court of her great uncle or— God be praised—her husband's court.

Suddenly one of the women, long dark hair cascading over her shoulders, sat on her brother's lap and laughed. He laughed back!

Margaret rose to her feet, deeply unsettled. She walked around to where Malcolm sat and whispered in his ear. "Why are these women here?"

"Entertainers," said Malcolm. "I think."

"I've not seen them play the flute or sing or juggle hand-kerchiefs," whispered Margaret. "Are they...women of the night?"

Malcolm now turned to her. "I suppose they're hired as a diversion for all the men who spend their lives at court or away in battle."

"My brother should not be touching a woman he isn't betrothed to," she hissed.

"Perhaps you should go tell him that," said Malcolm, with a raised brow.

Edgar was shiny-faced and laughing uproariously at something the woman had whispered in his ear. If she approached him in this state she'd be mocked at best, ignored or insulted at worst. Such a thing was beneath her dignity as queen.

Anger grew inside her that Malcolm didn't seem to see anything wrong with this debauchery, and in the days before her sister's wedding! Now one of the girls was laughing with Fingal, refilling his cup and leaning over so that her long hair brushed against his shoulder. "This is not fitting company for my sister or myself, we shall retire."

"Good idea," said Malcolm. "I'll join you soon." He put down his cup and started clapping to the rhythm of the music.

Furious, Margaret tugged Christina away from the table. "How is my husband not offended by this depravity?"

"Perhaps he was used to this sort of revelry before you joined his court."

"It's undignified and ungodly."

Christina looked like she was about to cry. After hovering over her all day, Fingal didn't even seem to notice she'd left the table. "Will this be what my evenings look like once I'm married? Women of low morals hovering around my husband like flies?"

"He's hardly swatting them away." He'd probably invited them here. But why would he display such behavior right before his marriage to Christina, and in front of Malcolm? Was he setting expectations so she'd be unable to lodge complaints about similar behavior once they were married?

"As I've said before, I have my doubts that this man is a suitable husband for you."

Christina looked like she wanted to protest, then frowned. "I fear that you might be right, sister."

Hope swelled in Margaret's heart and she felt guilty for it. Even before they came here she'd been afraid of losing her sister to marriage. She'd tried to warm to the idea but Fingal's courtship had done nothing to reassure her. Yes, he'd wooed Christina like an ardent lover, but with an intensity and purpose that didn't feel genuine—and that dissipated after a horn or two of ale.

"I can't shed the fear that your intended might be involved in the deaths of the two young women."

"Impossible. He was with us here in this hall when they were killed."

"Do you think great men do the deed themselves? They have loyal warriors to take care of their dirty deeds and keep their secrets."

Christina shook her head like she wanted to rid her mind of this idea. They'd walked away from the table and into a darkened nook where Margaret and Malcolm's bed sat. The music—drums, pipes and strings all at once—thumped and thudded and hid their words easily. "Why would he want them dead?"

"I suspect it might be because they both had a claim on his affections. Remember how the first girl came here to confront him? And the second girl's father told me he nurtured hopes of her marrying a noble."

"I still...no...I can't." Christina pressed a hand to her head. "Despite some inappropriate behavior—which, you must admit isn't uncharacteristic for a lusty bachelor—he's been so kind to me, listening to my stories and showing me his realm." She drew in a breath. "And surely every women in the region covets his hand in marriage. He's so handsome as well as powerful and…" her voice tailed off.

Margaret didn't find him handsome at all. Especially now that she'd got to know him. He was tall, yes, but his disposition showed in his features—arrogant, careless, with an air of the brute that never disappeared even when he whispered sweet nothings in her sister's ear. "Each girl was living proof that he'd stray from the bonds of marriage and sully a girl's innocence with no thought for her future. He swatted those flies to silence them."

"I don't believe it." Christina's defiance had returned. "You're jealous."

"Jealous?" Margaret didn't even understand her sister's thinking. "I'm only anxious for your happiness and fearful that you'll be stuck married to a man who cares nothing for your feelings."

Tears now shone in Christina's eyes, visible in the dim light from the candle in a nook on the wall. "I don't expect my husband to be a virgin."

"But do you expect him to be chaste after marriage?" asked Margaret.

Christina seemed to think about this. "I imagine that would be too much to hope for."

Indignation rose in Margaret. "I'd be devastated if Malcolm took a lover. He knows this. I have full faith in his loyalty and fidelity. I want that for you as well."

Tears rolled down Christina's cheeks. "I'm not as pretty as you."

Margaret put her hands on her sister's arms and shook her gently. "Please, sister, don't settle for a man who won't treat you like the royal princess that you are! Your beauty is inner as well as outer. The Raven is not the last man on earth. We shall find you another!"

"I think it's too late. Guests are arriving for the wedding feast."

"Until you've said your vows, it's not too late."

CHAPTER 19

Margaret was still lying awake when Malcolm came to bed. He undressed, lay down, then took her in his arms. For once she had trouble relaxing into his warm embrace.

"I don't want Christina to marry."

"Shhh. Get some sleep." His voice was thick with drink. They'd been laughing and throwing back ale for hours to the cacophony they called music.

"I can't sleep when I'm worried about my sister's future. Do you really think our host is a man who takes his marriage vows seriously?" She whispered as loud as she dared. Anyone could be listening at the bed curtains.

Malcolm wrapped his arms tight around her. "He'll have me to answer to if he doesn't."

"I think he's the killer."

Now Malcolm pulled back from her. "Why would he take such a risk?"

"What risk? When you're the ruler you can get away with anything. You're judge, jury and executioner. He could simply accuse someone else and hang them for it."

Malcolm didn't even try to argue with this. He knew it was true. He could do it himself if he wanted.

"And he has a roving eye," she continued. "I learned today that he'd given false hope to the murdered woman. Her parents were cherishing fantasies that he might marry her."

"I struggle to believe that he promised to marry either of these low-born women." Malcolm sounded tired but at least he was listening.

"When does a man promise to marry a woman? When he wants to bed her."

"I'm afraid he could do that without any promises."

"Not and have her smiling and cooing. I admit he doesn't seem like a cold-blooded killer, but he's careless and pleasure seeking like a spoiled child." She hoped no one could over-hear her.

Malcolm's chest rose and fell. "You're not wrong. He did have a woman sitting on his lap for the last few songs."

"These women are prostitutes of some kind."

"Aye. They're an elevated sort, to be sure. Perhaps even fallen noblewoman who were taken captive. But they're not behaving the way a good woman should."

Margaret's heart suddenly ached for them. If Osgifu were older she might have found herself forced into such a role. "Why would he invite such women into his hall under the gaze of my sister—under your gaze!"

"They're to entertain his men. I agree that he should not be enjoying them himself."

"You can see that he's a terrible choice of husband for Christina. We must break the engagement at once."

Malcolm sighed again. "How does your sister feel?"

"She's torn. When he charms and woos her she's a blushing bride with dreams of babes in her arms. When he forgets her to sweet-talk another, she's crushed. As her older sister I must take responsibility for her future. This man will destroy her."

There was a very long silence. "I need him as an ally against William."

"Even if he murdered innocent women?"

"Not then. No."

"So if I can prove that he murdered Agnhilda and Catriona, Christina will be free?"

"Yes."

IN THE MORNING Margaret awoke before dawn filled with determination to provoke Fingal into some sort of confession. He was a careless man, she'd seen that often enough. He felt invincible, like he could do anything he wanted without consequence, including permanently dispose of two women he'd led on and defiled and now had no further use for.

When he arrived at the table to break his fast, she accosted him from across the table. "I don't think it's safe for my sister to come to live in a place where two young women have been murdered within the space of a few days. I think that she should return home with us until the murders are solved." She watched his face closely.

His gaze met hers with fierce intensity. "You're not wrong. Whoever killed these women must be brought to justice. Someone knows who did it. Perhaps I should threaten to kill everyone in the villages until the culprit confesses."

Margaret stared at him. This was not at all the response she'd expected. "I'm not sure that would endear you to your people."

His hollow laugh chilled her. "Then, my lady, what would you suggest?"

"Someone knows who did this. It's possible they've even confessed it to a priest in an effort to expunge their sins."

"As I understand it, even the King of the Scots can't extract the secrets of the confessional from the mind of a priest."

"Perhaps you might offer a reward of sorts for such information."

"Bribe the priests? These Culdees have sworn a vow of poverty and I suspect they'd take a dim view of my attempting to turn their heads with gold." He seemed amused by this prospect.

"The reward might be increased alms for the poor, or supplies for a project dear to their hearts."

Malcolm had joined them at the table. "My wife has a pure heart indeed to imagine that a murderer would confess his sins to a holy father."

Margaret sighed. "Do you have a better idea?"

"How many people are within this general area?" Malcolm asked Fingal.

"My steward has counted them," he replied. "Four thousand and nine in this land between the rivers, not counting babes born since last summer, and one hundred and sixty two Culdees."

"No babies born there, I'd wager," quipped Malcolm.

"Don't be so sure," said The Raven, with a lifted brow. They both roared with laughter.

"Less than five thousand in total and one of them is a murderer. A cruel and cold hearted murderer of young girls. Surely this fiend can be rooted out."

"I would like nothing more, my lady," said The Raven.

Unless it's you. "I'd imagine you take it personally since you knew the two victims." She watched his face closely. Would he deny it?

"I did indeed, and two lovelier young ladies could not be

found in all these isles. Their loss pains me as if I lost a daughter."

This response, which gave every appearance of being genuine, surprised Margaret again. "Have all the victims found dead in water over the years been young girls? It might be helpful to compile a list of their names and particulars, to see if we can find links between them that might tie them to the murderer."

"One who was killed about seven years ago was a widow of thirty or so. The rest, as far as I know, were young unmarried girls. I shall have my steward find out their names."

Margaret nodded. "What kind of man would want to kill unmarried women on the brink of starting their lives?" She looked from Malcolm to their host. "And what would his motivation be?"

"He wants them and can't have them," said Fingal.

Malcolm murmured agreement. "Aye. A spurned lover can be filled with fury."

"What man might be spurned by so many women over a period of three or more decades?"

"A very ugly one," said Fingal.

"A very poor one," said Malcolm. "A man who can't support a wife can't take one."

Margaret found herself feeling sympathy for this poor and ugly man, deprived of affection and the company of a woman. "I could see that such a man might feel rage in his heart. But what would turn that anger into the violence required to kill a living woman?"

"Lust that has never been slaked," said Fingal. "Every man has desires and they can turn into a raging fire in his heart and loins if left untended." He looked around, perhaps expecting them to laugh, but Margaret found his words striking in her heart and mind like a hammer to an anvil.

"A holy man, perhaps," she whispered. "It pains me to say

it, but…" She let her words hang in the air. "A man who perhaps didn't want to devote his life to God but who was forced into it by a lack of other life paths available to him."

"Younger sons of noblemen are sometimes pressured into joining the church when the family has not funds or land enough to divide between all their offspring," said Fingal. "I'd prefer the lads to become soldiers, but some aren't capable of the training or education required to become a fighting man."

"A cripple wouldn't have that option, to be sure," said Malcolm.

Margaret's mind went to the man whose gnarled hands sat in his lap while he foretold of the long and fruitful marriage she'd share with her husband. "What about Brother Sechnall? He's known for making predictions of love and romance while he sits hunched in his chair, alone in his cold damp cave."

"Brother Sechnall can't walk," said The Raven. "Crippled from birth. And his fingers are curled over on each other. He's hardly capable of killing a mouse, let alone a woman."

Margaret's heart sank. This was true. Whoever had killed the woman had not only strangled them but also somehow carried them to a stream or river and left them there. "If not him, then someone like him but more able bodied? Are there other priests with infirmities that would keep them from a more active life but would still permit them to carry out a murder?"

The Raven shrugged. "I can't say I know all the Culdees. I find them an odd lot, living alone in their little huts."

Margaret now felt guilty for accusing them. "I'm sure most of them are pure in heart, I don't mean to cast aspersions. But perhaps we could meet with the abbot and ask him a few questions."

MARGARET PROPOSED ANOTHER ALMSGIVING FEAST, but Fingal pointed out that he'd hardly have provision for the wedding feast if they kept giving all the food and drink away.

All the more reason.... Still, she was content to cross back over the river in the ferry and ask more questions. To her surprise Fingal didn't insist on coming with her. Malcolm and Aidan escorted her and Grizel.

This time she had a different question for the boatman. "Do you ever carry the Culdees across the river, or do they stay in their little caves and huts?"

"I carry them regularly. Some of them have wives and bairns in the villages round about and go home to see them in between bouts of prayer and fasting."

This reply left Margaret stunned. She looked at Malcolm. "Have you ever heard of such a thing?"

"Yes," he said simply. "Many of them are not ordained or pledged to the church. They simply take up the life of an ascetic and live it for as long as it suits them."

"And have relations with a women when they're not at their prayers?" she couldn't seem to wrap her mind about this. "Are they married to these women, or living with them in sin?"

Malcolm shrugged. "I confess that I've never seen it as my business."

Margaret tried to keep her voice calm. "Do the Culdees at Dunfermline behave in this outrageous manner?"

"Oh no," he replied. "The bishop runs a very tight ship more akin to a Romish monastery."

She sighed with relief. "And what about the men at St. Serfs on Loch Leven?"

"I believe they live the chaste lives of monks as well, at

least in theory. But once you get further off the beaten path, out here in the western wilds, for example, practices vary."

"I hardly think this is what Saint Columba had in mind for his followers," said Margaret, truly shocked. The boatman jumped out on the far side.

"The Culdees don't necessarily consider themselves acolytes of Columba's church," said Malcolm. "But as hermits who walked away from the rules and restrictions and corruptions of the institutional church to commune directly with God. That's why they like to live alone."

"I find it humorous that they live alone in a large community of like-minded hermits." Malcolm helped her down from the boat. An awful thought occurred to her. "Do they have women and children living in those huts?"

"Oh no," interrupted the boatman. "The woman and children live outside the religious settlement."

"And how do these men support their wives and children, if they spend their days in prayer and communion with God?"

"That's a very good question," said the boatman. "And I don't know the answer." He bid them adieu and set off back across the water before she could ask anymore awkward questions.

"I've never heard of such nonsense," said Margaret, as they walked toward the Culdee settlement, which was still out of sight behind a cluster of hills. "These men supposedly devote their lives to prayer and ascetic living, then travel home for a hot meal at a hearth sustained by some poor woman who lives without his protection but who must welcome him into her bed whenever he wishes?"

"I'm sure it's not quite like that," said Malcolm looking ahead.

"Then how exactly is it?"

"I don't know but I do beg you not to ask them directly, my pet, as we are guests in this territory." He lifted a brow.

"I was raised for diplomacy," she replied. "Have no fear on that score. But I do have many questions burning in my mind."

As they approached the settlement, Margaret found herself scanning the scene for women—or children—but saw nothing but men. They did at least seem to support themselves with a measure of husbandry judging from the animals, gardens and storehouses. Perhaps they raised and grew ample produce to support their families even if they chose to live separate from them.

"I would never agree to live separately from my husband," she said as they approached.

"So you'll be riding into battle with me, then?" asked Malcolm cheerfully.

"Perhaps I shall."

They were greeted by a young man who led them to the abbot. Margaret silenced all the questions in her mind except those that might help her find the dead girls' killer—or killers.

"Such an ill wind blows among us," she said. "It seems that the lifted prayers of all the men in his holy settlement are not enough to catch and stop the evil killer who preys on innocent young women."

The abbot blinked. "Indeed my lady. Our prayers are unceasing that the murderer may be discovered and punished."

"Are you aware of any men in this settlement who might harbor hostilities toward unmarried women? All of the dead women were either maidens or widowed. None of them was married."

"Perhaps he thought to take advantage of women who had no husband to protect them."

"That makes some sense, but the two latest victims have a father or brother. They were hardly alone in the world. But somehow they were alone with this man who killed them. Who—other than the ferryman, who shares his boat with all —would spend time alone with a young girl? A priest who takes her confession?"

"Most of us in this area, clerics and laity alike, confess directly to God. We do not hold with whispering our sins in the ears of an intermediary."

"Why? Surely a priest has the power to offer absolution."

"God alone can offer absolution, my lady." The abbot spoke simply, as if to a child. At that moment she felt like a child. She wanted to argue that God had given priests the right to forgive and pronounce suitable penance here on earth but decided that would be a fruitless argument under the current circumstances. These people were strange indeed!

"I've learned that the Culdees sometimes take a wife. Are there any among them who you think would like to take a wife, but have been frustrated in their efforts?"

"One man you could ask about that is Brother Sechnall, who has become known in these parts—not with my approval, mind you—as a sort of spiritual advisor when it comes to marital matters."

"My husband and I visited him and he pronounced that our marriage would be long and fruitful. I found the experience odd. How is it that a holy man is playing the role of a pagan soothsayer?"

"As I said, it's not something I endorse but he's been here longer than any of us. It seems that over the years many of his pronouncements and warnings have come true so he's gained a measure of respect from the people."

"Do young girls go to visit him to consult him about their marriage prospects?"

"Indeed they do, my lady."

Margaret looked at Malcolm. "Let's go visit him again."

CHAPTER 20

When they came within sight of the hermit's cave, Malcolm grabbed Margaret's wrist. "This man may be a murderer who's killed countless women over the course of several decades and you think I'm going to let you go in alone?"

"I wish to test him—to see how he behaves with a lone woman. I can't do that if you're standing there. You and Aidan will be right outside the cave so I'll be in no danger. You seem to forget that he's unable to walk and his hands are like claws."

"Then how could he possibly be the killer?" asked Malcolm.

"I'm following a trail. Have patience, my king."

"Patience is not my strongest virtue, but I shall endeavor to cultivate it."

"Pray for justice for the dead women, and that this scourge of murder shall cease."

Margaret left them a short distance from the mouth of the cave. She decided not to knock. Her instinct was to surprise him and perhaps find him out of his chair. She pricked her ears as she approached the door and pushed it.

The trickling sound drew her attention to the font as she entered. As her eyes adjusted to the dark interior, she made out the hermit in his usual seat in the back of the cave. He didn't say anything.

"I've come to see you again," she said, unnecessarily. The silence felt so awkward. Being a queen, and before that a princess, she was used to the air filling with sounds of welcome and offers of assistance as soon as she entered any room. "I have some questions for you."

Her heart beat faster as she approached him. Something about this man unnerved her. "How long have you lived here in this cave, Brother Sechnall?"

He cleared his throat. "More years than I can count. My mind is no longer as sharp as it was."

"I do wonder how you take care of...necessities, if you're unable to rise from your chair." She had no wish to mention the indelicacies of human functions but unless he lived without partaking of food and drink...

She watched his heavy brow furrow. "I can move around enough for such activities as are essential. And the lads who bring me my food are kind enough to help me."

So he could stand. And even walk. "Which lad is that?"

He didn't answer right away and she could feel his eyes boring into her. "Whichever one has the kindness in his heart to help an old cripple."

"It's a relief for me to hear that, as I was concerned for your welfare. You're such a treasured member of this community."

He didn't respond. She could tell he was wary, wondering why she'd come here again.

She wanted to disarm him. "I come because I have questions about my sister's upcoming marriage. My sister is Christina, who's to marry—"

"I know who your sister is. I only give advice to the one who asks me about their own situation, not to their relatives."

"So if a mother wanted information on which of two men her daughter would marry, you'd refuse to give it?"

"Aye. The daughter must come herself."

"And you can advise her on which man would be a suitable husband for her?"

He didn't answer, which she took as a yes.

"And how do you have foreknowledge of whether two people are compatible or not?"

"The Lord puts it into my heart."

Such a mystical assertion was hard to dispute. "And why do you think the Lord gives you a gift of divination that seems pagan, rather than Christian?" she asked boldly. She studied his face carefully in the scant light. His skin was very pale, not much lined perhaps because he'd spent his life in a dark cave rather than out in the wind and sun.

"It is not my business to question the work of the Lord."

"The Lord commands you to give marital advice to the people of this district?"

He didn't dignify her question with an answer. No doubt he felt himself bound to answer only to a higher authority than the Kingdom of Scotland, which he did not even live in. Such unfamiliar rudeness stung her.

"How do you know it's the Lord and not the devil who gives you nuggets of wisdom for these hopeful young people?" She watched a flash of fury brighten his eyes and stir his bent body. "For the Lord does not command his holy men to function as soothsayers."

His gaze darted suddenly to the side and she followed it. Her eyes rested on the stone font tucked against the wall of the cave, where water dripped down into it. The carved font was the size of a cooking pot. Large enough to press someone's face into and hold it under the water until they were deprived of air and their lungs filled with fluid.

Margaret stared at him. Why had this gruesome thought suddenly flown into her head? She felt almost as if she'd seen the image in his mind's eye.

He's thinking that he could kill me.

She looked at his gnarled hands. They didn't look like they'd have the strength to hold a cup of ale let alone choke the breath from a healthy young girl.

"I think you like to feel powerful," she said slowly, looking into his angry eyes. "You like to feel that you can determine the course of a life." She studied his face. His blocky features bore a disconcerting asymmetry, one eye slightly larger than the other. His lips were so thin as to be almost invisible. His chin receded into his neck. He had not likely been a young man that any girl would swoon over.

Still standing, Margaret loomed over him. "Perhaps you wanted to marry and have children but no woman wanted to go on that journey with you."

His lips twitched for an instant before he spoke. "The Lord called me to serve him."

"I've heard that many Culdees like yourself are not ordained. That they can simply call themselves men of God without any special training and even without oversight by an abbot or bishop. Perhaps even Satan could declare himself a Culdee and pass unnoticed if he appeared to devote himself to a life of solitary contemplation.

"Your words are offensive to God and man," he hissed. She could tell he was almost trembling with fury under his tattered habit.

"I wonder," she said slowly. "Does the presence of a particular young woman ever offend you? Perhaps she's so pretty and so conscious of her own charms that she dreams of marrying a man far above her station?"

This seemed to be the case for both of the dead women. The Raven had filled their heads with fantasies so he could seduce them. He had no intention of marrying either one, but they didn't know that. "What advice would you give to such a foolish girl?"

He seemed to consider this. "I would caution such a creature to chastise her vanity and seek the advice of her father."

"Her father on earth or her Father in Heaven?" asked Margaret.

"Blasphemy!" His curled hand clenched into a fist.

"How so?" She moved a step closer. Since the only source of light came through the cave entrance behind her, her shadow now fell on him.

"You think our Holy Father whispers advice in the ears of foolish girls?" He spat the words at her.

"You seem to believe that he whispers in your ears, so how is it different?"

"I spend my life in close communion with the Holy Spirit," he rasped.

"It seems to me that you portray yourself as something akin to the Oracle at Delphi, a priestess of the pagan god Apollo. But perhaps you've not heard of such a person? She is mentioned in the works of many Greek authors. I've had the good fortune to read their words in the library of my great uncle, Edward the Confessor."

"Blasphemy!"

"Do you find my words blasphemous because you consider yourself to be some sort of sacred object or personage, above all criticism?"

"Blasphemy!" he roared again, louder than ever. Margaret stepped back as he rose from his chair.

Noise at the entrance to the cave made her turn and she

saw Malcolm and Aidan silhouetted against the daylight. "What's amiss in here?"

"I seem to have evoked the ire of Brother Sechnall," she said softly. "By wondering how he feels qualified to give advice on love and marriage to innocent young girls."

Malcolm stepped into the cave and stood next to her. "You risk much to raise your voice at the Queen of the Scots."

The grizzled Culdee seemed to shrink under Malcolm's gaze. "Begging your pardon, King Malcolm."

"You should beg it from my wife, who has shown the patience of a saint in listening to your rantings. I've stood outside all the while and heard the nonsense you've spouted. You have no business telling people how to live their lives when your existence resembles that of a patch of moss growing on a rock."

The cave was so dark, especially with the one source of light now blocked by their bodies, that Margaret couldn't fully gauge the Culdee's reaction—but she could feel fury simmer off him like steam from a stew.

She'd like to see just how much movement he was capable of, if pushed. She'd gathered that he could stand and move around, but how far? How much strength lay in those claw-like hands? Might he even be capable of choking the life from a sturdy young girl and dragging her half a mile or more while walking at least part of the way within the flow of a stream or river?

"I beg your pardon, my lady," he said quietly. "May God have mercy upon us all."

"Let's go," said Malcolm, taking her arm. She wanted to protest. She'd pricked the man's composure and stirred him into rage. But now was not a time to argue with her husband. She let him lead her out of the cave.

Blinking outside under the white sky, she took in a deep breath and her body shuddered. She looked at Malcolm and raised her finger to her mouth signaling that he not say anything until they were out of earshot. Malcolm shot her a glance that seemed to ask if she'd taken leave of her senses, but he stayed quiet as they marched away from the mouth of the cave.

"I didn't even get to ask him if Agnhilda Finnsdottir or Catriona Maclean came to him in the days before their deaths," she hissed, once they'd gone far enough away.

"He's a hundred years old and can barely move," said Malcolm. "What were you thinking?"

"I'm almost sure he's the one who killed them. He said he can move enough to attend to his bodily needs outside the cave. Perhaps he's far more agile than anyone thinks? We must find a way to test him."

"If he's the murderer you think he is, you were probably a hair's breadth from feeling his wizened fingers pressing on the veins in your neck," said Malcolm. "You provoked him to call you a blasphemer! For a reclusive holy man to shout at a queen must take quite a good deal of provocation."

"He's not a holy man. He pretends to be one because it gives him a sense of power and control. Think about it, both the Lord of the Isles and the King of Scotland stood at his feet and listened to his rambling pronouncements."

"Seeking marital advice from a cleric is hardly unusual."

"He's not offering marital advice, he's offering prognostication. There's nothing Christian about that. If anyone is a blasphemer, it's him."

"Should I arrest him, your grace?" Aidan looked from one to the other so she couldn't tell which of them he was asking.

"We cannot arrest one of Fingal Mac Gofraid's subjects without consulting him," said Malcolm. "Imagine if he came into my kingdom and decided to take Bishop Fothad prisoner without a word in my ear first."

"Understood, my lord."

"I think this old man may be the very devil in human form," said Margaret softly. "But he's gained a reputation in these parts, so to accuse him we need to be sure of his guilt and have at least a grain of proof."

"We must be able to demonstrate that he can walk," said Malcolm. "Let alone haul a body across the countryside. Or do you suppose he has an accomplice?"

Margaret drew in a breath. "An accomplice? I hadn't thought of that. But who?"

"It would have to be someone very intimate with him," said Malcolm.

"He did say that a lad brings him his meals and firewood. Whether he can walk or not, he's certainly cultivated a belief that he's close to helpless." Margaret frowned. "Why would a man do that?"

"He's lazy?" said Malcolm.

"Or because early on in his life he was accused of a horrible crime and had to convince everyone he was too infirm to have done the deed. Perhaps he escaped here from somewhere else and hid away in the cave…and then he got trapped into the performance for the rest of his life? No one would believe it. If he can move, it must be shown in front of an unassailable witness."

"Like The Raven himself," said Malcolm.

Unease tightened Margaret's shoulders. If Brother Sechnall was the killer, and she was now almost certain that he was, then Fingal was innocent. Which meant that she had no cause to call an end to her sister's betrothal.

She glanced behind them to make sure the guards were out of earshot. "I dread the prospect of The Raven's marriage to my sister."

"He'll give her a life of ease and comfort, father her children, give her the leisure to spend time at prayer," said Malcolm softly. "And she'll be close enough to visit regularly.

Perhaps she can even spend much of the year living in our household."

"While he's left at home with a whore on his lap," said Margaret quietly.

Malcolm looked at her. "I can't deny that is a possibility."

"It's more than a possibility. It's a probability. He can't even stay away from them while my sister is under his roof. This marriage is impossible. He'll make her miserable and ruin her life."

"They're officially betrothed and the date has been set. Ending the engagement could create hostility between our two kingdoms."

"You told me that if The Raven was a murderer, we could call off the wedding."

"Any promises would certainly be void in that circumstance," said Malcolm, barely above a whisper. "But you no longer seem to think he's the killer."

"I admit that I don't, more's the pity." She looked at him and saw a flash of wry amusement cross his face. "But he's not a good man, either. Not a good husband, anyway. I can't believe you still seem to want this marriage to take place."

"This match provides peace with our neighbor, an ally against William and a husband of rank for your sister."

"There's more to a marriage besides rank and diplomacy. I would never marry a man I could not respect and I don't want to inflict the same on my sister. I married you because, despite rumors to the contrary, I believed you to be a good man."

"Rumors to the contrary? Whose head must rest on a pike?"

"I first met you not long after you'd killed your predecessor to seize his crown."

"A man can't be king without a little blood under his fingernails," said Malcolm softly.

"Not in these dark times," she admitted. Her poor dear father was likely too gentle a man to have ever worn the crown. "And I didn't expect Christina's prospective husband to be a peace-loving abbot. But I do expect him to forsake other women to enjoy the honor of her presence under his roof and in his bed."

Malcolm sighed. "I shall talk to him, man to man, and convey my expectations."

"And will you believe what he tells you?"

"I shall ask in such a way that invites him to tell the truth, one way or the other. Then I shall believe him."

"Be wary, because my sister's heart rests in your hands."

CHAPTER 21

*B*ack at the hall, Malcolm told their host he was dying for a good gallop across the countryside after all the walking they'd been doing back and forth from the ferry crossing. Fingal needed no encouragement and soon he, Malcolm, and Edgar were mounted and trotting away, with four guards in tow.

Margaret approached the women where they sat outside at a pretty spot near a copse of trees. "This weather is sweet, almost summery," said Christina as they approached.

"We can hope for fair weather for your wedding," said Margaret, as if holding a finger up to the wind to see which way it was blowing. Was Christina now back to being enthusiastic about her impending marriage, or wanting to run from it?

The hush that fell over the group gave her an answer.

"We're not leaving without Oswin, are we?" asked Aelgith, putting her stitching down in her lap. "Even if the wedding doesn't happen?"

"No we won't!" snapped Christina. "Why does everything have to be about your son?"

Aelgith's mouth dropped open. "I beg your pardon, my lady." She shot a pleading glance at Margaret. "I'm just so anxious that everything will fall apart."

"You are not the only one who's anxious," said Margaret calmly. "But rest assured, all will be well, one way or the other."

"What am I to do?" asked Christina, her face a mask of anxiety.

"Malcolm has gone out for a ride with him." She looked around. Their intimate group was just Christina, Aelgith, Osgifu, Grizel, and the wet nurse with little Edward at her breast—no prying ears. "He intends to have a discussion with him about...fidelity."

"And he thinks this inveterate charmer will do anything other than tell him what he wants to hear? He's almost talked me out of my gown a dozen times. I can hardly blame the poor foolish women of the district that he's cajoled and seduced. But I no longer trust him."

"I admit that I don't either. Still, all must be managed in a diplomatic fashion." She moved in closer. "If he were to fly into a rage, and perhaps even decide to side with William against us, that could unleash disaster."

Christina huffed. "Why must the fate of the Kingdom of Scotland suddenly hinge on my willingness to be a quiet pawn in these games between men?"

"That's how these things work. Enemies to allies with the exchange of vows."

"I do understand it. And I admit I grew enthused by the prospect of motherhood. But I didn't realize that I might be called upon to sacrifice my happiness to maintain peace in these cold northern lands."

"You shall not be called on to do that. Until the vows are made we can ride away, but it must be handled carefully." She looked at Aelgith's worried face. "And we shall leave with Oswin."

"God be praised for your kindness, my lady." Aelgith took Osgifu's hand and squeezed it.

Grizel had brought over a chair for Margaret and she sat in it. "I don't wish to leave until the man who murdered the two girls has been found and accused."

"Sister! Why must you get involved in this local matter?" Christina raised her voice a little too much. "Do we not have enough problems to disentangle ourselves from?"

"If I thought that anyone would bother to take charge, perhaps I would leave it in their hands. But women have been dying for years...decades. The families are desperate, with no recourse, because the killer has covered his tracks so well."

"I suppose that's why he leaves them in water. To literally cover his tracks," said Christina slowly. "So he can walk away in the water and no footprints remain nearby."

"I'm sure you're right," said Margaret. "And I'm beginning to think that water is involved in their deaths as well. And it's possible that they were drowned as well as strangled. In a font."

"In a church?" asked Christina, clearly shocked.

"In a cave." She studied Christina's face. "A hermit's cave."

Christina blinked. "Brother Sechnall?"

"Who goes to visit him?" asked Margaret.

"Couples," her sister replied.

"And young girls," said Margaret. "Young, romantic girls with stars in their eyes. Girls who've already given their lips and hearts—and who knows what else—to a scoundrel eager to touch their flesh."

"But why would he want to kill them?"

"Because he hates them. He resents their youth, their beauty, perhaps even their foolish dreams or lusts that led them to consult him. I suspect he's a man who hates women and who wishes to destroy their happiness for his own craven purposes. Perhaps he even gets a visceral pleasure from the act of killing them."

"We encountered such a man in Northumbria," said Osgifu suddenly, looking up from her sewing. They all turned to look at her, since she rarely spoke unless directly asked a question. "Do you remember, mama?"

Aelgith hesitated for a moment, then nodded. "One of the younger sons of the family who owned us."

Osgifu blinked, as if the images passing before her eyes disturbed her. "Elfrid, his name was." She shook her head and shuddered. "He lived in the hall with us, walked and slept among us. At night he would go out and murder prostitutes." She looked up at Margaret. "I suspect that most of them were ordinary women like us forced into unaccustomed work to survive in the wake of the invasion."

"How did he kill them?" asked Margaret.

"He strangled them and then stabbed them, they said. I think they could tell because he never got blood on his clothes or in the surrounding area." She frowned at the memory. "They said that the blood stayed in their bodies because they were already dead when he cut them."

Aelgith drew in a ragged breath. "He would lure the women away from the settlement out into the woods, and do the deed there. How many were there? Three?"

"Four, I think," said Osgifu.

"Why did women keep going into the woods with this man after the first one was killed?" asked Christina, sounding incredulous.

"No one suspected him," said Osgifu. "He was young, not even twenty. Not tall either. His brothers were both knights and well respected. His family ruled the region. He didn't have the skills and talents of his brothers and no one seemed to think much about his prospects. He spent most of his time out hunting, alone. There was talk of him going away to join a monastery."

"I remember that," said Aelgith. "We would sit in the hall not far from the family where they discussed such matters. He didn't want to become a monk or priest but they told him that he had no business being a knight because he couldn't wield a sword or ride a horse with any skill."

"They had no idea he was creeping out at night and going to consort with fallen women. The women themselves would have looked at him and thought him easy money for a few minutes of holding their breath and thinking of their next meal."

Margaret crossed herself at the suffering of women who had to sell their bodies, their honor, to survive in these dark times.

"When the first body was found they thought she'd been killed by a vagrant who lived in the woods. He was hanged for the crime though he protested his innocence," said Aelgith.

"When the second body was found, killed the same way, they blamed a local miller who was in a dispute with the lord over tithes that he owed. I don't think any of us thought he was guilty but he was a convenient scapegoat and there was no one to stand up to the man who owned all the land and most of the people on it."

"Was the miller hanged as well?"

Osgifu nodded. "And his wife and children sold to pay his debts."

"By the same man that owned both of you?" said Margaret, horrified.

"Aye. He's dead now, too," said Osgifu. "Murdered by Mac Duff and his men when they raided and took me to Scotland."

"Justice sometimes arrives from an unexpected direction," said Christina.

"I would hardly call that justice," said Margaret. "So how did they find out who the true murderer was?"

"There was a witness to the third or fourth killing," said Osgifu. A young lad tending pigs at the edge of the forest who saw him hasten away just before dawn. His pigs led him to the body and he raised the alarm and told others what he'd seen."

"And this younger son of the lord was hanged as well?" asked Christina.

"He protested his innocence, and his mother tried to defend him. No one wanted to listen to the words of a peasant lad not even ten years old. But ultimately they put the pieces together and knew it was him. When they realized what a monster he was, even his family saw him as a blot on their name. I confess I'm not sure what happened to him," said Osgifu. She looked at her mother. "Do you know?"

"The last I know he was imprisoned, but I don't remember him being put to death. Everyone in the household was afraid to speak of him. I dare say he died when the Scots invaded, if not before."

Christina hugged herself. "Imagine if such a man survived because his powerful family allowed it."

"Perhaps he repented and changed his ways," said Margaret.

"Such a fiend is always a fiend," said Christina. "It would be only a matter of time before his cruelty surfaced again." She looked hard at Margaret. "You're right. The killer here must be stopped. He must be removed from this earth and sent to face his final judge." All the women nodded and murmured in agreement.

"To seek justice we need to demonstrate that this supposedly crippled and ancient man has both the means and desire to kill these women," said Margaret. "He's covered his tracks for years—decades—and no one seems to suspect him. Worse yet he's a revered and treasured member of the community—a man of God, they think!"

"He's had an excellent disguise, to be sure," said Christina. "If it is indeed him."

"You still have doubts?" asked Margaret. Hers had evaporated.

"I do. There are no witnesses, no evidence beyond our speculation. And you must admit that you even suspected my intended—our host—of being the killer."

Margaret didn't want to confess it aloud, especially on his own turf, but this was certainly true. She'd even secretly hoped he was the killer so she'd have good reason to get her sister out of the promised marriage. "We need to find a way to prove he's a murderer."

"You say he hates women and girls," said Osgifu. "And has a horror of licentious women. Perhaps I could go to him and pretend to be in love with another woman's husband—"

"No!" cried Aelgith. "You're a child." Osgifu had filled out and even grown since they'd rescued her from captivity and privation last winter. At fifteen she no longer looked like a young child and might even be tempting bait for the cruel hermit. But the prospect of giving the poor girl more horrors to carry in her heart was too awful to contemplate.

"Your mother's right," said Margaret. "I'd like to tempt him myself that I might see his iniquity with my own eyes but I'm afraid that I infuriated him enough with my last visit."

"I would think that makes you more tempting bait," said Christina. "But he'll hardly believe that the Queen of the Scots is there alone and unprotected." She frowned. "Am I right in thinking that the two women he murdered were suspected of having…aspirations toward Fingal Mac Gofraid?"

"Yes," said Margaret. "Agnhilda spoke of promises he'd made to her and her family seemed to think there was hope of a marriage between them. Catriona's father also seemed to dream of a marriage for his daughter."

Presumably Fingal had already deflowered their daughters. Under most circumstances that would be enough for the girl's family to force a man to marry her.

"I am also promised to Fingal, which puts me in their company," said Christina. "Perhaps I should go to him and—" She broke off. "And what? What is it that they say that enrages him to the point of wanting them dead?"

"I doubt it's anything they say," said Margaret. "Though I certainly got under his skin by accusing him of being a pagan soothsayer."

"You didn't!" said Christina.

"He is, isn't he? He told you that you and Fingal would have a long, happy marriage…how would he know that? Even God himself does not dabble in prognostication, as far as I know."

Christina seemed to contemplate this. "You're right. I suppose he told me what I so badly wanted to hear that I chose to believe it. I never even thought about how or why he—a crusty old hermit in a dripping cave—would be privileged to have such information."

"And that's his game," said Margaret. "He's enjoyed a stream of people coming to him for years—decades—bringing tributes in the form of food or coin or valuables of some sort. He wields power over them and their future with his predictions, which he likely makes up off the top of his balding head."

"Something about these two women must have set him off, though," said Christina. "Because from what I've heard the murders are few and far between. Why two so close together?"

"This district is remote and not well populated," said Margaret. "I doubt there are that many maidens seeking love-advice at any given time."

"I could go." said Grizel suddenly. "I'm young enough and with no husband. He won't know I'm a servant, will he?"

Margaret studied Grizel. Her clothing, suitable for a Queen's closest aide, was similar to that of a provincial noblewoman. Margaret didn't think her accent marked her as a rustic, though she was still learning the language herself. "It might be dangerous."

"No it won't, because I'll be wary. Those other girls had no idea he was about to try to kill them. I'm quick as a mouse and I'm a lot stronger than I look." Grizel looked positively excited by the prospect. "I could—" she broke off and looked at Christina. "I could tell him that The Raven held me close and made me promises and ask if I can expect a proposal of marriage from him?"

Margaret was about to protest—since Christina had made no reply and looked rather stunned—but the possibilities of this risky approach intrigued her. "This does seem to be very similar—almost exactly similar—to the situation the two dead girls might have presented him with."

"He'd have to think I was there alone. Perhaps I should even go at night? I think they did."

"Why would they go there at night?" asked Christina, who looked as if she was waking from a trance.

"Secrecy," said Margaret. "Perhaps they didn't want everyone in the area to know they'd been to visit him."

Christina nodded. Grizel looked excited enough to spring from her stool.

"We must have men with us," said Margaret. "Armed

guards, close enough to arrest him if even the slightest hint of an attack is made."

"How will we keep these unruly Scotsmen quiet?"

"They can be quiet if needed."

"I suppose they must be able to. They murder each other all the time, after all" said Christina drily. "They hardly march in with pipes and drums to slit their neighbor's throat in the dark."

Margaret bristled. "They are trained warriors and will do what they're commanded to do." She wondered if it would be difficult to get Malcolm on board with this plan. And she wondered how things were going in his conversation with The Raven.

CHAPTER 22

That night's dinner was a far quieter affair than the raucous drunken festivities of the previous nights. Malcolm's stern chat with Fingal had made him realize that his last-days-of-bachelorhood abandon was souring his intended bride on the marriage.

Margaret watched as he fawned and cajoled and tried to feed Christina delicacies—and while she sat wooden and wordless. She'd grown impervious to his charms.

"Let us offer a prayer for the souls of the poor murdered women of this parish," said Christina, at one point. It was about the longest speech she'd made all night. "That their evil killer may be brought to justice."

"I didn't kill them," said The Raven, looking directly at her. Margaret almost spilled her drink.

"I didn't accuse you," said Christina, looking rather startled.

"You think it's me, though, don't you?" He shoved a hand through his hair. "I admit that I knew those women. I may have even taken liberties with them, but I had nothing to do with their deaths. I swear it on my mother's grave."

Margaret could tell Christina was wondering whether to share their suspicions about the identity of the true murderer and their plan to ensnare him. "I think all the women of your realm, including us, would feel much safer if the culprit was captured and punished."

"I told you I'm willing to hang every man in the district if need be!" cried their host.

"That certainly won't be necessary," said Margaret. "And would be most un-Christian since all but one are likely innocent. Perhaps instead we should follow my sister's advice to offer prayers that the Lord might intercede to help us find and capture the fiend who's terrorized the women here for so many years.

She was hoping to buy time until she could share their plan with Malcolm and get his approval. The Raven, clearly chastened by Malcom's warnings and Christina's unwelcoming attitude, nodded in agreement and offered for Christina to lead them.

"Dear Lord," said Christina, whose face suggested that she regretted making herself the center of attention. "Please deliver the cruel and evil man who killed these women into the hands of those who can bring swift justice here on earth, that he may then stand at your feet ready to face justice before your throne."

Murmurs of agreement rose around the table. "By God's grace we'll have his head on a spike by this time tomorrow night," said The Raven cheerfully.

AT LAST, Margaret found herself alone in bed with her husband. She wasn't sure whether to share their plan to trap the killer or to inquire about halting Christina's marriage.

Before she could utter a word, Malcolm pressed a finger to her lips.

"I can feel your mind bursting with words, ready to shoot them at me like a hail of arrows," he said softly, right into her ear. "But first let me tell you what passed between myself and our host."

"Tell me," she whispered, into his finger.

"He admitted that he's always had a weakness for women and tries to confine his interests to…uh, professionals in that field so as not to upset the local families by tampering with their daughters."

"Well, he's done a horrible job of that. And consorting with whores sounds like an excellent way to become poxed. Everyone knows that."

"I said the same to him. He was contrite and promised that all such foolishness would cease and that he would have eyes and hands only for your sister."

"Did you believe him?"

"Not for an instant."

"He'll ruin Christina's life."

"He won't, because he won't be marrying her."

"He agreed to end the betrothal?" Margaret could hardly believe her ears.

"Not exactly. I want to give him time to sit with the idea and to realize—to admit—that he's not man enough for your sister."

"He's not."

"Indeed he isn't. He's not likely to prove a worthy leader and ally either, in my estimation, but I can't risk making an enemy of him—not with William on the rampage."

Margaret frowned. "What are you saying?"

"I need the dissolution of the marriage to come from Christina herself. She must tell him that she wishes to forsake the world and take the veil."

Margaret's heart sank. Christina had finally warmed up to the idea of marriage and children, and now they'd be snatched away from her again. "If she's to say that—and to stand by it—it must come from her heart."

"Speak to her tomorrow, and then we'll talk again." He kissed her softly on the lips, then rolled away from her as if to go directly to sleep.

"Wait, husband. We must discuss something else."

Malcolm rolled back toward her. "What is it, my dove?"

"Have you forgotten about the two dead girls and their killer?"

His silence was not encouraging.

"I have a plan to trick the old man into revealing that he can move."

Malcolm's chest rose and fell right next to hers. Still no words.

"Grizel has offered to be bait. She'll go into his cave and tell him that our host has seduced her and she wants to know if she has a future with him. As far as we can figure it, that's what the other two girls must have said."

There was a long pause, then Malcolm spoke. "And you think he's going to rise from his stool and wrap his hands around her neck."

"That's the hope."

"You hope that he will strangle your maid and closest companion?"

"Do you have a better idea? It would prove that he can move and also that he killed all the women over the years. Grizel is agile and will be expecting it, so she's confident that she can jump out of the way in time."

"And what if she can't? This man apparently has years of experience in overwhelming and murdering women far younger and fitter than himself. It could end in disaster. Why not publicly accuse old Brother Sechnall and ask Fingal to arrest him and bring him in for questioning?"

"You make it sound so easy. What if Fingal refuses?"

"He will hardly refuse it if I request it. Then you can question him yourself in front of everyone."

"Am I to say, in front of all gathered, that the two dead women are victims of Fingal's licentious activities?"

"Perhaps not in those words, my dove. But you can see how it would kill two birds with one stone."

Margaret nodded. "Once we know when he's coming, I'll call for the girls' families to attend as well. Surely they'll want to seek justice. I'm rather surprised that they're not here baying for it."

"Perhaps they really think their daughters were killed by a kelpie."

"I'm not sure anyone's that gullible, but it is odd that they're not asking The Raven to do something to find the killer."

"I shall speak to him first thing in the morning," said Malcolm sleepily. "Now can we get some sleep?"

Margaret wanted to comment that for both Malcolm and Fingal "first thing" was likely to be half way through the morning, but instead she kissed him on the cheek. She then turned her pleas to God in a prayer that justice would be served.

THE NEXT MORNING, Grizel was disappointed that their daring plan had been changed to something far more…sensible. Margaret herself wasn't entirely thrilled with the new plan, either. She suspected that the holy man would just sit there like a bump on a log and convince everyone that he was a mystical hermit with God whispering in his ear and no ability to move, let alone take a young woman's life.

When Fingal finally rose to break his fast he was dead set against the idea. "Absolutely not. The Culdees will rise up in a holy fury!" he said when Malcolm proposed the arrest and trial.

"Do you rule your lands or do the Culdees?" asked Malcolm, with apparent good humor.

"They've been here a lot longer than I have, truth be told," said Fingal. "And I've learned to leave them be. They're as persistent as the foolish legends. Some things are better left unmolested."

"Young girls are also better left unmolested," said Margaret quietly. "But since two have been murdered you must act. If Brother Sechnall is innocent then he shall return to his cave and recommence his mystical mutterings."

"He can't possibly have killed them," protested Fingal. "He's a lifelong cripple. His hands don't even open enough to strangle someone."

Margaret hated dangling Christina as bait, but since she hoped this fishing expedition would free her for good, she took the risk. "You can hardly expect my dear sister to come live in a place where two young women have been cruelly murdered and the killer walks free."

Fingal's brow lowered. He clearly still hoped to claim his prize of an English princess and close family ties to the King of the Scots. "I want to catch the killer as much as anyone else. I just know it can't be him."

Malcolm cleared his throat. "My wife obviously has a flea in her ear about old Brother Sechnall. He may well be innocent, but I shall only be satisfied of that if I have the opportunity to question him myself. I propose that he be brought here this morning—carried all the way if need be—and examined. If he's found to be blameless he shall return home at once."

Fingal fumed for a moment. "I shall go with my men and fetch him myself."

Malcolm looked triumphantly at Margaret. "Excellent."

ONCE FINGAL MAC Gofraid and three of his men had left to fetch the old mystic, Margaret sent Aidan and Grizel to convince the families to come to the hall. She thought Grizel would help her cause by reminding them of their young daughters or nieces, which might quell any hesitancy about coming forward.

In Fingal's absence, Margaret and Christina ordered the servants to arrange an area outside the hall where the hermit could be questioned and everyone could have a good view of him. "Don't you think it's odd that Fingal himself went to fetch the man?" asked Margaret.

"I'd imagine he wants to make sure his men don't seize him roughly and stir up ire among the Culdees. Which makes sense, I suppose, since Brother Sechnall is revered by the people."

Fingal returned with one guard, and some considerable time later the other two guards appeared, carrying the holy man in their arms as if he were sitting in a chair.

"Could he not have sat on a donkey?" asked Malcolm, looking like he was trying not to laugh.

"He's too crooked for that," said Fingal. "And I don't have all day and all night to wait for a donkey to cross the river."

The elderly hermit looked furious. His skin, in the unforgiving light of day, was pale as a toad's underbelly but also grubby, with dark lines in its wrinkled surface. His ancient and colorless woven garments were equally dirty and disreputable in the daylight. His halo of yellowish-white hair stuck out in all directions around his mostly-bald scalp.

"He looks every bit a cave-creature," whispered Christina. "The stuff of nightmares."

"If I'm right, he's even worse than he looks. But we shall see," said Margaret quietly.

Fingal fussed and fumed and ordered his men about. The appearance of the girls' families, not just the small groups who'd visited before but grandparents, aunts, uncles and small children, seemed to infuriate him further. "Who told you to come here?" he demanded of Agnhilda Finnsdottir's brother. The man pointed at Aidan and Fingal turned a hostile glare on Margaret.

She lifted her chin. Why is he so furious? Why would he not want to see the guilty accused? She reasoned that perhaps he truly believed the man was innocent and holy and that in addition to disturbing the Culdees, they might be enraging God himself by summoning him here to face accusation.

Dark clouds gathered overhead as they drew into a sort of circle around the hermit, who sat hunched on a stool not far from the hall. Margaret prayed the inevitable rain would hold off for a while longer.

Malcolm prompted The Raven to question him first.

Their host began by apologizing for disturbing Brother Sechnall's peace and thanking him for his long service to the community and praising his holiness and devotion to God. Margaret tried not to roll her eyes. Is he truly in awe of this toad-like creature? It was hard to believe.

"Did you—and I hesitate to ask this as I know it's preposterous—but did you, an elderly and infirm holy man, a life-long cripple and devoted servant of God, kill these two young women and leave their bodies in a stream?" He asked it as if such a thing was beyond ridiculous to suggest.

"I did not, my lord," said the hermit. He did not appear to be looking at The Raven. In fact he was squinting and staring at the ground as if the unaccustomed daylight was too much for his eyes to bear. Fingal looked around at the gathered crowd, as if this provided incontrovertible proof that he was innocent.

Margaret glanced at Malcolm, who stood next to her. She'd whispered all her questions in his ear that he might ask them for her. She'd explained that his first duty was to undermine the local perception that Brother Sechnall was a holy man on speaking terms with God.

"May I ask some questions?" said Malcolm, in deference to their host.

"Yes, King Malcolm," said Fingal, perhaps in case some of the assembled locals didn't know this tall, bearded man in fine clothing. "Though I fear you'll be wasting your time."

Again Margaret thought it odd that Fingal seemed to be so reluctant to have the man questioned. She looked around at the assembled peasants and farmers and tradesman. People must have heard something was going on and come from miles around. There were almost as many gathered as when they'd offered free food to the people. Could one of them be the true murderer?

Malcolm cleared his throat. "When I visited you with my queen, you informed us that we'd be blessed with many children and enjoy a long and happy marriage." He paused, and Margaret watched the hermit's face. He seemed to be peering up at Malcolm, head slightly tilted, like a tortoise peering out from under its shell. "How did you come to have such seemingly un-Christian foreknowledge?"

The hermit blinked. "I cannot say how or why, but I've been blessed with a gift from God." He croaked out the words as if they caused him pain.

"How can you be sure it's God?" asked Malcolm. "Perhaps it's a gift from the devil."

The hermit's mouth opened, then closed. Margaret could swear she saw his gaze dart to Fingal.

"How long have you been advising people on marital concerns?" asked Malcolm, walking closer.

"Since I was a young man," he rasped.

"Have you ever been married?"

"Never. I devoted my life to God at age fourteen."

"So what makes you think that you, of all men, have any business telling people who to marry or what their marriage will be like?"

Again, the hermit's mouth opened, and there was a long pause. Malcolm waited patiently. "I cannot say why the Lord has given me this work."

"Might I suggest that you've found it expedient to bring a stream of people to your cave to bring you food and money?"

The hermit looked like he might be about to say something, but Fingal cut in. "The Culdee community supports all of its members. They grow crops and raise livestock so that even the elderly and infirm are supported."

The hermit seemed to sag with relief.

Margaret looked at Aidan, who'd been sidling closer to the stool where the hermit sat. She nodded. Aidan reached under his cloak and untied a leather bag from his belt. He undid the strings and released a good sized adder onto the ground near the hermit's feet.

The serpent—no doubt confused and dazzled after being furled up in a leather bag—raised its head and surveyed its surroundings, then slid toward the old hermit as if to shelter under his robes. Brother Sechnall gasped, flung himself backward and fell off his stool. In front of everyone he scrambled to his feet and plunged away into the crowd.

Margaret looked at Malcolm in triumph. "It seems he can

move," said Malcolm, in a voice loud enough to be heard over the sudden hum of chatter. "Our ancient and crippled hermit can stand. Where is he?"

Aidan had dived into the crowed after him and now brought him forward. The hermit was back to pretending that he could barely move and Aidan had to drag him, but Aidan brought him right up to where the snake still sat, stunned, on the bare earth. Panicked, the hermit fought against Aidan with considerable force. Aidan let go of him and allowed him to run off to the side.

Now the snake started moving and a woman screamed in the crowd, which had shuffled back away from the serpent. "The bite of an adder is painful but harmless," said Malcolm, above the din. Aidan stepped forward and grabbed the snake by its tail and dropped it back into his bag. "But this snake has shown us something important. This man, supposedly so holy and sacred, is not a cripple but has been pretending to be one for all these years. Why?"

Two more of Malcolm's men had seized the hermit and now brought him back to his stool. Perhaps he was still unsettled by the snake—which had clearly ignited an irrational terror in him—but he no longer wanted to sit on the stool and resisted their efforts to put him back there.

"Has he kept his ability to move secret because it allows him to murder innocent women and evade suspicion? No one would suspect a crooked cripple who can't even unfurl his fingers of choking the life from a sturdy young girl."

Margaret watched as the old man crunched his fingers back into fists. That too had been a ruse.

Malcolm walked right up to him. "How did this charade start, I wonder? Did you kill a girl early on in your life—perhaps not even here but somewhere far away—and find it expedient to come live here as a hermit in a cave with a reputation for being barely able to rise from your stool or uncurl your fingers to eat?"

The old man's face had also tightened up like a fist. "No."

Malcolm walked right up to him and loomed over him. Margaret had warned him not to ask the man directly if he had killed either of the girls, because if he simply said, "no," the crowd might side with him due to his longstanding reputation. She held her breath as she worried he might do just that.

The old man shrank back, obviously also wondering what Malcolm would say next. But instead of talking to him, Malcolm looked over his head at the brother of Agnhilda Finnsdottir. "Your sister came to the hall here to plead her case that promises were made to her by The Raven. Did she go visit this man to ask for advice on her prospects of marriage?"

Agnhilda's brother and his wife looked at each other. They seemed to be hesitating. Why would they want to protect this man? Or did they just not know?

"Don't let your sister's death go unpunished," said Malcolm. "Speak for her, since she can no longer speak for herself."

Agnhilda's sister-in-law suddenly covered her face with her hands and blurted out, "Two died that day. She was pregnant."

CHAPTER 23

The woman's words hung in the air. *The Raven seduced her and got her pregnant, which is why her family urged her to risk her reputation and her dignity to come into the hall to confront him.* Her seemingly foolish behavior now made sense. Margaret glanced at Christina, who stood off to one side. She held hands with their mother and had her eyes closed.

Did Fingal know that Agnhilda was pregnant? She wasn't far enough along for it to be obvious through her clothing, or at least they hadn't observed it when viewing her clothed body. If she'd told him, he might have wanted her—and his unwanted offspring—to disappear.

And if it was The Raven who'd be inconvenienced by her pregnancy, was she accusing the wrong person?

"I'm so sorry for your double loss," said Malcolm. "It compounds the killer's guilt. It would give her an extra incentive to want the protection of marriage that may have brought her into the damp cave of Brother Sechnall. Do you think she visited him?"

"I begged her to," said her sister-in-law, through tears. "I shamed her for her sin. For allowing a man's embrace without any firm promises." She broke off in a sob. "She'd asked me if she should go to Brother Sechnall and said she should. My husband told her to go directly to Fingal Mac Gofraid's hall to plead her case first."

The hermit man now stared down at the ground as if trying to block out everything going on around him.

Margaret watched, heart pounding, as Malcolm approached Catriona Maclean's family where they stood in a knot off to one side. "Did your daughter go to visit Brother Sechnall, in the days before her death?"

Her mother was already weeping, and her father and brother looked like they were holding back tears with all their might. But her father shook his head and said he didn't know.

"Was your daughter, by any chance, pregnant?"

They all shook their heads vigorously. Which didn't mean much. Agnhilda's sister-in-law had sullied the dead girl's reputation by admitting it, and they perhaps saw no reason to do the same, if it was true.

"So one girl did go to visit this man, Brother Sechnall. Another was in a very similar position, led on by hopes—perhaps promises—of marriage and suddenly seeing her planned future vanishing before her eyes. Why would she not go seek counsel from the man revered by all as a font of wisdom?"

He looked down at the hermit, who—grotesque in the bright light of day—looked like the last creature on earth who should be giving young women advice about their love life.

Malcolm now loomed over him again. "You killed them both. I'm sure of it." It wasn't a question but it still begged an answer. Margaret held her breath.

The hermit seemed to shrink.

"Go on!" roared Malcolm. "Admit it. You killed them with these thick, gnarled hands of yours, forced their faces into your holy font and then—somehow, I have no idea how—hauled them into a nearby river." He pulled his sword from its scabbard in a single dramatic action and now held the point against the man's neck.

The hermit let out a tremulous quivering cry.

The Raven, who'd been silent up to now, strode forward, drawing his own sword. "I'll cleave his head from his shoulders right now!"

The hermit let out another cry. "He made me do it!"

"Who made you kill them?" asked Malcolm.

"The Raven," rasped the old man. "Fingal Mac Gofraid."

"Lies! Evil lies in a desperate attempt to save his sniveling, wretched life. He's a canker on the face of the earth." Fingal raised his sword sideways as if to strike the man's head clean off.

Margaret felt a scream rising in her chest at the sight of The Raven so close to her husband with his sword drawn—worse yet, Malcolm stepped in between him and Brother Sechnall. "Stop. The girls' families deserve to hear why he killed them."

The Raven dived around him, still holding his sword over the man's head. "He doesn't deserve to breathe air. I shall end his miserable life."

Margaret was increasingly convinced that The Raven played a role in the killings. He had motive: he'd hardly want women growing heavy with his bastards while he was wooing and wedding the King of Scotland's sister-in-law. Now he stood accused of murder—what if he decided to try to fight his way out? His armed men surrounded them and their own guards would be easily outnumbered.

She pressed her hands together and offered a prayer for

her husband's safety. Aidan and two other guards had surrounded Brother Sechnall, so in order to take a swipe at him with his blade, The Raven would have to attack them too. He hovered, clearly furious at being thwarted. Margaret wished someone would disarm him, but how, when he stood there as ruler in his own lands?

"Why did you kill them?" asked Malcolm of the hermit. "Were you ordered to?"

"They were whores," he replied a crabbed whisper. "They didn't have any right to ruin the life of a good man."

"The Raven wanted them dead?"

"Yes," he said, holding Malcolm's gaze with his rheumy eyes.

"Had he asked you to kill women before?"

"No."

"Then why were women being killed in a similar fashion for years, decades even?"

The hermit shifted on his stool, hunched over, then looked up at The Raven. "Because I did the same for his father. And for his father before him."

Stunned silence reigned for a few moments, then morphed into a hum of chatter from the crowd. Margaret could hardly believe her ears. This grizzled old hermit, living alone in a musty cave, had been killing women to order since before most of them were born?

Malcolm held up his arm. "His forbears had you kill women they no longer wanted?"

"A pregnant woman—or even a needy, mouthy one—is an inconvenience to a man who's promised or married to another. The unwelcome babe of a king may live to become his rival," hissed the hermit. "My time on earth is coming to an end. I'm already older than most men in the land. The Lord anointed me! He gave me the power to squeeze or choke the life from disgraced wenches and their bastards these many years. I cleansed the land of their filth and perversion!"

"How did you carry them to the stream?" asked Malcolm in disbelief.

"I didn't. The guards did that."

Now it all made sense. Margaret stared in horror. How many men, over the years, knew exactly what was happening to these local women and kept quiet about it? The Raven, like all leaders in the region, had local warriors in his household but also foreigners, from Norway, Ireland, Denmark and other distant places. They would owe no allegiance or even excuses to the devastated local community as one women after another disappeared over the decades.

"Which guards? Are they here?"

Fingal launched into a volley of abuse against the old man, calling him a liar and all manner of insults that scorched Margaret's ears. He surely would have cracked his sword down on the hermit's skull if it wasn't for Malcolm's guards bravely defending him with their own bodies.

"I don't know," growled the hermit. "These ruffians all look the same to me. I don't know where they put the bodies or why."

"I suspect they carried them in a stream, either by boat or on foot," said Malcolm. "So they could conceal the fact that a man was moving each young girl's slight body."

Margaret glanced at their families. The women were sobbing. Agnhilda's brother was also red-eyed and her father stared in mute horror. Catriona Maclean's father glared at The Raven. He'd now had confirmation that his chief, his leader, the man who controlled his land and his life, the noble he'd hoped to see his daughter married to—had snuffed the life out of her as if she were an insect buzzing around his ale. Margaret wondered if the families suspected something all along, which is why their cries for justice were muted.

"Why did they have you kill the girls?" asked Malcolm of the hermit. "Why not order the guards to do it?"

The old man peered up at him and let out a harsh laugh. "They wouldn't do it! Wouldn't kill an *innocent* young girl." He said the last words in a mocking fashion. "But these hussies weren't innocent. They were craven and pathetic sinners who didn't deserve to hold their heads high among decent people. And when their lord and master told the hussies to go to me…to ask for my counsel…."

Margaret shuddered. The Raven—or his guards waiting outside the hall—had sent the girls on a fool's errand into the hermit's dripping cave. And this disgusting old "holy man" saw himself as meting out some kind of grotesque justice on unfortunate young women who'd been seduced by powerful men.

Christina could hold off Fingal's lascivious advances because she had the full force of Malcolm and his court behind her. Agnhilda and Catriona had been led to believe that there was a prospect of marriage—probably only because Fingal wanted them pliable and willing in his embrace. If they'd had any sense they'd have known there was no betrothal coming, but they likely still couldn't have refused him without consequences for themselves and their families.

Malcolm now looked directly at Fingal. "Did you send the girls to this man? Perhaps to get his blessing to marry you or some such thing?"

"It's all lies," said Fingal with a scowl. "Do you believe this crabbed old wizard?"

"I do," said Malcolm. He stood steady as an oak tree,

despite having an armed and angry warrior only a few feet from him. Both of them knew that if they took a swipe at the other, their opponent's guards could fell them before they drew their next breath. Margaret tried to convince herself that this gave them both a measure of safety—as long as they both kept their heads.

Malcolm continued. "He's confessed his guilt and knows he'll die, either by the rope, or the sword, or perhaps even in the same manner that he used to take the life of countless young girls. He has nothing to gain by falsely accusing you."

The Raven seemed to consider this. "I demand a trial by the Brehons."

"That is a very reasonable request. Except that if Brehon men live in your kingdom and are beholden to you they can hardly be expected to take a disinterested approach to the case. I shall summon Brehons from Ireland." Malcolm strode around him. "And your betrothal to Princess Christina is hereby suspended until such time as judgement is passed on your guilt or innocence."

MALCOLM'S GUARDS secured Brother Sechnall. While Malcolm wanted the evil old man killed at once, Margaret persuaded him that the families of the dead girls deserved a chance to get their own measure of justice by confronting him. Guards were sent out to find local families who'd lost a daughter or sister in past years.

The Raven retreated into his hall, calling for ale and his musicians, even though it was far from dusk. "We can't just let him walk around a free man!" hissed Margaret, after he disappeared from sight. "He sent these last two girls to their deaths. Even if he wasn't responsible for killing them with his own hands, he gave the instructions that they must die.

And he swore on his own mother's grave that he was innocent!"

"Aye, but he's the ruler in these parts and as such is a law unto himself."

"And you think a judgement by the Brehons will change that?"

Malcolm gave a hollow laugh and looked around. They stood outside, away from the others. "Nay, but there are men in Ireland who'll be glad to exploit this opportunity, so I doubt he'll be drinking at this table much longer."

Margaret frowned. "You think they'll invade and snatch power from him."

"I guarantee it. He's young, arrogant and foolish. He's only in power at all because he inherited the title from his father Gofraid Mac Sitruic, who was a fearsome warrior. He'll barely be remembered in the annals of history."

"And you think you'll be able to make an ally of his successor—preferably without promising my sister in marriage?"

"I shall do my best."

Malcolm's guards stood watch over the next few hours while the girl's families, some of them now aged, had their chance to scream at the old hermit and hurl insults. He bore them silently and would provide no further details about either his own actions or the thoughts behind them. He also said nothing further about his orders from Fingal's father Gofraid Mac Sitruic or his father before him.

"A king or great lord having hired assassins to do his work is hardly unusual," said Malcolm softly. "But I've never heard of a case where discarded mistresses are killed. Usually, if they're not just kept quiet and happy on the side, they're paid off or sent away, sometimes to a convent. In this case The Raven and his forbears had the dubious luck to stumble across a man who thought the girls deserved to die and took pleasure in the task."

"It was hardly the fault of the girls that they were seduced and defiled by a powerful man."

"I'll grant you that. And rest easy in the knowledge that revenge shall be had, even if not in the most conventional manner."

They determined that The Raven's guards had sent Agnhilda Finnsdottir to Brother Sechnall's cave, even escorting her there but taking the route through the river on horseback so she was seen alone on the ferry. They'd then been on hand to remove the body.

Margaret wanted these guards identified and tried before the Brehons for their part in the killing, but Malcolm convinced her that because they hadn't committed the murder with their own hands—and they had acted on their lord's commands—it would likely be a waste of time and a diversion from their main goal of leaving with Oswin.

The hermit was put to death the following morning. His head was separated from his hunched shoulders by the cleaver of a local butcher, whose niece Deirdre had been found drowned in a stream fifteen years ago.

The gathered crowd dwarfed anything that Margaret had seen at thus far, for people had come from miles around as the story of the hermit's grisly reign of terror spread throughout the region.

The abbot had ordered the hermit's cave exorcised and searched, and they'd found a great quantity of women's jewelry, gold and silver and gemstones, buried under a layer of sand in the font cut into the cave wall.

The Raven himself was not present, since he was inside, drunk and morose at his table even though it was only halfway through the morning. When people asked—in hushed tones—what punishment he might face, Malcolm,

Margaret and Aidan murmured about the Brehons and the course of justice—and God's final judgement.

THEY LEFT the lands in the shadow of Fort Dunnad the same day. Food and drink gathered for the planned marriage feast was piled onto the pack horses and they set out not long after noon. To Aelgith's great relief, Oswin was secured and mounted on his favorite horse.

When Margaret expressed reservations about leaving an unpaid debt in the form of the horse—a tall and powerful dappled gray destrier—Malcolm assured her that The Raven would not be long burdened by his anger over the loss. The wet nurse rode sidesaddle on a donkey led by Aidan, so she could attend to little Edward's needs on the long journey.

Margaret and her mother and sister rode astride, with Margaret back on her new black palfrey, Maud, who'd already proved herself as a sturdy and trusted family member.

Christina rode in silence. "You've had a lucky escape," said Margaret, trying to coax some enthusiasm from her mute sister. "I'm so glad that you're coming home with us rather than staying to live the rest of your life in that wet and windy place."

"And you don't have to become a nun," said Agatha cheerily. "Since we didn't need that excuse to break the betrothal. You can still marry and have babies of your own."

"I'd rather die," said Christina harshly. "I feel foolish for even daring to dream that I might have a measure of ordinary happiness."

"Don't be silly, darling," said Agatha. "We shall find you a lovely husband like Malcolm."

"Please, don't. I almost got bargained away into the bed of

a debauched murderer. I'd rather be locked in a stone cell with a prayer book for the rest of my life."

"Then you shall be like a second mother to Margaret's children," said Agatha. "Think of how much little Edward already dotes on you."

Margaret saw her sister's face soften. "If I can't devote my life to God, then I shall devote it to protecting Margaret's dear babes from harm at the hands of evil men, as God is my judge."

"I think that's my duty," chimed in Malcolm. "Though I'd be glad to have you as my lieutenant."

A light drizzling rain pursued them all the way to the border of her husband's kingdom, where it finally lifted. Margaret's heart felt heavy. "It pains me that the man who ordered the deaths of two young women walks free and sleeps in his own bed."

"You know I couldn't arrest him unless I was willing to conquer and rule his entire territory—which I have no interest in doing since it would stir the kings in Ireland and cause trouble I don't want or need. I had no choice but to leave him there for the time being."

"Perhaps I might be King of the Isles," said Edgar, from the back of the group. "I could get used to the weather. There's decent hunting and—"

Malcolm silenced him with a laugh.

Margaret didn't see anything funny about the current situation. "What if Fingal gathers allies and seeks to attack you for accusing him?"

"I've already sent messengers to Ireland. Godred MacCrovan will be most interested to hear that the King of the Scots supports his ancient claim on the Kingdom of the Isles."

"You think he'll invade?"

"I'm sure of it. They're relations of some kind, he and The

Raven. He's had his eye on this territory. I suspect he'll be glad to relieve his cousin of it and possibly remove his head from his shoulders in the doing of it."

"I suppose that would be justice of a sort. And this Godred MacCrovan would be a good ally to you in any future fights against William?"

"God willing."

unfermline, September 1071

"Who are you to say that kelpies don't exist?" asked Malcolm. He was helping Margaret onto the boat that would ferry them across the firth on their journey from Dunfermline to Edinburgh. They were traveling there to conduct the knighting ceremonies for several young men, including Oswin. "The people here have believed in kelpies for many centuries."

Margaret glanced at the dark water swirling around the boat. It was easy to imagine a strange, horse-like creature emerging from the murky depths. "There's no mention of kelpies in the bible," she said brightly. "Not even one. And the Bible is a collection of writings gathered over a long period of time."

"They weren't writing it in Scotland, though, were they, my love?" Malcolm balanced her as she stepped off the dock down into the belly of the boat. "No one asked the Scots for their contribution to the Bible. Perhaps we should write an addendum." His mischievous grin provoked her as much as his suggestion.

"The Culdees would love that," she replied. "Since they've rewritten half the church's teachings for their own purposes."

Malcolm held her arm as she settled onto the cushioned bench. "I don't see anything wrong with a man having a personal one-to-one relationship with God."

"I don't either. I cherish my freedom to pray directly to Him. But I don't support a lot of lone hobgoblins living in caves and making up new rules for themselves."

"Said the woman who prays in a dripping cave in the dark hours before dawn."

"I didn't say there was anything wrong with praying in peace and quiet. There's much I admire about the Culdees and I still have more to learn from their contemplative approach. But there's a reason that the Church of Rome has rules. I don't support heresy any more than I support one bitter hermit choking the life out of young girls who've had the misfortune to be led into sin."

Christina settled on the bench next to her. "I offer up prayers of thanksgiving every day that I didn't end up being his next victim."

"That would never have happened," said Margaret. "Because your presence in Fingal Mac Gofraid's household would give him power and security. Besides, if we weren't all there and making delicate negotiations, he'd likely have whisked you off to another court on Man or Islay, and you'd have heard no more of the disappearance of any inconvenient young girls."

"God forbid." Christina crossed herself. "I hate that the man himself still walks and breathes so I might unwittingly share a breath of the same air as it blows across Scotland."

"The Brehons condemned him, but since Godred Crovan is his cousin he didn't want him put to death. He's been exiled to the most miserable outcropping in his former kingdom. If the rough waves and steep cliffs don't keep him prisoner, Crovan's guards will."

"And this Crovan is a friend to you?" asked Christina.

"Aye, sometimes a Crow bests a Raven," he said with a wink. "A steady and powerful man is a better ally than a chimeric wastrel like Fingal. Godred Crovan joined with Harald Hardrada against William, so he's fought him once already. He's still rankling from the loss and he'll help me fight him again if need be."

Her brother Edgar stepped down in the boat, little Edward in his arms. The lad was getting stronger, sometimes too strong for the wet nurse to hold him if he wanted to be put down.

"Let me take him," said Malcolm, seizing the lad. Edward settled onto his lap, then pointed at the water and let out a loud shriek.

"Aye, lad. That's where the kelpies live." Malcolm winked at Margaret.

"Don't teach our son nonsense," she said. It was bad enough that the boy would learn about the non-existent monsters from the servants.

"He'll hear plenty of nonsense before he's grown," said Malcolm. "But we'll teach him to be a man of honor who respects the traditions that matter."

Oswin stepped down into the boat, then held out a hand for his mother. Aelgith sat on the bench opposite Margaret and Malcolm, and her daughter Osgifu joined her. Both rosy with health and arrayed in courtly finery, it was hard to even remember the desperate state they'd been in when she first encountered them.

Oswin sat next to his mother. Like his sister, the boy was quiet and circumspect, made wary by the violent course his life had taken. Since arriving in Dunfermline he'd proven himself adept with a sword as well as a horse and easily earned the respect of Malcolm's men. Malcolm himself had declared that it was time to make him a belted knight.

The men on the dock threw the rope to a boatman who furled it neatly as the oarsmen pulled away from the shore, out onto the deep, dark water of the Firth of Forth.

Malcolm sat next to Margaret and opposite Oswin. "You'll be a fine addition to my fighting forces. And your skill with the horses is valuable indeed. Once again, England's loss is Scotland's gain."

"Are you not worried that so many English men and women will overwhelm your Scottish culture?" asked Christina. "Insisting that kelpies aren't real, for example."

"Never. My own people are relative newcomers from Ireland, if you look back at the old annals. This country is a medley of Gaels, Norsemen, Danes, Picts, and yes, the English. I have no doubt that we Scots will always be distinct and different."

"I notice you didn't include the Normans in that list," said Edgar. "Aren't you worried they'll try to invade sooner or later?"

"If they do then we'll send them running home with their tails between their legs."

"God forbid." Margaret grasped his hand. "Let's pray for peace. An end to war."

"And have my knights sitting around idle with all their good horses going to waste?" asked Malcolm cheerfully.

"Yes!" said Christina and Margaret in unison. "For the love of God, yes."

THE END

AUTHOR'S NOTE

What little we know about the life of Christina, Margaret's sister, comes from testimony before a council of bishops by Margaret's daughter Edith, as she pleaded for her right to marry, insisting that she was not a nun. The controversy arose because Margaret and Malcolm had sent Edith to be educated at Romsey Abbey, where Christina lived first as a nun and then as abbess. When a group of Norman knights arrived to view and inspect the young Edith—perhaps as a suitable bride for William II—Christina hid her behind a veil and insisted that she wasn't available for marriage because she'd taken vows.

Christina had apparently hoped to hide her niece from "the lust of the Normans." According to Edith's testimony before the bishops, Malcolm was furious when he heard this, and tore the veil from her head. Her father wanted her to make an advantageous marriage, not be buried in a convent. Edith herself also said she'd ripped off the veil and stamped on it after the incident, causing her aunt Christina to beat her and scold her. I can easily imagine Christina's fear for her niece: a cadre of macho Norman knights striding into a monastery to get a look at King Malcolm's pretty young daughter must have seemed quite alarming—especially since Edith was born in 1080 and Malcolm died in 1093, so the girl would have been under thirteen at the time. However since Edith was the daughter of a king and a prospective bride to a king, it's hard to imagine her virtue and safety were truly in danger.

In 1100, seven years after her parents' deaths, Edith married Henry I. Her name was changed to Matilda, to better fit the Norman court. She went on to give birth to— among others—Henry II and is thus the matriarch of many of England's monarchs.

Christina lives on as only a footnote in history—the bitter nun who beat and scolded her pretty young niece for wanting a husband. How did she become that person? Why was she so afraid of these knights, rather than encouraging her niece to make a potentially advantageous match? Even when girls were betrothed or wed very young, they were not usually expected to consummate the marriage until they reached a suitable age. In this book I decided to imagine a story where Christina finds herself tempted and almost drawn into marriage—and then turned off it in a very final way.

The story of a betrothal and flirtation between Christina and Fingal Mac Gofraid is entirely a product of my imagination, as is the murder mystery. Fingal Mac Gofraid is, however, a historical figure who was Lord of the Isles briefly starting in 1070. He then disappears from the historical record and no one seems to know what happened to him— did he die? Was he conquered and exiled? All we know is that Godred Crovan became Lord of the Isles in his stead.

I chose Dunadd Fort as the location because it would have been within the territory of the Lords of the Isles (which roughly corresponds to modern Argyll and Bute), yet close to the border of Malcolm's kingdom. A seat of ancient kings, it would make sense as a familiar haunt for the ruler of The Isles. Google maps insists that you can walk there from Dunfermline in two days (and nights), and bike there in twelve hours, so a royal party on horseback could have managed the journey fairly easily despite the complex terrain since they no doubt knew which routes to take.

The Culdees (also written as Céilí Dé and Kelidei) must have both fascinated and provoked Margaret. She surely admired their deep spirituality and close personal relationship with God, but was also wary of their non-conformity. During her time as queen, Margaret hosted numerous religious councils to try to hammer out differences between the religious communities in Scotland and the Church of Rome. She's usually described as trying to convince the rustic clerics of Scotland to abandon their ancient and unorthodox practices—such as celebrating the Sabbath on Saturday—but I suspect she was also intrigued by their beliefs. No doubt she was initially suspicious of solitary hermits living and worshipping in caves, but she famously crept away from the royal court to pray in a little cave downhill from the stone tower in Dunfermline. It's still there today, and can be visited seasonally, despite being paved over for a town car park.

If you have questions or comments, please get in touch at jglewis@stoneheartpress.com.

BOOKS BY J. G. LEWIS

The Margaret of Scotland Medieval Mystery Series

Book 1: Spoils of War
Book 2: The Raven's Price
Coming soon: Book 3: The Devil's Due

The Ela of Salisbury Medieval Mystery Series

Book 1: Cathedral of Bones
Book 2: Breach of Faith
Book 3: The Lost Child
Book 4: Forest of Souls
Book 5: The Bone Chess Set
Book 6: Cloister of Whispers
Book 7: Palace of Thorns
Book 8: A Surfeit of Miracles
Book 9: The d'Albiac Inheritance
Book 10: Unholy Sanctuary

AUTHOR BIOGRAPHY

J. G. Lewis grew up in a Regency-era house in London, England. She spent her childhood visiting nearby museums and riding ponies in Hyde Park.

She came to the U.S. to study semiotics at Brown University and stayed for the sunshine and a career as a museum curator in New York City.

Over the years she published quite a few novels, two of which hit the USA Today list. She didn't delve into historical fiction until she discovered genealogy and the impressive cast of potential characters in her family history. Once she realized how many fascinating historical figures are all but forgotten, she decided to breathe life into them again by creating stories for them to inhabit.

J. G. Lewis currently lives in Florida with her dog and her horses.

For more information visit www.stoneheartpress.com.